The Mid Witch

The Mid Witch

DJ Bowman-Smith

Illustrated by
DJ Bowman-Smith

Edited by
Anna Sharples

Copyright © 2023 by DJ Bowman-Smith

All rights reserved.

No part of this book may be reproduced in any form or by any electronic or mechanical means, including information storage and retrieval systems, without written permission from the author, except for the use of brief quotations in a book review.

❦ Formatted with Vellum

This book is dedicated to women of maturing years who ever
felt - as they ploughed headlong into midlife -
invisible, frustrated, slightly angry, tired, hot, confused,
ill-informed, redundant and overweight.
I wrote this story to remind myself, and you dear reader, that
wisdom, humour, adventure, love and even magic
also belong to us - women of a 'certain age.'

Foreword

Hello dear Reader. Thank you for being here on this journey with me. If you enjoy reading The Mid Witch please take the time to leave a review. This really means a lot and is a massive help to an independent author like myself. Reviewing this book on Amazon will make a huge difference. More reviews mean others will find The Mid Witch and it will not sink into the depths of obscurity. Even if you only have time to leave stars - I am grateful.

I hope you enjoy reading this as much as I enjoyed writing it. For updates on the next in the series and to grab your free bonus Mid Witch short story, please hop over to my website:

www.djbowmansmith.com

Many thanks,

Deborah

Chapter One

A feather has blown under the kitchen door. I pick it up and admire nature's perfection as I wait for the kettle to boil. Outside, a magpie hops about in the apple tree. 'You've dropped your feather,' I say, opening the window and throwing some raisins onto the path. The magpie glides down and cocks her head to eye me as she eats. She's been living in my apple tree for three days now. There's still no sign of her mate in the other trees. I know how she feels. The feather shimmers blue, black and green, and there is a buzz in my fingertips as I poke it into the soil of a red geranium on the window ledge.

I am groggy. Desperately in need of tea and annoyed that on such an important day I have slept the night in an armchair. Again. I scratch my itchy scalp, and as my fingers meet the plastic bag wrapped around my head, memory returns. The hair dye!

Twenty minutes later, I stand naked in front of the bathroom mirror. 'Fuck,' I say, examining my bright orange hair. Why today of all days? Why now? I wish I'd bought a hat. Do people wear hats at graduations? Maybe it will look better dried. Not so angry. Not so bloody vivid. I'm wrong, of course. It's worse. Vibrant is the word that springs to mind. My son is graduating, my estranged husband will be there and my hair... my hair is brighter than a synthetic pumpkin. I tie it back, looping it over into a sort of bun, and get dressed.

With no money to buy something new, I plan to wear the same frock I bought for my daughter's graduation. However, ten years takes a toll on a woman. The dress is too tight and too hot, though it matches my hair. How ironic. The only other garment I have ironed is an old blue polka-dot sack of a dress, which is cool and loose-fitting. At least I have the new strappy sandals I bought on sale, which is something. Let's

The Mid Witch

hope people notice my feet and not my hair. The shoes came with a sweet little matching handbag. What a bargain. I grab it from the kitchen table and run.

I don't drive. Never learnt. Mike and I started dating when I was seventeen, and he used to collect me in his plumber's van. It felt romantic and grown up. We'd have sex on a pile of old blankets in the back. At nineteen, I was married and pregnant. There was never any money for another car, and Mike was always good about chauffeuring me.

The bus driver, Stan, knows me and, bless him, he is waiting at the top of the road. I run as quick as I can, boobs bouncing, orange hair escaping. By the time I climb on, I'm a woman on fire.

'I was about to drive to your house and knock on the door,' he laughs, and I hang on as the bus lurches along the lane.

'Thanks. Thanks for waiting. I don't know what I would have done,' I pant.

Sitting in the front seat, I try to calm myself. I ride the bus most days, and he never asks for my bus pass, but the train is different. My train pass is safely in the side pocket of the tiny handbag. I feel smart with this neat little thing on my lap, even if it's entirely impractical unless all you want to bring is lipstick. Somehow, I have managed to squeeze in my phone, house key, bus and train passes and a graduation card for

Jason. No lipstick. Well, I can easily borrow a bit from my daughter.

'Thanks, Stan,' I say when the bus pulls into the train station.

'Have a great day, love. Doesn't seem two minutes since they were going to school. Give him my best.'

'I will.'

The train is busy. I have to stand for most of the forty-five-minute journey. My feet are furious. I hate these shoes already. When I arrive, I text Bel to see if she can collect me. My phone is full of angry messages from her. Where am I? It's about to start. These days I can't think straight. My head is full of cotton wool. I must have the wrong time. By the skin of my teeth, I get a taxi. It's massively expensive, but he drops me off in exactly the right place, and I am so grateful I could kiss him. Or cry.

Barrington University is old and huge. The red bricks glow in the summer heat. The courtyard is empty, and there's music playing somewhere inside. I text Bel again, and in a few moments, there she is. A big scowl on her pretty face. She waves me in and leads the way along the oak-panelled corridor into Barrington Hall. The music has stopped, and there is a general air of anticipation. The ceremony is about to start. Our seats are in the middle of the row. A horrible shuffling embarrassment ensues as we squeeze past everyone's knees, whispering 'Sorry' and 'Thank you'. Once seated, I go to hug her and am met by a stern glare. These days I mostly feel like a child in her class. She teaches primary school. I try to sit still and will my body to cool down. Sweat trickles down the backs of my legs. Even my handbag on my lap is making me hot. I put it on the floor between my feet and steal a glance past Bel. Her husband, Brian, also a primary school teacher, gives me a friendly smile. Next to him is my husband, Mike. Last time I saw him was about two months ago. He's had his hair cut short, which suits him. He smiles, and I smile back. Good. He definitely seems pleased to see me. Later, at lunch, I will ask if he will give me a lift home, and then... and then, well, we shall see. I take a deep breath.

We sit through a whirl of speeches and then the long procession as the young people file onto the stage to shake the principal's hand and get their certificates. We all cheer when we hear the name Jason Turner. He smiles at us as he leaves the stage, and I have a pang of regret that I was not here early enough to see him put on his cap and gown.

Afterwards, the sunny courtyard is full of chattering graduates in their academic robes. We look for Jason. As soon as he spots us, he comes over and gives me a hug. 'I'm so proud of you, darling,' I say into his shoulder. He's taller than Mike now.

Mike comes over with a big grin on his face.

'This is Charlotte,' he says.

A well-dressed woman, much younger than me, steps forward. 'Call me Charlie,' she says, 'everyone does.'

'Lilly,' I say, forcing a smile. I hope I don't look as shocked as I feel.

We hang around for photos, and Jason is keen to introduce his friends. Charlotte, Call Me Charlie, chats effortlessly with everyone, including Bel. Brian is speaking to one of the tutors.

I need a minute to get myself together, so I slip away to the toilet. I wet a paper towel and put it on the back of my neck. I'd like to run my head under the tap, and I wish I had Big Bag with me, which is always full of useful stuff like lipstick and a hairbrush. My hair. Oh my god, my hair. Any other day I would have laughed. I look crazy. Leaving the dye on all night has given it a new texture. It is both gleaming and incredibly dry, and where the chemicals have grabbed onto the white streaks, it is iridescent. I could easily get a job as a party clown. I splash my face with water, then take a few deep breaths and remind myself that this day is about Jason and his achievements. Nobody will be looking at me.

We go to lunch. Mike has booked a fancy restaurant for us all, and I manage to sit as far away from Call Me Charlie as I can. Jason is chatty. He always is. I always thought he would go on stage, but he has taken a degree in graphic design. Two of his oldest friends have joined us with their girlfriends. They all went to different universities, but it seems only days ago that they were coming back to the cottage together after school.

I sit at the edge of the table, an outsider in my own family.

The Mid Witch

It's clear they know my husband's girlfriend. She's not here by chance. So why didn't somebody warn me?

Everyone laughs at one of Jason's many impressions. I am immensely proud of my son, and I try to think of only that. To watch him as he smiles and laughs and regales the many amusing moments of the day. Jason sees the funny side of everything.

I try not to notice Call Me Charlie and Mike – although she calls him Mitch. The way he looks at her, how close they sit. When she laughs, she throws back her head and her perfectly highlighted bob swings like a silk curtain. She's fun. Joins in the chat with some funny stories of her own. As I listen, I learn she is a hairdresser. The owner of the fashionable salon in Market Forrington, named, predictably enough, 'Charlie's Hair Design'. She's hoping to open 'Charlie's Two' very soon. This explains Mike's smart new haircut. I wonder how much younger she is than me. Ten years? Fifteen? Another hot flush flares up my body, gathering heat as it burns my neck and then my face. Would anyone notice if I put the ice from my diet coke down my cleavage?

When the lunch is over and we are standing outside in the warm summer evening saying our goodbyes, Mike seeks me out. 'Well, that was quite a day,' he says, sighing deeply and arranging his jacket over his arm. He hates creases. We both look at our children. So grown up. An icy shiver engulfs me. A cardigan is something else I always have in Big Bag.

'I've been meaning to call in,' he says, looking at me properly for the first time. His gaze slides over my hair and I try not to cringe. 'Now the kids have properly flown the nest, I think it's time to put the cottage on the market. You know, move on with our lives. Don't you?' As he speaks, he smiles at Call Me Charlie. She's giving him the 'time to go' look. 'Good, well then. Lovely to see you,' he says, as if I am an acquaintance he has encountered on the pavement. Then he's off. Waving to the kids and putting his jacket around his girlfriend's shoulders as they walk away.

Belinda and Brian rush off because they want to pick the twins up from friends. Jason is clearly itching to party with his mates. I assure him I am quite happy walking to the station on my own.

Even after sitting in the restaurant for so long, my feet have not improved. Swollen flesh is pressing against the straps. My feet are being grated alive. Big Bag always has spare shoes. Flip-flops in the summer and trainers in the winter. It's a slow walk to the train station. The carriage is empty on the way back, and I cry ugly tears then find I have no tissues. Beyond caring, I wipe snot on my dress. God knows I can't look any worse.

Chapter Two

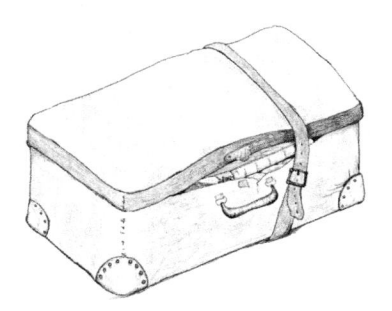

The next day is Sunday. I'm up early, which is unusual. I am always wakeful on bright summer nights when the sky is clear and moonlight shines on the garden. In the morning, I have no trouble sleeping. Last night, though, I slept well, exhausted from the emotions of the day.

I shower, put on some comfy shorts and a baggy T-shirt and make a big pot of tea and an immense pile of toast. On the kitchen table is an unopened letter, official and boring. I'd been so busy cleaning the cottage for my imagined reunion with Mike that I'd just left it. I open it now. Inside is a letter from Mike's solicitor stating that he will no longer be paying me an allowance. I pour more tea into my mug, but it's stewed and lukewarm. It's time to take stock. Be honest with myself. Face up to reality.

My marriage is over.

I am moving house.

I have no money.

Whenever I feel low, I favour action over thought. Best to keep busy, my mother told me whenever things got bad. Before the cottage goes on the market, I should clear out the attic. I rinse my mug and plate, toss some raisins to the magpie and go upstairs.

The best idea is to empty the attic entirely, though it seems a shame to make a mess when the cottage is so clean and tidy. Never mind. I find the old shepherd's crook at the back of the wardrobe that pulls open the hatch and releases the steps. I can't think when I last came in here. Stacking the loft was always Mike's job. He'd initiate a clear out and we'd end up storing everything we no longer needed but I couldn't part with. That's the trouble with me. I'm sentimental.

I work all morning, hauling down old suitcases and cardboard boxes. I can't believe there is so much stuff. The sitting

The Mid Witch

room and narrow hallway are crammed, and I am overwhelmed by the task I have taken on.

Dust-covered and sweaty, I go into the kitchen, drink a glass of water and tip some into the red geranium plant, which I'm sure has grown since yesterday.

The magpie jumps onto the window ledge and tilts her head to look at me. I put a raisin in my hand and hold it out to her. She hops closer, pecks it up and swallows it whole. Will the people who come to live here feed her? I am filled with so much sadness I go into the garden and stand in the apple tree's shade.

Apart from a few years when Mike and I were newly married and had a second-floor flat in Barrington, I have lived at North Star Cottage all my life. My mother and grandmother were born here. When my mother got cancer, it was easier to live here with the kids. She loved the kids. After she died... well, we just stayed. Jason was a toddler and Belinda was at the school in the village. It was cheaper than paying rent, and Mike needed money for his plumbing business. Whenever he got the time, he tried to bring the cottage up to date. New bathroom, obviously. An ensuite in the bigger bedroom. He painted the walls tasteful shades of grey and insisted on getting rid of anything chintzy. He was full of ideas. The kitchen with its old pine cupboards and battered table was always on his 'sort the cottage out list', but time and money never came together enough for him to make a start. It gives me a pain in my chest to think of new owners renovating the place even more.

My skin itches from the dust. I'd like to lie in the shade in the long grass and look at the sky through the branches, but I decide to press on. The attic is almost empty. I will bring out the last few boxes and then take a shower.

It's late afternoon when I stand under the eaves in the empty space. I'm hungry and tired. I have not stopped to eat lunch, which is unlike me. Now I'm a bit wobbly. 'Right. That's that then,' I say, and my voice echoes. Then I notice one more box, tucked under the slope of the roof. I hook it out with the shepherd's crook. At first, I think it's a large shoe box, but when I put it on top of a pile of old coats in the spare room, I see it is a small suitcase made of leather. An old belt holds the lid in place.

After a shower, I pull on a comfy track suit and eat some cheese on toast. Then I walk about, looking at all the junk. Flip through old books and unwrap forgotten toys. A bag of baby clothes brings me to tears for the joy of motherhood and the passing of those unrepeatable years. I sift through photographs and pull out discarded clothes. Recollections rise to the surface with each item I find. The love my children had for favourite teddy bears. Tents we used to pitch on the lawn and child-sized deck chairs. Hats, now squashed, that I wore at weddings, and piles of their school books I could never bear to throw away. Celebrations and daily life all carefully stored.

My own childhood is here, packed in boxes and neatly

The Mid Witch

labelled with my mother's writing. I leave them unopened. So many memories. My whole life represented in a stack of rubbish that needs to be thrown away. My heart aches, and I wish I could feel that this was a new beginning and not an end. I am an empty nester, and soon I must leave North Star Cottage and start a new life.

It's work tomorrow, so I go to bed. Sleep claims me instantly. But five hours later, I am awake. I don't bother trying to get back to sleep. I put the kettle on, make a mug of cocoa and sit in the moonlit kitchen. The leather suitcase is on the table. I thought I had left it upstairs. Never mind. I pull it to me, undo the crescent buckle and lift off the lid. Inside are packets of crisp brown paper tied with string and many small leather pouches. There is also a brown and faded book, which I lift onto the table.

Carved onto the thin leather cover is a spindly star. The pages inside are fine as silk and handwritten in black ink. There are drawings of plants and animals. Recipes to cure headaches and sprained ankles. Love potions and soup to mend sadness. The language is strange and the spelling peculiar. I can hardly make out the meaning. How old is this? How long has it been hiding in the attic? Maybe I should cook something from this book before I leave. The writing is very hard to read, but I open it at random, persevere and discover a recipe for curing gout. As I thumb through the delicate pages, I find cures for bunions and teething babies, bone aches and backaches, bee stings and snake bites. How fascinating. A book of herbology. I wonder if the museum in Barrington might be interested and if they could tell me more about it. There is an inscription on the last page:

Whosoever use this, my book of shadows,
do so in good heart and pure intent,
pleasing faith and spirit.
Bethany Blackwood.

Wood is my maiden name, and I wonder if I am related to this woman and if our last name was shortened.

I get into the big easy chair in the lounge. Old and squashy with faded flowery covers, it's out of place alongside the smart, low-backed pair of grey sofas Mike bought. We call it the easy chair, but it is almost a bed, long enough to lie on. It is where my grandmother and mother both liked to relax. Moonlight comes through the window, and I pull an old blanket over myself and sleep.

In the morning, I am so late I miss breakfast and run for the bus still buttoning my polyester work shirt. I hang on the grab rail and talk to Stan about the graduation. I don't mention Mike, and he doesn't ask. Then I sit and muse about my situation. Now Mike has stopped my allowance, I should ask for a pay rise. See if I can take on more responsibility at work. Or maybe I could get another job on the weekends.

The bus is almost full when we drive into Market Forrington. I make a point of not looking at Charlie's Hair Design as we go past. No point in torturing myself.

The bus stops at the end of the high street, and off I get. I

The Mid Witch

work in Dunwicks Department store. The staff entrance is in a side alley, and I'm glad I'm not late. All things considered, I'm doing fine, I tell myself. Orange hair is safely secured in a tight bun. Uniform of skirt and shirt in pale blue with pink piping is clean, and I've remembered my name badge. On the bus, I dabbed on some makeup to disguise red eyes and general blotchiness. I have Big Bag to cope with whatever else life might throw at me. My stomach rumbles, and I feel weak. I may need to see the doctor about my blood sugar or something.

Recently I have worked on the ground floor in the gifts and ornaments section. This is one of the coveted positions in Dunwicks Department Store. I'm surprised they gave it to me, as I have only worked here since Christmas. To be honest, I was much happier working with my friend Tina upstairs in haberdashery.

Monday is a quiet day. Brenda, the floor manager, is keen to get all the 'jobs jobbed', as she puts it, and sets the six of us to our tasks. I have drawn the short straw and must dust the locked cabinet that contains the expensive china and crystal. 'Now take your time,' says Brenda, handing me a key on a lanyard and frowning at my hair. She is half my age and speaks to me like I am a wayward teenager.

This large glass display cabinet is at the back of the store, and with any luck, I can fuss about here all day in peace. I unlock the first door, slide it across and begin moving everything onto a holding trolly so I can clean the glass shelf. Each piece and its price tag must be put back exactly as I found them. This is Brenda's method. And we 'girls' know if we stick to her method, nothing will go wrong. Brenda has a method for everything.

The top shelf is easy. It has only three large crystal vases. They have been here as long as I can remember. Perhaps today will be the day when someone buys them. The next shelf is trickier. A plethora of bone china animals and a few figurines stand in neat rows, smaller objects at the front. As I replace them, I am struck by how boring everything looks, and a terrific idea pops into my fuzzy head. I will rearrange the entire cabinet into an eye-catching display that everyone will love. There has been a lot of staff gossip about opportunities in Dunwicks lately. Perhaps this is my chance. I will show a bit of initiative and then ask if I can train to do window dressing or something.

Because they remind me of ice, I group all the crystal vases together. Locked drawers at the bottom of the display case contain more stock. I try the key. It doesn't work, which is a shame because my idea is excellent. I really wish the key worked. In frustration, I twiddle it again, and the drawer opens. I am thrilled and carefully unpack all the polar bears and penguins from the drawer and set them about my frozen crystal world. There are some glass snowflakes in the stock drawer, and I add them to the scene. I am so enthralled, I miss my coffee break and start unwrapping all the porcelain crinoline ladies. I give each lady a horse and a dog or a cat and

The Mid Witch

arrange them in a parade. Some of their faces are snobby or sad, and I wish they were cheerful. As I organise them on the newly polished shelf, the light catches their faces, and they look pleased. It is as if they always wanted a horse and a pet. I chuckle as I gather all the porcelain birds and put them on a perch I have made from upturned mugs. This is great. I have not enjoyed work so much for years. Perhaps shop display is my calling? Maybe I could work for a window dressing company. It would be nice to have a fun job.

All around my feet are boxes and bubble wrap. I should sort this out, put everything neatly in the drawer and organise price tags alongside the ornaments. There is only one more shelf to arrange, though, and I've saved the best until last. Dragons. There are two large and three smaller ones. A dragon nest is my idea.

I am distracted by a customer looking at my creation. A sale would be terrific. 'Can I help you?' I say.

His face is contemptuous, and he ignores me and carries on perusing the ornaments, studying each shelf until he stands next to me. My trolly prevents me from moving away, and the sleeve of his expensive dark suit brushes my arm as he points at the polar bears. His scent, citrus and pine and something else I cannot place, is so alluring I have to stop myself from gulping in a deep breath. He runs his finger slowly along the glass to the shelf below. Until his head is level with mine. Tanned and freshly shaved, he has black hair greying at the temples and a few characterful wrinkles that enhance his handsome face. He turns his head. We are almost nose to nose. His eyes are dark, and they meet mine with an intense gaze. Does he fancy me? We are a similar age. A thrill runs through my core, and I smile. It's such a long time since anyone has admired me. For a woman, middle age brings invisibility.

'You look a mess,' he says, standing up and tapping the glass. 'Get this one out.'

Shocked, I fumble for the lanyard around my neck. It's not there. Annoyingly, I have an awful bruised feeling in the centre of my chest. I can't find the key on my trolley, so I rummage about in the packing at my feet. At last, I find the purple lanyard under his expensive polished shoe. I look up.

'Could you please move your foot?'

He tilts his foot just enough so that I can pull the lanyard free. 'Is this going to take much longer?'

A hot flush sears my neck as I try to unlock the cabinet. Will the key work? I drop it twice, and this man just stands there with his hands in his pockets and sighs. Finally, the key turns and I slide the door open.

'There, now that wasn't so difficult, was it?' he says.

This man really is a condescending prick.

'Which one?' I ask.

'The one at the back.'

The hardest one to reach. 'Certainly, sir.' My face is hot, and I know I look like a sweaty tomato. Reaching the large polar bear from where he peeps behind an expensive crystal vase entails moving everything. I take my time and try to ignore the customer. He's actually tapping his foot. I force a smile as I lift the polar bear out. It is almost as large as a cat. He takes it from me in his well-formed hands and examines it, and I wish I was a person who could chat with strangers. A little sales patter would be helpful right now. And I really need this sale to validate my display. This polar bear is the most expensive item in the entire department.

'What is going on?!' Brenda appears from behind the scarves carousel. She sees the customer and immediately goes into charming shop assistant mode. 'Is there anything I can help you with, sir?' she says, her voice smooth and gracious.

'How much?' he asks, fixing me with those dark, dark eyes.

'Erm?' The display is wrecked, and there are piles of plastic price tags on my trolley. I cast a beseeching look at Brenda.

The man tuts, hands back the polar bear and says to Brenda, 'Perhaps I'll come back when you're not in such a mess and have some competent, polite staff.' He deliberately squashes some boxes under his big feet as he leaves.

Brenda glares at me, speechless. My hands are sweaty. I clutch the polar bear tighter, and, as if in slow motion, Brenda's mouth opens as the ornament slips from my grasp. I try to catch it as it falls, only to send it spinning onto the corner of the trolley, where it smashes into smithereens.

Chapter Three

Turns out there were no 'staff opportunities' for me at Dunwicks. Recently employed and still in my probationary period, I am thanked by the store manager and told that if I leave immediately, they will overlook the cost of the breakage. Could I please return my uniform (laundered) as

The Mid Witch

soon as possible? I am so mad I nearly strip it off in his office.

It is the middle of the afternoon when I step, somewhat stunned, into the blazing sunshine. All I want is to go home and lie in the shade. I have forty-five minutes until my bus, so I buy some groceries, a meal deal and more hair dye. The nice girl in the chemist has assured me that this will return my hair to a medium brown. Then I sit in the bus shelter and eat my sandwich. I am beyond tears.

The bus I catch stops in Foxbeck and does not go all the way to Church Lane, where I live. I am glad of the walk. I need to do some serious thinking about my life. Or, more accurately, about money. Mike's allowance and my job just about covered the bills. Without qualifications of any kind, I am restricted in what I can do. Over the years, I have cleaned houses, served school dinners, worked in various shops, picked fruit and washed dishes. Mike was always keen that I worked part time, not full time. He liked a wife at home, and homemaking was my primary occupation. This arrangement worked and provided my kids with a bit of stability when Mike was absent. Which was most of the time, if I'm honest. The thought crosses my mind that I probably need a lawyer. I've raised our children and kept house, and now what? Can I support myself without him?

Foxbeck is tiny. We have a post office and a general store, a café with a gift shop that shuts in the winter and a veterinary practice. The Fox pub looks over the quaint village green with a cricket pitch and a village hall. Both of my children attended Foxbeck Primary. Now I wonder if Bethany Blackwood, the author of the shadow book, went there too.

Church Lane is tree-lined, and I am glad of the shade. A long, hot summer is a trial for women of a certain age. Middle-aged menopausal old bags like me long for the cool days of autumn.

Halfway along the lane is St Gutheridge and All Angels. It is the only church in England to have a stained-glass window depicting ten magpies. Curious gargoyles carved like pigs peer from the roof. As I walk past, there are a few tourists wandering about in the old graveyard. They are probably looking for the headstone of Galahad Thornbury. My family headstones are behind the church in the far right-hand corner. When I visit next, I will look for Bethany Blackwood.

North Star Cottage is the only house on Church Lane, and a small path winds ten yards among the trees to where it nestles. From the lane, it is hardly visible, and I expect people in cars drive past without noticing it.

The magpie is sitting on the gate and swoops about as I walk to the kitchen door. I fancy she is pleased to see me. I put away the shopping and switch on the kettle. To make ends meet, I will try to sell some of the stuff from the attic. Isn't vintage all the rage these days? Some of this must be worth a few quid. I sort old coats and clothes into a pile I could sell, then sit with a cup of tea and look for a local job online. The packet of dye is on the table, and I should try to sort out my hair, but I can't face it. Instead, I pull the old leather suitcase toward me.

Inside the lid is a seven-pointed star. I carry it to the door and compare this star to the one scratched on the doorstep stone. Both are roughly drawn, and although the one on the lid is smaller, it seems to me that the same hand made them. Kneeling in the last rays of the summer day, I am taken back to my childhood. I used to sit here on nights such as these while my mother made blackberry and apple jam. She'd give me a hunk of bread she'd wiped around the jam pan, all warm and sticky, and I would trace my finger over the lines of the doorstep star as I ate.

I am an only child and fatherless, yet I never felt lonely here. We had chickens, a scruffy black lurcher called Rufus and a large lazy cat with pale orange fur called Gabriel. My mother did not mind how many friends I brought home or how long they stayed. North Star Cottage was where everyone came. There was always food, and the old wood-fired range cooker was ever hot, keeping us cosy, drying the laundry and cooking dinner. If I close my eyes, I can see the pets warming themselves beside it and my mother in her apron shooing them away to open the oven door and check on her baking. Now the old range sits cold and redundant. Mike put in a small electric oven when we took over the cottage, but he never got round to doing anything else to renovate the kitchen.

After I've changed out of the hateful uniform, showered

and eaten beans on toast, I look inside the old case and take out the first thing on top. Brown paper, crisp with age, rustles as I unwrap a smooth, white, palm-sized stone. On one side is a seven-pointed star – the same uneven shape in red and green paint. Faded gold lines give the impression of starlight. So lovely. I press the cool marble to my forehead, my temples, the back of my neck. I sit there for a while and fancy the hot flush that was brewing has abated. I take the stone to bed with me.

In the morning, I am secretly glad I do not have to rush off to Dunwicks for another long and boring day. Today my first job is to sort out my hair. I read the instructions carefully, mix the foul-smelling mixture and daub it on with the plastic brush provided. Half my head is covered in dark brown goo when I hear banging. From the bedroom window, I see a large estate car parked in the lane and a man hammering a post outside my gate.

I know what this is, and I am so mad I rush out in bare feet.

'Wait!' I shout.

The man turns, and it's him. That bastard from the shop yesterday. He's draped his expensive suit jacket over my garden gate and has his shirt sleeves rolled up as he hammers a post into the ground. On the grass beside him is a For Sale sign.

'Mrs Turner?' He looks me up and down, taking in my scabby feet with chipped nail varnish, my hairy legs and the vile, stained old nightie I always wear when I'm colouring my hair.

A blob of congealing hair tint drips down one cheek, and I wipe it off and flick it in the grass. What I'd like to do is wipe it on his jacket.

'Your husband has instructed me to put this property on the market,' he says and makes to swing the hammer again.

'Stop!' I say.

He raises one eyebrow and swings the hammer. The sound, as it hits the post, vibrates through me. I'm not sure whether I'm hot from sheer anger or the menopause, and right now, I don't care. 'I'm not ready. The attic. Everything's a mess,' I wave a hand toward the cottage.

'I can imagine,' he says drily.

He throws the hammer into the grass and picks up the For Sale sign. 'I'll need to take pictures. For the website. Mr Turner is keen for a quick sale. I'll take some of the outside.' He looks over my shoulder. 'No need to worry about sorting out your chaos. I expect a builder will buy it and pull it down. Probably for the best.'

He fixes the sign to the post and gets his camera bag, and I stand by the gate, blocking his path. 'What is your problem, Mrs Turner? Your husband gave explicit instructions about his property,' he says.

I hold his dark gaze. I am defiant even if I have no underwear on and my boobs are drooping round my waist. 'He's not my husband. Well, he is, but we're separated. And it's not his house.'

Again, that annoying eyebrow lifts, and I have to fight an urge to slap his handsome face. 'Not his house? Mrs Turner, I don't have time to stand here and argue. Why don't you sort out who, exactly, owns this property, and then we can all move on.' He leans across me and plucks his jacket from the gate, and I get a whiff of his scent again. Fresh and manly. I hope the misogynistic bastard can't smell me.

I shut and bolt the kitchen door, then stand at the window while he drives away. He leaves the sign, which makes me furious. I call Mike. Of course he doesn't pick up, so I text and then ring again and leave a voice mail.

Out of sheer frustration, I scream at the top of my voice. I clench my fists and scream again and again until I am spent. This makes me feel better, and when I open my hands, tiny sparks float up.

I go upstairs, shower and wash my hair. I turn the water to cold, stand under the cooling stream and breathe in. I need time to adjust and get the old place sorted and ready for the new owners. That's all. Three weeks. That's what I will tell Mike if I ever get hold of him. When I step out of the shower and grab a towel, I see the tub of hair dye in the sink. I never did the other half. I rub my head on the towel and wipe the steam from the mirror. One side of my hair is still orange, and the other is now green. I'm probably going to have to cut it all off and start again. I tie it back wet. At least it will help keep me cool. Then I put on a comfortable bra, some big knickers and the sack dress I always feel happy in.

My phone rings in the kitchen, and I rush to answer, hoping it will be Mike. It's Jason, and he's got a job with an advertising firm in London. He tells me all about the interview and what the company does. I'm thrilled for him. Yet the thought of him living far away is so sad. Barrington was far enough. When he asks how I am, I tell him I'm fine and babble some nonsense about it being a good year for apples.

When he's gone, the pain in my chest is awful. On my ancient laptop, I look up 'seeing sparks'. Stress and possibly a migraine or exhaustion seem to be the cause. So I go into the garden and lie in the cool grass under the apple tree.

The magpie is high in the fruit-heavy branches. Maud is a perfect name for her. Maud the Magpie. 'Hello, Maud,' I call softly, and the bird hops through the branches and swoops down beside me. 'Maud,' I say again, and she cocks her head to one side and then preens her feathers. I watch her and fall asleep. A car in the lane wakes me, and before I can run inside the cottage and hide, my visitor is striding along the path and opening the kitchen door. 'Theo!' I say.

She is already putting on the kettle, and she gives me a big hug. 'I heard the news!' she croons. 'You must be so proud.'

'Yes,' I say, realising she is talking about Jason's new job.

'I was passing and thought I'd drop off this for Jason. I

expect you'll see him before me. Just a little something.' There is a large, beautifully wrapped parcel on the draining board. 'So sorry I couldn't make the graduation.'

'How was Portugal?' I say, sitting at the kitchen table.

'Fabulous, darling.'

Her bracelets jangle as she stirs the tea and puts a mug in front of me. She finds a packet of biscuits in the cupboard and gives me some on a plate. Before she sits, she puts the old book in the suitcase, closes the lid and pushes it to one side. Then she wipes her dusty fingers on a tea towel.

'I was going to leave this on the doorstep. Why aren't you at work?'

She eyes me over the mug. Theodora Grimshaw is the closest thing I have to family. We call each other cousin, but she is, in fact, the daughter of my mother's closest friend. She's a few years younger than me, and it shows. She never married or had children and instead had a prestigious career working as a personal assistant before starting her own company. She's organised the lives of the rich and famous and is currently writing her memoirs. She is one of those women who always looks dressed up even when they're not dressed up. Theo is effortlessly glamorous.

No wonder she's always so cheerful.

'I got sacked.'

'Because of your hair?'

'No. But it may have been a contributing factor.' We

laugh, and I tell her the whole sorry tale about work, Mike and the estate agent. I don't get into Mike's new girlfriend. There's only so much you can tell a person in one go. Also, Theo doesn't do tears, and I know if I open that door, the waterworks will start.

'Well!' she says when I have finished speaking. She puts the mugs on top of all the other dirty dishes in the sink. Theo's smart town house in Market Forrington has a dishwasher, and she has the sort of fingernails that don't do dishes or cook. Today they are painted a tasteful grey.

'I think when this is all over, you will see it was the best thing that could have happened. It's time to move on. From your marriage and this old place. A new start is just what you need.' She looks at her watch. It's one of those fitness trackers. Theo is always fabulously thin. 'This is the moment you make a new life for yourself. New job. Buy a little flat from the proceeds of this sale.' She waves a manicured hand to encompass our surroundings. 'You could even travel, darling. Now come on. Show me the damage this loft clear out has made, and I'll give you a hand.'

That's the thing about Theo. She always puts a positive spin on everything. 'Organisation with a creative outlook' was her company motto.

With Theo's expert help, I sort out my tidal wave of rubbish. We relegate some of it to plastic sacks ready for the tip and make a pile for the charity warehouse (which I'd never heard of – 'You can just drop the whole lot off at once, darling') in Marswickham. She puts an app on my phone so I can sell various odds and ends online. There is a stack of books and toys that Bel might like for her school. By the time I walk Theo to her car, there is a pile of black bags ready for the tip outside the kitchen door. I am feeling optimistic and, crucially, much more in control.

'I'm sorry I can't stay longer, darling. But I have this thing at the County Hall. Are you sure you don't want me to take a load?'

Her neat red sports car is no place for my junk. 'No, it's fine. I'll call Bel later and get her to give me a hand at the weekend.'

She gets in and closes the door, and the roof glides away with mechanical perfection and drops out of sight. 'You know, you could always call that useless husband. No reason he shouldn't help.' I nod, but we both know that is the last thing I will do. She ties a silk scarf around her head and puts on fashionable sunglasses. 'You should try that hairdresser near me. The one in the middle of the high street. Charlie's. I've heard they are very good and not overpriced. Yet.'

I bend and give her a kiss. 'Thanks for all your help.'

She starts the car, which is surprisingly loud, and looks at the For Sale sign. 'And if that cunt of an estate agent comes back, tell him to fuck off until you're good and ready,' she shouts over the engine. Her posh voice makes music of even the worst words. I'm laughing as I close the garden gate. Theo was just the tonic I needed today.

As if sensing my good mood, Maud the magpie swoops past, white wing tips flashing in the late afternoon sun. Could I take her with me? I head for the kitchen door, then stop short. A sleek black dog is sitting on the step.

Chapter Four

I bend down and hold out my hands, and the dog sniffs me and wags her tail. I stroke her soft head. She is entirely black and without a collar. I'm not very good at dog breeds. She looks like a greyhound. Streamlined and thin.

'What happened? Did you get lost?'

The Mid Witch

The dog wags her skinny tail and gazes at me with big brown eyes. Upstairs, from the spare room window, I can see the woods at the back of the cottage and the public footpath across the fields. Nobody is looking for a lost dog, as far as I can tell. I call the police, who advise me to take her to the vet tomorrow to see if she has a microchip in her neck. The dog follows me back into the kitchen, and I find something for her to eat. A tin of tuna is all I have. After checking on the internet to see if dogs can eat tuna – they can – I tip it into a dish, fill a basin with water and put the two together near the kitchen door where my mother used to feed Rufus and Gabriel. She eats, laps some water, goes into the garden, has a pee and then gets into the easy chair in the sitting room and goes to sleep as if she has lived here all her life.

It's been quite a day, so I leave her there and go to bed myself. In the night, she creeps in, lies beside me and sighs. When I get up to pee and cool my hot flush in front of the open window, she watches from the bed.

In the morning, as soon as I'm sorted and dressed, I fashion a collar and lead from a dressing gown cord and walk with her to Foxbeck Veterinary Practice. She trots neatly beside me, her black coat gleaming in the early morning sun. A short woman and a tall dog.

I'm hardly through the door when Becky comes to greet me. We went to school together. All her family are vets, pretty much.

'Well, who's this? Aren't you beautiful!' She's on her

knees, making a big fuss of the dog, and the dog is doing skinny wriggles all around her.

'She's not mine. She wandered into the garden last night. I informed the police. Anyone lost a dog?'

'I'll have a look,' says the young man at the reception desk.

'Come on in. Let's check her over,' Becky says, leading the way into her consulting room. 'She isn't chipped,' she says, putting the scanning device down. 'Sometimes if they were a racing dog, they have a tattoo in their ear. Nope, no tattoo here.' She gives the dog a quick examination. 'She's young. She's not spayed, and my guess is she's abandoned. Happens all the time with black dogs.'

'Why?'

'They seem cute as pups, but they don't photograph easily on social media.'

'That's crazy!'

'People are bastards,' Becky says, fingering my makeshift lead. She roots about in a drawer and finds a collar. 'Here, have this. It's old, but it's the right thing for a greyhound. They need these wide ones because of their long necks.' Then she finds a lead and clips it on. The waiting room is already full when we go back out. We have a quick chat about old times. Then I leave my number at the desk, just in case, and buy a small sack of food Becky recommends.

School holidays are still in full swing and there is a group of older kids hanging about on the village green. One of them calls out as we walk past. 'What do you call that haircut? Port and starboard?' The others have a good laugh and shout, 'Hello, sailor!'

At home, I spend some time photographing items and getting them online to sell. I send a text to Bel to explain what is happening and ask if she could give me some help. I text Jason as well to keep him in the loop, but as he doesn't have a car, there is not much he can do. I send them pictures of their childhood belongings and ask if they want any of them. But I know in my heart that it's only me who is overly sentimental about this stuff. Will they be sad to see the cottage go? Probably not. They are young and have lives of their own. Everything moves on, and so must I, I tell myself.

After Theo's help yesterday, I am in charge of the situation. I am on track to begin a new life. In the kitchen, I make a pot of tea. Stretched out on the grass in the sun is the greyhound. Her coat is beautiful, and I take my tea outside and kneel to pet her. She's such a tame and relaxed hound. I can't believe she is an abandoned pet. Even if she is black. 'Someone must miss you,' I say, smoothing her as she stretches out with a big doggy grin. 'Ink,' I say, and her head snaps up. 'That's what you remind me of. Old-fashioned black ink we used to put in fountain pens.' Her head flops down. 'I'll tell you what, Inky dog. If no one claims you, you can stay with me.' She sighs as if to say she knew that all along.

I go inside to get my laptop so I can search for a job. The

old laptop is on the kitchen table where I left it, but the little leather suitcase is no longer there. It can't be far away. I search under the table and all over the kitchen, looking in places where it can't possibly be, like the cutlery drawer. Theo has most probably tidied it away. I check every space in the sitting room. In the hall, the cupboard under the stairs is crammed with coats, boots and long-forgotten shoes and bags. I crawl to the back in my quest, which is something I have not done since the days of lost school shoes. There is a universe of forgotten junk in here, and it will be up to me to sort it all out.

It is not there, so I go upstairs and search high and low. The dog finds me sitting on my bed with the stone with the star on it in my hand. She gives it a good sniff, and I pat her smooth head. 'Come on, Inky dog. We'll have to go through the rubbish.'

Theo would most definitely have classed the old suitcase as rubbish, not donatable. I stand next to the pile of stuffed black bin liners by the garden gate. Ink sits beside me as if she, too, is deciding where to start and what method to employ. I don't want to undo all our hard work, yet the rising sense of panic I have regarding the suitcase is most odd. Ink goes to the back of the pile and sniffs enthusiastically at a bag. I lift it up and she moves in, nudging the next. Can she smell what I am searching for? I move bag after bag aside until one, deep in the middle of the pile, has a greater significance than the rest. The dog spins around, wagging her tail and growling excitedly. What is even more odd is that I also know this is the right bin liner. Why? How? I have no idea.

Moments later, Ink and I are in the kitchen with the suitcase on the table. I check inside. Everything is in there, including the shadow book. What a relief.

I make a nest for us under the apple tree. In the heat of midday, it is the best place to be. Some old rugs and cushions. Water for Ink. Tea for me. I settle back to read the *Book of Shadows* with the greyhound stretched out beside me. The book has sections, although it is hard to navigate without a contents page or an index. 'Problems of the Body' is at the beginning. This comprises various cures – herbal remedies with accompanying words to speak while making and applying them. To my amusement, I find one entitled 'Hair in Ruins'. The list of ingredients is long, and some of the more unusual plants have accompanying drawings. I take a handful of hair in each hand and hold it in front of my face. The orange and the green. Both handfuls are like straw, and anything that will restore some of the condition before I dye it again will help. I have no money and I can make this for free. What have I got to lose?

Some plants are hard to find. Many seem most odd. I have a pestle and mortar that belonged to my mother, and at the back of a cupboard there's some coconut oil I didn't know I had. Ink follows me, sniffing my herbs with interest, rummaging in the flower beds and then sleeping under the tree. I pound, sieve, boil and strain the mixture through a cotton tea towel. I mutter the words, paste the warm, thick mixture onto my poor hair and then bandage my head 'sundial wise', which I decide means clockwise. I read more words out. I'm not sure if these are made-up or an old dialect, but they feel most pleasing on the tongue. When I am finished, the last instruction is that everything remains on the head until the sun comes up. Well, I'm not going anywhere, and short of falling out, my hair cannot get any worse.

The next morning, Ink and I lie in bed for a bit. My head is strangely hot, and I remember the bandage. I hope the weird gunk has not damaged my hair even more. I imagine unbandaging my head and my hair falling out in orange and green clumps. It would be just my luck.

At the bathroom sink, I peer into the mirror as I peel away the wrappings. I'm not sure whether it is the effect of the goo, but the orange and the green seem to have gone. Even if it is like straw, at least strangers won't shout at me. Today I plan to go to Barrington and apply for a job. Neutral hair would be a huge bonus.

After a shampoo and shower, I am standing at the mirror, combing out my grey locks. I have dyed my hair since my teens, everything from blonde to brunette. Anything to cover my natural mousey shade. Now I am grey with streaks of pure white. I dry it off with the hairdryer and fancy it is longer. It falls in soft waves past my shoulders. Was it this long before? Was there always a natural wave lurking beneath the weight

The Mid Witch

of the dye? Inspired, I grab my epilator and apply it to my face. It is the only way to combat the galloping facial hair of middle age, even if it makes me wince. A quick swipe over my legs and then my arms. Epilating my arms is a new job. Something I have done for the last two years after my arm hair changed into some weird, white Santa Claus fluff. In the light from the window, I pluck anything else on my face that has escaped the epilator – a couple of resilient chin hairs and a long curly fellow who likes to appear on the end of my nose from time to time. Ink, who had been lying in bed with her legs in the air, is now in the garden. She is a shadow moving through the long grass, her tail curved in a happy hook and her ears flat to her narrow head. I must have left the back door open. I should be more careful. If there is a burglar in the kitchen, I hope Ink will bark to let me know.

I moisturise my body, face, eyes and scraggy neck with various creams. Bit of lipstick, and then I get dressed. It's going to be hot again, so I find another floral sack that's cool and comfortable. Jeans would be nice, but they would boil me alive. For once, I look okay. Funny what a difference a good hair day makes.

The kitchen door is shut. I blame this on the breeze. I feed Ink, put a bowl of water in the garden for her and lay the old rugs under the apple tree. 'Got to go out for a bit, Inky dog. But you'll be alright in the garden. When I get back this afternoon, we'll have a big walk. And if I get a job, I'll buy you a nice collar and lead and lots of treats.'

Ink stands by the garden gate mournfully when I leave, and I feel awful. But I can't take her to a job interview. I console myself that she cannot get out of the garden and she will be happier outside on such a hot day. Also, vet Becky can easily come and get her if her owners turn up. Secretly, I hope they don't. I have already fallen in love with the dog.

Chapter Five

When I get to Barrington, I walk to the University from the train station. The advert said 'casual jobs and walk-in interviews this week only', and I hope there is something I can do. When the cottage sells, I will move to Barrington. Probably. There is more chance of finding work in the city, and I could not bear to stay in Foxbeck and witness others living in my home. Because wherever I live, North Star Cottage will always be where my heart is. I push these thoughts aside as the red bricks of the old University come into view.

Today, there is a light breeze, and a few clouds skid across the sky. I am glad it is not so hot. The University campus is large, but I know my way because both my kids came here. Term does not begin again for a few more weeks, and the walkways echo around the sleeping buildings.

At the main reception, I push open the heavy door. Inside the oak-panelled room, there is one woman at the desk. Usually, this room is a clamour of activity.

'Can I help?' she asks.

'Yes. Well, I hope so. I'm looking for a job. Saw your advert online.' For some reason, I feel like a fool.

The young woman slaps a hand on her forehead. 'Oh god! Is that still on there? I meant to take it down. Sorry, all the casual stuff's gone.' She turns to her computer and brings up the Barrington University website so she can take off the advert.

'Don't suppose they have any other vacancies?' I sound desperate. Then again, I am desperate.

She glances at me and smiles. 'I'll check.' I put Big Bag at my feet while she flicks on another screen. 'Can you tutor pure mathematics?'

I laugh. 'Sorry, no.'

'What about stone masonry? We need repair work on the east wing. Knowledge of abseiling is useful but not essential for this position.'

'Not good with heights,' I say.

'Shame. What about a biology lab technician?'

'Will there be dead rats?'

'Probably.' She's laughing now, and I am glad she's here with her bonhomie. So many people on welcome desks are less than welcoming. Something flickers on the screen. I can't make out the words from where I stand. 'What about life modelling for the art class?' She's still reading. 'Sounds like their regular woman has gone sick. The post is just until she gets better.'

'Yeah,' I say. How hard can it be? Standing about while people draw you.

'Really? That's great. Thing is...' – she picks up an old-fashioned telephone and presses in a number – 'today's art class is about to be cancelled because we have no model.'

'I can start today?'

She gives me the thumbs up. I imagine gold coins clinking into a china piggy bank.

'Hi, Phil? Guess what? I've found a model, and she can start straight away.' She laughs. 'Well, I aim to please. Yeah, no problem. I'll send her over right now.' She puts the phone down, then rummages about on a shelf under the counter and finds a form. 'Here's some preliminaries. Could you sign this, please?' She's still smiling. I tick various boxes and sign, and she hands me a map and explains how to get to the fine art department's life drawing studios. As she speaks, she draws a path with a yellow marker pen. Then she hands me a lanyard and explains how the security doors work. I put it over my head. 'When you're done, come back here.'

The next thing I know, I am marching across the campus to the art wing. This is my lucky day. It is a temporary position, but it is a start. The map and her explanation were perfectly clear, but I am completely confused now. Jason did not do fine art, and I am unfamiliar with this part of the campus. And I hate maps. I am standing outside what I think is the correct building according to my map reading. The sign over the door says Natural Science.

'Lost, love?' A young man in overalls carrying a crowbar smiles at me.

'Fine art building?'

'Yep. See that turret? Head for that. Can't go wrong.' Now he mentions it, the receptionist said something about a turret. These days my head is full of cotton wool.

I thank him and get going. This place is enormous.

Barrington University is a historical institution, and the art department is in the original buildings. I climb two flights of stone staircases, find the oak door with the brass plaque marked A24 and go in. The room is lit by long skylights and tall windows. Around a circular dais are easels and tables. A man hurries over, weaving between the easels. He is tall and thin with sandy-coloured hair tied in a skinny ponytail.

The Mid Witch

'Hi! Hi! So glad you're here. You've literally saved the day!' He holds out his hand, and we shake. 'Well, not only the day. Also my skin. Possibly my reputation!' His hands are warm and smooth, and his eyes are blue and full of mirth. As he speaks, a woman comes in carrying a large plastic toolbox, which I assume is full of paints and brushes. 'I'm Phil. Phil Landy.' It is hard to tell how old he is. I imagine he's been wearing the same skinny jeans and beaten-up clogs for years. He could be late thirties or early forties. 'So sorry to rush you. Five minutes to go. Just through here,' he says, leading the way. He opens a door and ushers me into a small room. Inside stands a large woman.

'Morning, Phil!' she calls out.

'Top of the morning to you, Cressida!' he replies. She smiles at me as he says, 'Ava's got the flu. This is? So sorry I didn't ask your name!'

'Lilly.'

'Lilly, Lilly. Lovely Lilly. White in the sunlight. Pure in the morning dew. Sweet perfection the whole day through. Yet I love thee best, sweet Lilly, when your blooms are bright from moonlight,' he trills as he goes out and closes the door.

Cressida comes over and shakes my hand. 'Take no notice of him. He's got verbal diarrhoea.' Then she takes off her shoes, puts them neatly under a chair and begins unbuttoning her blouse.

The room has two doors. From each side, voices of art students setting out their equipment filter in. 'First time at this Uni?' she asks, hanging her blouse on the back of the chair. I am not a slim woman. Who is at my age? But Cressida is twice my size. She's all voluptuous curves and smooth dark skin. Her bra is red and silky, with a diamond clasp at the front. She takes it off and drapes it over her blouse.

Realisation is crashing in on me. In the space of thirty-five minutes, I have become a nude model. Almost. I open the door a fraction. The fine art students are organising their paints and brushes. Phil is drifting about, chatting and helping. My knees are weak. If I leave, I will let everyone down. And if I stay? If I stay, I will have to take my clothes off and go out there for scrutinization. All those eyes focused on my naked, middle-aged, menopausal mum body. Bile rises in my throat. Maybe I could make a run for it through the other door. I turn. Cressida – completely and fabulously naked Cressida – is smiling at me as she adjusts the coloured scarves around her head. 'First time?'

'Yes,' I croak.

'First time's always the worst. But you know what?' She chuckles deeply and comes over, then takes Big Bag from my shoulder and sets it on the floor beside a chair. 'You're going to be fine.' I let her pull my sack dress over my head. I take off my horrible shabby bra, big pants, trainers and socks.

'Now the trick is, don't stare at the floor. It'll make you dizzy. Look out the window and around the room. And relax.' She fluffs my hair over my shoulders and stands back. 'You're a beautiful woman. You've got this.' She lifts a flowered

The Mid Witch

kimono from a hook and shrugs it on. Then she takes a grubby towelling dressing gown and hands it to me. 'Best to bring your own,' she says. It smells a bit, but I put it on anyway. She leads me by the elbow to the door. 'Now be sure to say if you feel cold or hot.' A hot flush is already brewing. 'Don't sit with your legs crossed. You'll get cramps. You only pose for twenty minutes and then have a five-minute break. If you feel funny, just say. Happens to the best of us.' I already feel funny. Horrified, in fact. This is like one of those dreams where you find yourself naked in a public place. 'Remember, you can move your eyes and your ears and breathe.' She opens the door and gives me a gentle push. 'See you for lunch,' she says.

I pick my way between the easels and step onto the dais, which is only a foot higher than the floor yet seems like a stage. 'This is lovely Lilly, our model for the day,' Phil introduces me. The students all say hello, and Phil steps forward and holds out his hand. I stand there like a rabbit caught in a car headlight until I realise he is waiting for me to give him the dressing gown. I take it off. And that's it. I am totally naked in front of thirty strangers.

'How would you like me?' I say.

'Sitting, please, Lilly.'

I sit on the chair and cross my legs. Then uncross them and place my feet together. I should have trimmed my pubic hair. Or shaved. Isn't that what modern women do? Shave it all off? I'd like to fold my arms over my naked breasts. Not wanting to look ridiculously modest, I rest them on the arms of the chair.

'Everybody happy?'

The students mumble yes. Some adjust the angle of their easels. Many are already drawing. Phil hops onto the dais with a cushion, which he puts at my back. 'Hot? Cold?' he says quietly.

'Hot.'

He's across the room, opening windows, and cool air wafts over my naked flesh. I'm glad of the cushion. There is already one on the seat, and I can't help wondering how many naked bums have sat on it. We are on the top floor, and out the window there are birds in the sky and horse chestnut trees. I breathe.

'What do we think about the radio?' asks Phil. There is a general murmur of consent. Classic FM plays Ride of the Valkyries. Perfect. This is the most outrageous thing I have done in my life. Oddly empowered, I lift my chin a little, and Phil smiles at me.

At the first break, I put on the dressing gown, and Cressida pops her head around the door. 'We're taking ten,' she says, flicking her head for me to follow. 'I bet nobody showed you where the toilets are?' I follow her into the corridor. 'How did you get on?' she says, holding open a door marked 'staff only'. She is wearing gold flip-flops, and her toenails are red and glossy.

'Erm. Okay, I guess.' Then I'm grinning.

The Mid Witch

Cressida's laugh is throaty. 'Well done. Knew you could do it.' She pats my arm, and we go into the cubicles and pee.

The morning goes quickly. I am not sure if I am 'sitting' this afternoon, and in true middle-aged woman style, I am afraid to ask. At lunch, Cressida puts on her bra and knickers and then her kimono. 'Can't bear eating with my tits dangling,' she says. Disliking the dressing gown, I get dressed, and she takes me to the refectory. All the students, Phil and another tutor, who I learn is Martha Dee, are sitting at the long tables. 'Lunch is free for us. Perk of the job,' says Cressida, handing me a tray. We take our sandwiches and sit with some students. Everyone is friendly and chatty. And for someone who has spent the morning butt-naked in front of half of them, I am oddly at home with myself.

The afternoon lasts until four, and I am yawning as Cressida and I get dressed. 'Strangely tiring, isn't it? Sitting still all day.'

'God, I'm knackered,' I laugh.

'I've had a text from Sally.'

'Sally?'

'On reception. Reminding me to bring you back so she can sort out a proper pass for you and get you on the rota. They've signed Ava off for three weeks.'

Cressida waits for me while we get the paperwork sorted and then gives me a lift to the station. In the car, I look at the rota. For the rest of the week, I will work all day. I'm glad of the money and surprised at how well paid it is, but I'm worried about the dog.

'Problems?' she asks.

I tell her about the dog who is not actually my dog but is, for the time being, my responsibility – and that I am moving house and have loads of stuff to sort out. Cressida parks at the train station. 'Just bring her. Phil won't mind. And normally, we only model for half days. This whole day thing is because these students are doing an extra fine art module. It's the only way to fit it all in before term starts.'

On the train home, I worry about Ink. Dark clouds have gathered, and when I get off, it is raining hard. I hope she has found a sheltered spot and is not getting too wet. If only I had left the shed open so she had somewhere to go out of the rain. Worse than anything, I worry she has run away and is wandering about looking for someone who will care for her properly. Poor dog. The short bus journey takes ages, and the rain is lashing down with streaks of lightning and rumbles of thunder as I run along Church Lane. My flowery sack dress is stuck to me, and I'm sure Big Bag is half full of water when I reach the garden gate. Sodden blankets lie under the apple tree, and there is no dog. As I trot along the path, I peer into the shrubbery in case she has sought shelter there and call her name. But how can she know that name yet? She is only a dog.

A massive thunderclap frightens me as I fumble for the key, searching through pockets and feeling around among the

The Mid Witch

many items I lug with me daily. At last, I have it in my grasp. It slides out of my hand and hits the doorstep star. When I pick it up, there is a flash of silver sparks. I turn the key in the lock.

Inside, the cottage is safe and warm, and I cannot bear the thought of that animal out in the storm. I chuck Big Bag on the table and head for the under stairs cupboard for boots and a coat. I will go along the lane and see if she has run into the woods.

There she is. She lifts her head from the arm of the old easy chair and thumps her skinny tail. I go over and pat her with my wet hands, and she stands and shakes herself from nose to tail as if wet through.

'Who let you in?' I laugh. 'Was it Bel? Jason?' She follows me into the kitchen and watches as I tip dog food into a bowl. 'Mike, my bastard husband?' She eats, wagging her tail every time I speak. 'I mean Mitch!' I spit out his newly adopted name.

I'm shivering and don't bother to check whether my daughter or son has popped in and taken some of their things. I go upstairs and run a hot bath.

In the night, Ink creeps into my bed. I am still cold, and she lies against me so we are back to back. I can feel her heart beating and hear her soft breath. It is so soothing that I sleep deeply. I wake hours later, my skin on fire and the room stuffy and hot. Ink stays where she is and watches as I strip off my nightie, stand in front of the open window and fan myself with a magazine. Moonlight illuminates the garden, and an owl swoops over the wood. It's beautiful, and if I was asleep, I would miss it. As I fan myself, silver sparks flick into the air and float away into the garden. Ink sighs on the bed. The owl hoots. I have a powerful urge to go outside and wander about. But I must get some sleep. Otherwise, the students will need extra paint for the bags under my eyes.

These night flushes are the worst and last so long. I get a cold flannel, put it on the back of my neck and slurp water from the bathroom tap. Then I lie on top of the covers and think cool thoughts.

Eventually, I sleep, only to wake shaking cold again. I flick the blanket over me, and Ink returns with her warmth.

Chapter Six

The next day I am up early. Partly because I want plenty of time to get ready and partly because I need an appointment with my doctor. Seeing sparks is not good, and it keeps happening.

'We cannot answer your call at this time. Please hold,'

says a chirpy electronic voice. Then the automaton plays a reedy version of the Four Seasons. Just the same few bars from Spring before 'Your call is important to us. Please continue to hold' followed by more violins. I'm sure Vivaldi would turn in his grave if he knew what the modern world was doing to his masterpiece. I carry the phone with me as I eat breakfast, use the loo, pack Big Bag with a dressing gown and flip-flops, take a shower, apply the epilator, moisturise and then consider trimming my pubic hair. I am standing in front of the mirror, nail scissors poised, when 'Welcome to Marswickham Surgery. We may record your call for training purposes. Hello!'

I dive for the phone, which is on the bed. 'Hello, yes, is it possible to make an appointment to see Dr Flemming?'

The receptionist breathes in sharply. 'And what is it about?'

'Well, I'd rather talk to the doctor about it, if you don't mind.'

A sigh. 'How urgent is it?'

I'm not sure. Urgent enough for me to want to see a doctor.

'Are you in any pain?'

'No, not pain. But...'

'So it's not urgent.'

'Well, it might be.'

'Might be urgent. But you're unable to explain the problem.' I can hear her drumming her fingers on the desk.

'It's private.' I'm trying to stay calm.
'Might be urgent. And private.'
'That's right.'
'Name?'
'Doctor Fleming.'
'Your name?'
'Lilly Turner.'

She taps the keyboard. 'Dr Fleming could give you a telephone consultation at ten twenty this morning.'

'No. I'll be at work.' I'll be naked in front of a group of students younger than my own children.

'You're not off sick then?'

'Not yet. No. I'm hoping that a visit with my doctor will ease my symptoms.'

'You have symptoms? What are they exactly?'

'That's what I am going to tell the doctor and not the receptionist.'

She harrumphs. The line goes quiet. Has the bitch cut me off? 'I bet this isn't being recorded for bloody training purposes,' I say and am about to hang up when she speaks.

'You can see Dr Wilson on evening surgery at 6.10.' She hangs up before I can check if she means today. I do not know who Dr Wilson is, but I am so grateful I have an appointment, I kiss Ink on the head.

'Come on, hound. You're coming to work with me.'

I've been doing some research about greyhounds. Apparently, they hate the cold and sitting on hard surfaces. In the discarded things waiting to go to the charity warehouse, there is a stack of fleecy blankets that could be useful for dog beds. I pick a nice thick rainbow patterned one that was Jason's and drape it over Big Bag.

Ink is not afraid of the train and hops on and sits on her blanket as good as gold. I pet her head, which she rests on my lap. On the way to the University from the station, I make a detour through the park so she can stretch her legs. As soon as we arrive, she hunkers down and does the most enormous shit in the middle of the path. It's then I realise I don't have any doggy poop bags.

A man jogs past. 'Hope you're going to clean that up!' he shouts. I root about in Big Bag for a substitute. A tissue, a plastic wrapper, a bit of paper, anything. I keep one eye on the man so I can walk away when he's gone. But he is using a circular running track, and there is a sign: 'Fitness zone. No dogs.' So not even a chance of another dog owner to help me out. The man is back, jogging on the spot beside me. 'It's an offence,' he says, pointing at Ink's massive turd. 'Not clearing up after your dog.'

'She's not my dog,' I say.

'Bloody looks like your dog!' He shakes his head and runs on. I stay where I am.

When he jogs back, I hold up my hand. 'Stop!' He does, which surprises me. 'Look. I am just looking after this dog. And I don't have a poo bag. Now, why don't you help by jogging over to the dog part of the park, asking someone for a bag and then running back here?'

He's stunned.

'Well, go on!' He runs off. I stand there in the empty park. Ink lies on the grass and sighs. Being a new dog owner is a lot like early motherhood. There's a lot of unexpected shit that you don't quite know what to do with. I have another rummage in Big Bag because clearly jogging man has run home to tell his wife about the crazy woman he met in the park. I have nothing I can pick up a turd with, but I find a small piece of chalk in a side pocket and am about to draw a circle around the offence and write 'Dog shit don't tread here' when the jogger returns. He stops, puts his hands on his knees and pants, and then hands me a dog poo bag.

'Thanks,' I say.

'You're welcome.' And away he runs.

I sort the problem, and we head to the University. 'Soon as we get finished, we'll find a pet shop and buy supplies,' I tell Ink. I'm nearly there when I hear pounding footsteps. The jogger has caught me up. In his arms, he has the rainbow fleecy blanket.

'You dropped this,' he says.

'Thanks.'

'Thanks for the workout!'

Ink is a big hit with the art class, and after she has said hello to everyone and let them pet her, she lies on her blanket beside me. Ink thinks nothing of the fact that I am naked.

That non-judgmental acceptance, I muse while Classic FM plays, is part of the nobility of dogs.

The day goes well. At lunch, Cressida and I sit with Phil and the other tutor, Martha. I tell them about the morning jogger and the turd. And they laugh, which is great. When I take Ink for a walk around the University grounds, Phil comes with me. He has found some small plastic bags I can use for the poop.

'You know, both my kids came here, and I've never walked through the gardens,' I say.

'They are lovely. I don't get out as often as I should. Spend most of my time locked in the studios. Always something to do.'

'Been here long?'

He laughs. 'Probably too long. My plan was to teach for a few years and then work abroad. Venice, Rome. You know the sort of dream, painting all day, eating a simple pasta supper and selling my work to local galleries.'

'Don't tell me. Real life took over.'

'Exactly that. The three m's, to be precise.'

'Which are?'

'Marriage, mortgage and money.'

'What does your wife do?'

'Ex-wife. Also a teacher. Ran off with a plumber.'

'My husband's a plumber.'

'I'm sure he didn't run off with Carol.'

'No. He ran off with a hairdresser.'

Phil re-ties his straggly ponytail. 'God, life can be shit.'

'Any kids?'

'No. Just one stepdaughter. It's complicated.'

'Fuck, I hope Mike doesn't have another family. The hairdresser is much younger than me.'

We've walked a circuit and are back at the fine art building. He holds the door and pats my back as we go in. 'Are you getting divorced or waiting for the storm to pass?' he asks.

'To start with, yes, I hoped the storm would pass. Because when you have kids, you try to keep the family together.' We go into the studio, and he fills a bowl of water for Ink. We watch her lap. 'But now, years later...'

'He's been with the hairdresser for years?'

'No. She's quite new. I think. Usually, he flits about, sewing the wild oats he never got the chance to when we were young. I had Belinda at nineteen.' He sits on the wide window ledge. Behind him, the sports pitches are parched and brown from the long, hot summer. 'No, the hairdresser is a recent development.' I am not sure why I am telling him all this.

'Lucky bastard – all those free haircuts,' he says, and I laugh.

'To be fair, his hair never looked better.'

The students come in, and I go to the changing room. The walk has made me hot, and I can't wait to get my clothes off. Maybe I have discovered the perfect occupation for women of a certain age.

After work, Cressida drops me off in Marswickham, where she lives, and I take Ink to the pet shop for supplies. Then we go to the doctors, where the woman on the desk frowns at Ink but does not tell me to tie her up outside.

The waiting room is busy. A worried mother sits with a toddler on her lap. An old man coughs frequently into a cotton hanky. An old lady and her carer happily read the magazines and chat. A teenager and his mother scroll their phones and look furious. All life is here.

My phone bleeps. It is a message from Mike. 'Get an extra key cut and give it to the estate agents. I've instructed Rutherford & Greys. They're in Marswickham. Thanks.'

Typical Mike. He has a key. Why can't he get an extra one cut? Everyone always assumes I have nothing to do. I don't know whether I want to scream or cry.

A young nurse comes in. 'Mrs Turner?'

I follow him into the consulting room. He sits behind the desk. This fresh-faced young man cannot possibly be the doctor. Can he?

'How can I help you, Mrs Turner?'

'Lilly,' I say. I've never really felt like a Mrs.

He glances at his computer screen, waiting for me to speak. He leans forward and pets the dog. This morning, seeing a doctor seemed like a sensible idea. Now I feel like a fraud. I imagine I see sparks, and I should let this young doctor attend to a proper patient, one who is actually sick.

A hot flush grasps my neck. My face is on fire.

The Mid Witch

'How are you feeling Lilly?'

'I'm fine, really.'

I search in Big Bag for a tissue to mop my sweaty brow.

He nods. 'How are you sleeping?'

Sometimes all it takes is the right question. Suddenly I am crying floods of snot and tears as I tell him about my hot flushes and the sparks. He passes a box of tissues, and I blow my nose and try to get it together. While I ramble on, he takes my blood pressure, shines a little torch in my eyes and feels my neck with cool fingers, checking for lumps. 'My emotions are all over the place. One moment I'm fine, then I'm in tears, usually over nothing. I never used to be this weepy.' Ink puts her head on my lap and looks at me. 'And I'm knackered,' I add, for good measure. 'I used to have so much energy. Now I can barely get through the day. I thought once my periods stopped, I'd feel okay again.'

'But you feel rubbish?' he says.

'Total rubbish.'

'What about trying some HRT?'

Ten minutes later, I am marching along Marswickham high street looking for the late-opening chemist.

Chapter Seven

On Saturday, I hope for a lie-in. No such luck. Someone is banging the knocker on my front door. Ink doesn't bark, just sleepily follows me downstairs. The front door is out of use because it is at the back of the house. The cottage faces the ancient road, which is now a public

The Mid Witch

footpath leading into the woods. I wrap my dressing gown around me, push my feet into trainers and go to see what all the fuss is about. The estate agent is tapping a rhythm on the frog-shaped knocker. The sight of him makes me angry. 'What?'

Ink pees in the tall grass that used to be a lawn and then greets him like a long-lost friend. He ignores her skinny wriggle dance, but when Ink rubs against him, pure delight on her face, he asks, 'Whose dog is this?'

It's none of his business. 'What do you want?'

'Mitch told me to collect the key that you haven't bothered to drop off.'

'Because I'm not ready. The house is not ready. And *Mitch* can get his own key cut.'

I stomp along the path around the house, back to the kitchen. He follows, and I hope he will walk right past and leave. No way. He stands firm, and I catch him looking at my hair, which is quite long now and falls in grey and white streaks well past my shoulders.

The dog is still flirting.

'Ink, come,' I say softly. She stops her nonsense and sits on the doorstep star with an adoring expression.

'A key, Mrs Turner. I need to get on with my job, and I need a key.'

'Well, I don't have a spare, so you'll have to wait.'

'I don't know why you old women have to be so bloody awkward. Maybe it's because you don't understand the situation you're in. Your husband is selling his house, and it's time to sort your life out!' He waves an arm at the overgrown garden.

'What! Sort my life out! This house was my mother's before it was ever his and... You know what, I'm going to call your boss. You've no right to come here and harass me in this way.' My fingers tingle, and I put my hands on my hips. Stress – that's what the nice doctor put the sparks down to. And I am certainly feeling bloody stressed with this jerk on my doorstep.

'Why don't you do that? Call the agency, Mrs Turner, and see what they say.' He flicks a business card at me. Actually flicks it. I'm fuming. 'And if you really think you own the property, Mrs Turner, then do us all a favour and get some proof.' He strides along the path.

'What's your fucking name?' I call after him. He carries on walking and ignores me until he is through the gate.

'Grant fucking Rutherford,' he calls back.

I pick up the embossed business card. Rutherford & Grey, Allingshire's Premier Estate Agents. I tear it in half. Sparks fly.

After a burst of anger, I am usually ashamed of myself. My natural response is tears of remorse. I make some tea and sit at the kitchen table. I feel fine. Perhaps I should insist that Mike – *Mitch* – put the house on with a different agent. That would show the cocky bastard. I will tell Mike how rude he is

The Mid Witch

and get it sorted. Once, although it is long ago now, he used to be protective.

There is a message on my phone from Bel. She's sending Brian over to give me a hand. The twins have a party to go to and she needs to pop into school for a meeting. My daughter and her husband are early birds, and I dash upstairs to get dressed. Brian arrives mid-morning. By this time, I have lugged all the boxes and bags that need to go to the charity warehouse to the garden gate. During the week, a slice of chocolate cake for Ron and Tony, the bin men, sorted out the rubbish pile. Nice to know that cake is still a popular currency.

Brian looks harassed as he gets out of the car. I steer Ink into the easy chair and close the lounge door so she cannot run into the road. Then I take the last two bags and go to meet him. 'Coffee?'

Brian shakes his head and picks up a couple of stuffed boxes. 'This for the charity place?'

'Yeah. Sorry there's so much of it.' We carry the donations to his car in the lane. He pops the boot, folds the back seats down and, together, we load up. 'There's some things in the house I thought might be useful for school. Toys and books.'

'I'll drop this lot, and then I'll call back,' he says, kissing me on the cheek. 'Can't believe you're going.' We both look back at the cottage.

'Me neither. Be odd not to be here after all this time. Shall I bring the school stuff down?'

'Yeah. I don't think it will rain.'

After I wave him off, I put the rest of the things by the gate. I suppose the new owners will cut the yew tree and make a new entrance. One that is big enough for cars. They will tarmac some of the garden, build a garage and put an extension on the cottage. The modernisation it has avoided all these long years is about to happen, and I feel like a traitor.

The cottage seems twice the size when the toys and books for school are by the gate. It is a shame to make another mess. However, I must tackle the cupboard under the stairs. I start with the coats and hats hanging on the back of the door and then the piles of shoes and boots. Soon the lounge is full again, and the mess is worse than before. Ink is enjoying herself. She goes in and out of the cupboard with me, sniffing and carrying old shoes into the garden to chew. She finds it exciting when I have to crawl in to reach the items under the narrow slope of the stairs. Pressed into the gap are a few boxes that are thick with dust. They must have been there for years.

Ink gives a quiet woof to tell me someone is here, and when I go to the kitchen window, Brian is driving away. He has taken everything, and for that, I am glad. But there is a pang in my heart. I would have liked to chat about the grandchildren. I wanted to see the twins and my daughter. But these days, kids are so busy. Spare time is an old-fashioned concept. Parents fill every weekend with activities and homework projects. There is no space in their lives for mucking about or visiting grandmothers.

The Mid Witch

I sit on the doorstep in the September sun with a hunk of bread and cheese and a mug of tea. 'It's no good feeling sorry for myself, Ink.' She looks up from the blanket bed I have made for her beside me. 'They're busy and have their own lives, and you know what? It's time I made my own life too.'

I go into the sitting room with its fresh pile of junk. I can't believe so much fitted into that cupboard. After I vacuum, I scrub the old, tiled floor on my hands and knees. Each square tile is a different colour and design. There are plants and many animals. Birds, cats and dogs, antlered stags and fish. Some of them I remember from games of hide and seek when I was a child. Now the cupboard is completely empty, I discover more. A dog like Ink, with long running legs, stretched out. A magpie carrying a branch. A star like the one on the doorstep. They are beautiful and must be as old as the cottage.

I hang the coats I usually wear on the hooks at the back of the door. Then I stack my wellies, boots and shoes in a neat row. The things that were right at the back are filthy, so I give them a wipe with the floor cloth. Two are deed boxes, and I put them on the kitchen table. The others are full of photo albums and other memorabilia. I make more tea and open one of the deed boxes.

Inside, it is dust free, and the labels are handwritten by my mother and grandmother. They labelled one section 'Lil', which is what my grandmother always called me. Inside is a pack of school photographs. Then a fat envelope marked 'birth certs, etc.' I take each birth certificate out and lay them on the table. A piece of family history all in a row. My mother. Her mother. My great-great-grandmother. And so on. Five generations of women. All the certificates have the surname Blackwood, including my mother's. Then there is a family tree written on thick paper in loopy writing. Only the women are named and dated. Details of their deaths are added. One woman is called Bethany. I am surprised to learn she was born in 1702 and died by fire in 1769. As far as I know, there has never been a fire in the cottage. Perhaps she died at her place of work. Only one of her children named on the family tree made it into adulthood. Infant mortality must have been heart-breaking in the 1700s.

Ink comes in from the garden, stretching her long legs and arching her back, and the magpie swoops onto the window ledge. 'It's that late?' I ask. There is a slight chill now the sun is going down, and I smell autumn in the air. I feed the animals – since I visited the pet shop, I have proper bird food – and watch them eat for a moment. Then I take out my own birth certificate. I am not surprised to learn that my surname is not Wood but Blackwood. But I am shocked that my name is not Lilly but Lilith. 'Lilith Blackwood. My name is Lilith Blackwood,' I say. Ink and Maud look up from their meals.

I pull out all the documents in a section marked 'North Star.' The deeds of the cottage are in my name – gifted to me by my mother. Then I find the most important paper of all, which I'd never known existed. It is a document signed by my

The Mid Witch

husband stating that North Star Cottage is mine, and that, after my death, it will become the property of my children.

The letterhead says 'Cranford, Holstein and Wigg; family solicitors since 1827'. The address is in Barrington. I look them up online. Their website is slick and modern. Further inspection of the deeds to the cottage seems to show that I also own the woods and the two neighbouring fields. All the land around the cottage is mine. This is most odd, as my mother never mentioned owning the fields or the woodland. Yet here it is in black and white. Two vast fields and a small wood.

I navigate to the contact page for Rutherford & Grey, Allingshire's Premier Estate Agents. With delight, I leave them a message that I do, in fact, own the property and that they can take it off the market. I try to call Mike, who, of course, does not answer, so I leave a message.

Ink and I walk along Church Lane in the dusk, and when we come back into the garden, the moon peeps over the trees. How cosy it all looks. Cosy and safe and mine. An immense weight has lifted from my heart. 'We'll need money, Ink. But we'll think of something.'

Chapter Eight

That night I go to bed early and sleep. I don't have a hot flush. I don't get up to pee. Nor do I lie awake wondering what the future holds. In the morning, I stay in bed with the dog curled beside me and watch the trees outside. They are mostly green, but a few leaves have

The Mid Witch

changed to orange. Summer is becoming Autumn, which I love. The coolness, the smell of rain and the long, moon-filled nights. I can't find my slippers. Ink has a thing for them, so I pad downstairs barefoot, pulling my old dressing gown around me, and let Ink into the garden, where she does her morning poop in the usual place on the grass near the path. Ink is a big dog; I'll easily find it later and clear it up when I've found my shoes. Ink also has a thing for my backdoor clogs.

I am amazed that I am up and don't feel tired when it is only six thirty. It must be years since I had an entire night's sleep, and I feel drunk. Sleep drunk.

After feeding the dog, I make tea and toast and eat it wandering around the garden. Ink drinks from the birdbath, which is balanced on a large stone. Rufus, my mother's dog, did the same. I once asked her why they did that when they had clean water in the house. She said they preferred this water because it was moon blest. Maud, the magpie, hops along the cobbled path. The greyhound mooches behind me.

An overgrown gate leads into the woods. This is a public footpath, but I cannot think when I last saw a walker pass this way. When I was a child, people often stopped at the cottage, and my mother gave them tea and cake for a small fee.

After pulling the ivy from the gate, I get it open and go into the wood. Maud takes wing and flies into one of the oak trees that stand like sentinels either side of the track that once was a main road. 'These are our woods, Ink. Who knew?' I walk for a while before I remember I am still in my dressing gown and have nothing on my feet. Also, the dog is not on the lead. Since she arrived, I have not let her off, afraid she will not return. She is, after all, a stray who does not know her name. While I've been musing about nothing in particular, she has wandered off. I turn about, looking for her. There she is – a dark shape moving through the grass of the field beyond the trees. So far away, she is a black speck. If she runs, there is no chance of me catching her, and a massive sadness washes over me. I love this dog, and in a few short days, I have come to believe she is mine. How could I be so stupid? She doesn't even have a collar on.

'Ink,' I call, and she ignores me. She is busy hunting a squirrel. I call again, 'Ink, Ink!' No response. Then I put a finger and thumb in my mouth and blow. Nothing happens, although I used to whistle like this when I was a kid. I try again, desperation rising in my chest as the dog trots away. I blow. Nothing. Then I adjust my fingers, and out comes a sound so loud that Maud flaps her wings in alarm in the branches above my head.

The greyhound's head snaps up, and I whistle in a sweeping loop like a builder on scaffolding. Then she runs. She lowers her head and stretches out her body in a great gathering stride. I have never seen her run before, and her speed takes away my breath. She leaps over the fence that encloses the wood and gallops through the leaves. When she gets to me, we embrace in a ridiculous hug. Rolling on the ground together, both of us grinning. And I know then that this dog is mine. She will always be mine.

We go home. As we come around the side of the cottage, Mike is walking up the path from the lane. He is an advert for washing powder in white jeans and trainers with a black hoody. He is always pristine, even when he's working. I'm sure few plumbers work in latex gloves. Not that he does much plumbing these days. Not since he started 'The Water Works'.

'Why don't you answer your fucking phone!' he says. His face is red above the beard he has grown. He is more tanned than normal.

I'm not sure where my phone is, now that I think about it. I say nothing. Brush some leaves out of my hair and re-tie my dressing gown, which is covered in dust, twigs and moss.

I mentioned the rude estate agent in my phone message, and my heart softens. Mike is worried. That's why he's rushed over. I smile, and he takes a deep breath. 'We need to talk,' he says.

Ink wanders past him and sticks her long snout into my tea mug, which I'd left on the path. 'That's got to go. Never going to get this place sold if it's a mess *and* stinks of dog.' Ink carries on drinking, big globs of tea flicking from her chops. I've never heard her make so much noise and I try not to smile.

'I left you a message. I found the deeds.'

'Yeah. I've been trying to get hold of you. Managed to sort

out a solicitor's appointment for tomorrow morning. It's a formality and won't take a minute. But you need to go in and be on time.' He's using his let's get down to business voice on me now like I'm his apprentice. 'Thorisson's in Marswickham. You need to be there tomorrow. At 9.30. They squeezed us in.'

'And do what exactly?'

Mike glances at the sky. 'Sign the papers so we can sell the cottage.'

'What papers?'

He breathes in deeply and answers in an unnaturally calm voice. 'Legal papers, Lilly, that say we both want to sell the cottage.'

'I'm not selling. North Star Cottage has belonged to my family for generations. That's why my mother had you sign that agreement when we moved in.'

I want to say more. That the cottage needs to stay with me, and I need to be here. Now more than ever. It is where I belong. But Mike is rubbing his face with his hands. 'Do you know how much bloody trouble I've gone to to get this appointment? Do you?'

There's a familiar sensation in the pit of my stomach and in my chest. Guilt. Everything is my fault. I'm nodding. Looking at my feet. Ink comes between us and gives herself a shake. A few globs of tea flick onto Mike's pristine jeans.

'For fuck's sake!'

He tries to brush it off with the sleeve of his black hoody.

The Mid Witch

Ink leans against my legs, and Maud swoops in and settles into the apple tree in her usual place, tail flicking up and down. Mike gives up, puts his hands into the pouch pocket and gets himself together. Patiently he says, 'It's time to move on, Lil. Sell this old dump and make a new start.' His voice is soft and kind now, and he steps closer. 'I'll send one of my lads over to cut the lawn. Give you a hand with the fallen tree. What about that?' He reaches out to pull me into an embrace like he always does when he has won an argument. Even now, after all these years, I am ready to fall into his arms. Grateful for any crumb of affection from the man I still love.

Ink barks. The sound is so loud and deep we both step back. I've never heard her bark before. She is standing between us. Head lowered. Lips curled – revealing long, hooked teeth. Mike is ruffled, I can tell, even though he ignores the dog. 'Are you looking after this mutt for a friend?'

'She's mine.'

'Well, it'll have to go, Lil. It's clearly out of control. You won't be able to look after a dog in a flat. Bel won't be bringing the twins over with that around. Have you worked out how much dogs cost?' His voice is all reasonable again as he organises me. Makes me fit into his way of thinking.

Ink's black coat is gleaming in the September sun. She has not moved. I'm not sure if it is the sleep or the hormones, but something in me clicks.

'No, Mike.' My voice is calm. Oddly, I am not angry or sad.

'Fine! Keep the dog,' he says as if it's up to him and he's doing me a massive favour.

'No, Mike, I am not selling my home.'

'You don't have a choice, I'm afraid. By law, we both own it because we both live here. I pay the bills. That gives me the right.'

'You haven't lived here for the past twenty fucking years.' He opens his mouth to speak, but Ink cuts him off with another colossal bark. 'You just visited occasionally. And the last ten years, you've not been here at all!'

'I think we both know...'

'Coming back for a comfort fuck doesn't count. I've been here raising our kids like a single parent for a bloody long time. You're right. We need to move on. It's time we got a divorce.'

The word divorce has never passed between us. We never officially split up. Mike just drifted away on the pretext of work and came back less and less. He'd leave a bit of money in a joint account for me, and the kids and I just carried on, always believing that we would sort it out. He'd see sense. Family life would resume as normal. Then the family was gone.

'A divorce lawyer will say I own half – or more than half.' He puts his hands back into the pouch. Even through the material, I can see clenched fists. 'Be an adult about this. We don't want to get the courts involved and go through months of nonsense and expense when we can sit down and get it all sorted out with a bit of straight thinking. Simple split down the middle. Easy-peasy.'

'No, Mike. Because I have the legal evidence to prove you have no claim.'

'Legal fucking evidence! Let's have a look at the legal evidence, shall we?' He strides across the lawn, and I wish I had kept quiet. I have no copy, and all the papers are still on the kitchen table.

Ink is on the doorstep before he gets there. She barks continuously until he takes a few paces back. Then she stops. 'Call this dog off!'

I walk behind Ink and stand on the doorstep. The stone is cool, and the star's rays press against my bare feet.

'It's time to go, Mike.'

Ink is growling. A long, steady, deep rumble. Mike walks away and then turns around. 'Just tell me one thing. How do you think you're going to afford to live here? You've no money, no job and, at your age, no prospects. Not that you ever had any prospects. You were lucky I married you in the first place!'

And that's when I first use magic.

I stretch out my hand, flick my fingers, and the dog poo rolls onto the path. Mike's white trainers squish into it. He tries to wipe it off on the grass, hops about and loses his balance, then falls. Now it is on his white jeans. His swearing is epic.

'I think he'll have to get changed,' I say to Ink as we go in and close the door.

I take a shower and wash my hair. Usually, if I have words with Mike, I am jittery for ages after. I go back over the argument and blame myself and shed a few tears. Today is different. I am different. I towel myself off, peel away the old hormone patch and apply a fresh one in a new place on my backside. It's a fiddly job. Ink is lying upside down on the unmade bed, watching me with a big doggy grin on her longhound face. I rub her tummy for her.

Chapter Nine

On Monday, I do my modelling stint at the University. This is the last session, known as touch-up day, and the students finish early. Before they leave, they present me with a bunch of orange roses and a collar for Ink. The new collar is wide and multicoloured. Each student has painted a motif onto it. I am really moved.

When I'm dressed again, I pop into the studio to say goodbye to Phil. Ava, the life model I have covered for, is better now, and I will fill in as needed – which won't be until a few weeks later, when Cressida hopes to take a long weekend.

As soon as I'm through the door, Phil comes over, all smiles. 'Thanks so much. I don't know what we would have done. Well, I suppose they could have painted me,' he laughs. Ink is still lying on the dais. I find her lead in Big Bag and clip it onto the new collar.

'Would you?'

'What? Take my clothes off? Sure. Wouldn't be the first time. But I think you make a better painting.'

This is a fascinating topic, and I would like to know more about Phil and his nude modelling. I wonder what he looks like without his clothes. Lean and bony, most probably.

'Did you ever have a look?' he says, changing the subject. I never have. Not once. I don't go to that end of the room if I can help it, and if I do, I keep my eyes on the floor. I'm not keen on my reflection standing, and that's when I'm sticking out my chest and sucking in my stomach. I certainly don't want to face images of myself seated with rolls of fat around my midriff and sagging boobs.

'At least come and look at your dog,' he says, taking me by the elbow. 'Always tricky, painting animals. They don't sit still, although, to be fair, Ink took her job very seriously.' Ink thumps her skinny tail at the sound of her name. 'Black fur is especially difficult. Very easy to get it wrong and make it look fake.'

I let him lead me over to the line of easels, which he has set out in an arc. There I am. Thirty times. Each different, and yet they are still me. 'They're so talented,' I say, and I can't help but forget the model is myself as I admire the way the light plays on bare skin. Somehow Ink's sleek black pelt emphasises my nakedness. And where my pose never changes, Ink is different in each one. Sometimes she sleeps curled in a ball or stretched out or lying on her back with her legs in the air. She stands, sits and walks behind the chair.

I am aware of Phil's gaze as I observe myself. I'm surprised at the depictions. It's just me – bespectacled, naked old me with stretch marks and greying pubic hair – and I'm okay with the truth of this. 'This is my favourite,' says Phil, tweaking the easel. Ink has her head on my knee. The dog and I are looking at each other, and I have the faintest smile. There is something sensual in the contrast of pale skin and gleaming black fur. I turn away, not wanting to know who painted it.

'Coming to lunch?'

'No. I've got an errand to run in town,' I say, putting Big Bag over my shoulder and picking up Ink's lead. She stretches and gives herself a quick shake.

'See you in a couple of weeks, then?'

'Yeah, going to cover for Cressida.'

'Be nice to see you before then?'

Our eyes meet, and I blush. He's walking over with his phone. Oh my god, is he going to ask for my number? I'm a giddy teenager. 'We should get together. Have a coffee. Walk the dog.'

He's obviously looking for some friendship. It's not as if he's asking me to dinner. In my stomach, a stone of disappointment falls.

'Yeah, that would be nice,' I say, looking up at him. He's smiling. Not the smile of pleasant understanding he uses in the classroom. This is a proper grin, and I grin back. Before I have time to process this mutual flirtation, he slips his hand under my hair, holds the back of my neck, leans down, and kisses me. He pulls me against him all tongues and passion. I drop Big Bag and Ink's lead. Phil is an expert kisser, and he smells nice. Some sort of lime and musk aftershave that is very subtle. Every time I break off, he nuzzles my neck with little nips and licks and finds my mouth again. It's the longest first kiss of my life.

When he stops, he laughs, then smacks his mouth with the back of his hand as if he has just quenched his thirst. 'God, I've wanted to do that for a while.' I stand there, embarrassed and excited. I thought the days of somebody fancying me were gone.

It's been so long since I've had a proper kiss, I step closer and, taking his shirt in both hands, pull him near so that we kiss again. God, it's blissful.

When we break off, Ink has settled back onto her pile of blankets on the dais. Phil takes me by the hand and leads me into his walk-in cupboard. I've never been in here. There are shelves of art supplies and books. Jars of brushes and bottles. He closes the door and slides a little bolt across. 'Welcome to my office,' he says. There is a sagging, two-seater sofa piled with sketch pads, and he clears them away with a sweep of his arm, sending everything crashing to the floor. He leads me over, and we sit down. He kisses my neck, and I breathe in the smell of linseed oil and turpentine while the rain patters on the skylight. The sack dress I'm wearing is not conducive to a good grope. There are no buttons to undo or dainty straps to pull down. Instead, it is a practical pull over your head garment in a flowery, stretchy cotton mix with long sleeves and a high neck.

'I want your skin, Lilly,' he murmurs.

'I will if you will,' I say with a laugh. He gets up and drags his shirt over his head, then stands there grinning. I stay where I am, eyebrows raised playfully, until he takes off his jeans, which he does in one motion, jeans and pants together. He's not wearing socks.

I don't know where to look. Well, I'd like to stare at his cock, but that feels oddly impolite, so I stand and take off my knickers. Then I slither my hands inside my dress and take off my bra. This is a tactical move. My underwear is awful. Amusing that this is what embarrasses me – the faded undies – and not being naked. I slip the sack over my head, and he steps closer, guiding me to him so our bodies touch. He's warm, and his flesh smells nice. The same lime and musk as his face. He's skinny and toned, not one bit of spare flesh, and as we kiss, his hard cock presses against me. Phil sits me back down on the sofa, pulls a seat cushion onto the floor for his knees and kneels between my legs. I run my hands down his back as he kisses my breasts. He's very good at this. Not so soft I can't feel it and not so rough it hurts. I pull him back to my mouth and reach for his cock, which is long and slim. Much longer than Mike's, in fact. That's when I realise I am about to have sex with a man who is not my husband. Mike is the only man I have ever been with. This is surreal.

Phil makes a low moan as I lightly stroke him. All the way down and over his tight balls and back again. He rests his head on my shoulder while I do this. Then he moves out of reach, which is easy as he is much taller than me. We're kissing again, which is the best, and his fingers are in my pubic hair and then amongst the folds of flesh. My clitoris is under the soft pads of his fingers, and as good as that feels, all I want is his cock inside me. His fingers find the entrance to my vagina, and as he attempts to slip them in, I remember that I am dry. A small intake of breath makes him stop, and he sits back on his heels. I am disappointed. Damn the menopause. He probably thinks I am not turned on because of my lack of wetness. He stands up, then goes to a drawer and finds a jar of petroleum jelly. 'Will this do?' he asks with a twinkle in his eye. He kneels again, and I take the pot off him and scoop some onto my fingers. I lubricate his cock in slow, easy strokes. Then he pulls my hips forward, and I help guide him in.

It's been a long time – years, in fact – but my body remembers. And Phil is very good at fucking. I am not sure if it is the rhythm or the angle he finds or the strange thrill of having a different cock inside me, but I'm soon moaning like a terrible actress in a porn movie. When his pace quickens, I come, which surprises me. Lately, sex has been so far from my mind, I don't even bother to pleasure myself. It must be the HRT.

His climax is soon after. I expect him to grunt like Mike, but Phil's release is accompanied by a long sighing 'Ahhhhh.' I bite my lip to stop myself from laughing, and we stay locked together while he gets his breath back. 'Oh god. This wasn't planned.' He looks around, and we just about manage, with a bit of shuffling together, to reach a kitchen roll on the shelf. He breaks off some so we can catch the mess. Then he washes himself in a small sink full of paint brushes and pulls on his clothes while I sit with my knees together. 'I'll check the dog while you sort yourself out,' he says.

When I emerge fully clothed, he is sitting on the edge of

the dais with Ink. He looks rumpled and sexy. I feel good. Sexy. Carefree.

'Are you sure you won't come to lunch?'

'No, I really need to run an errand in town,' I say, checking the clock on the wall. My god, we've been bonking for forty-five minutes. 'You should get a move on, or you'll miss lunch.'

'And I'm starving now!' He hands me a scrap of paper and a pencil. 'My phone's dead. Can you write your number down? I'll call.'

The corridor is crowded, and I stop a few times so students can pet Ink. She's popular and delighted to be made a fuss of. I smile and smile not so much for the love of a dog, although I do love this dog, but because of how I feel. I've just had crazy art cupboard sex with a much younger man. It's all I can do to stop myself from running back in there, taking all my clothes off and screaming, 'More!'

In Big Bag I have a sandwich for myself and something for Ink so we can walk through the park before I find the solicitors. I'm organised. That makes a change. The HRT has really helped with my brain fog. What's worse is that I did not realise I had it – the fog. Only now, after a few weeks of hormone replacement, am I acknowledging the many symptoms from which I was suffering. The sweaty flushes, constant peeing and fatigue have slipped away. I'm sleeping for the first time in years and am not overwhelmed by everyday tasks.

The Mid Witch

We quicken our pace toward the park, Ink beside me doing what I think of as her eggshell trot. I know now which area allows dogs, and as soon as we are in the open space, I let her off for a roam. She likes to hunt squirrels under the trees and run a few laps around the lawn. A light drizzle starts, and I find a plastic rain poncho – one of two that live in the depths of Big Bag, saved after a wet visit to the zoo when the kids were small. Both are animal themed. I pull it over my head and become a waterproof gorilla. Rain patters on my head, which I find oddly satisfying. 'No such thing as bad weather. Just bad clothes,' I say to Ink, adjusting the poncho on my shoulders so that I don't trip over. 'Come on. We'll eat our sandwiches on the bandstand.' The leaves are already falling after the hot, dry summer, and Ink chases a few across the parched grass as the wind takes them. The leaves are too slow. Ink dips her head to do what her body does best: run. She's crazy fast, and a couple under an umbrella turn to watch as she streaks past.

I put my fingers to my lips and whistle. The trill reaches out to her. It's like a thread between us. She always comes back. I whistle again, but Ink is deaf to my plea and carries on over the lawn and through the hedge arch into the forbidden fitness zone. I can't see her now, and I'm afraid she might run into the road. I chase after her in a panic-induced, panting, middle-aged, boob-joggling run. Unlike the dog, I'm not built for speed.

I joggle through the arch. Ink is cantering around the

track with a jogger, her mouth pulled back in a doggy grin, tail circling in an attempt to run and wag at the same time. The pair come closer, and I recognise her running companion. It's that bastard estate agent.

Grant Fucking Rutherford is shirtless, sprinting around the track in battered trainers and red shorts. What a prat. I hope he won't recognise me in my gorilla poncho and will jog on past. No such luck. He slows to a walk and stops ten paces in front of me. Panting. He has tattoos. Black and grey over his shoulders and biceps. Strange swirling patterns that glisten on his wet skin. For a man his age, he's in great shape.

'No dogs in the dog-free zone,' he says, and I nod, and when Ink comes back to me, I grab her collar, clip on her lead and walk on. He didn't recognise me. How could he? I'm entirely covered in a one-size-fits-all gorilla poncho. I keep my eyes on the hedge arch and walk with purpose.

I am almost through when he calls after me, 'Oh! Mrs Turner! Before you go back to the zoo...' He's alongside me and is jogging on the spot. What is it about joggers? Can't they stand still? I have a powerful urge to kick him in the nuts. I pull Ink under the poncho to keep her dry, and she presses against me. She needs a coat. 'I'll be over in the morning to re-instate the For Sale sign. I won't bother to knock.'

'I'm not selling. So you can come over and take your sign away.'

'Really? You better make it legal or have a conversation...'

The Mid Witch

'That's what I'm about to sort out, Mr Fucking Rutherford.' I march onward, leaving him there in the rain. All wet with his strange tattoos.

I can't stop myself from looking back through the arch. He's standing where I left him, his tilted-back face exposed to the downpour. He's obviously a nutter. All I can think of is getting out of the park and away from him. I don't bother going to the bandstand to eat lunch. I get the map I have saved on my phone and head for the solicitors, and Ink trots happily beside me under the poncho. Together, we are a six-legged gorilla.

Cranford, Holstein and Wigg are tucked away in a narrow side street. The door is black with a brass knocker in the shape of a hand. Pots of white cyclamen guard the steps, and I check the plaque on the wall to be sure this is not a house. A notice invites me to 'please knock and enter'. Inside, I take off the poncho and pack it away, and Ink gives herself a shake. The room is small, with a long empty desk in the middle. An old woman comes in. 'Can I help?'

'Do you mind the dog?'

'No, no, not at all.' She comes around the desk and pets Ink, and we chat about dogs for a bit. Then I tell her about finding the old documents and show her the letterhead. 'How fascinating,' she says, looking at me over her spectacles. Her eyes are bright blue. 'You must be Fanny's daughter!' She gives me a hug. 'I'm Joan. Gosh, you look like your mum. So sad when she died. Some people you never stop missing.' I look at her closely, trying to remember her. My mother had so many friends. I always wish I'd inherited her gregariousness.

Joan holds the paper to the light. 'They used to use a watermark, back in the day when good quality paper mattered. Before all this email nonsense. Can you see it?' Joan goes to the desk. 'Let me find my other specs. No, must be upstairs. There were several designs.'

'There's a snake and a rose,' I say. The watermark is intricate and beautiful.

'Lovely.' She presses a button on an intercom phone. 'Lilith Blackwood has just wandered in. Shall I send her up?' Joan is chuckling as she opens a small door, nods for me to go through and then closes it behind me. There is a narrow tunnel staircase with threadbare carpet and brass stair rods. As I climb, I remember. I've been here before when I was a small child. I recall the quiet stillness. The way no noise filters through from other parts of the building or from the town outside. My mother left me at the top of the stairs when she went through the door at the top, and I waited a long time with our dog, Rufus, for company. I traced the swirling carpet pattern with my finger and tried to listen to what was being said. When she came out, she was sad and worried for days. Even the dog knew something was wrong.

At the door, I hesitate. Perhaps I should go to another solicitor. Then an elderly man greets me. 'Well, well, well,' he says, holding me at arm's length. 'Lilith Blackwood at long last. Come on in.' No one has ever called me by my true name before today. 'I'm Walter. Walter Cranford,' he says. Sprightly is the best word to describe him. His office is a library. He leads me to a pair of leather chairs, and we sit. Ink likes him, which I take as a good sign. She puts her head in his lap and stands quietly while he mutters and strokes her shiny black head with his gnarled hands.

'Well, you wouldn't be here unless you'd found your mother's things. Show me what you've got.'

I hand him the big envelope, and he pulls over a side table on wheels and lays out the documents as he reads them. I wait patiently. Ink lies on the rug and sleeps.

When he's finished, he takes off his glasses and puts on another pair.

'Everything is in order. You must have questions.'

'Are these legal? I mean, do I actually own North Star Cottage?'

'Legal? Yes. Drew up these papers myself. When I wore a younger man's clothes.' He laughs at his own joke and then is serious. 'Yes. The cottage is all yours, along with the surrounding grounds. The wood, two fields and the church and its grounds.'

'The church?'

'Yes. Long since bought by one of your ancestors. For peace of mind...' His voice trails off as if he wants to say more. 'They're all there in the graveyard. The Blackwoods. Old family tradition.'

My mind is reeling as I remember the birth certificates

and the signature in the *Book of Shadows*. Bethany Blackwood. I have so many questions. Each one is clamouring for attention.

'The only thing is, you can't sell. If, for some reason, you don't want to be there, then it passes to your children.'

I think of the mounting bills and my overdraft. The electricity and water. The council tax. The many repairs that are needed. Mike used to pay for these. Now, with no savings or a proper job, I am in dire straits.

'I wonder if I can afford it. The cottage.'

Walter gets up with a grunt and totters out of the room. When he returns, he has a box file under his arm. He puts it on the table and roots through. 'I almost forgot,' he says, pulling out a wad of documents and changing his glasses to look at them. 'Fanny... Well, how to put it? Fanny had a very well-developed sense of forward perception.' He chuckles, taps the paper and then hands it to me. 'She was most concerned about – I'm sorry, what's he called, your wayward husband?' His eyes twinkle over his spectacles.

'Mike.'

'Ahh, yes. Michael Turner. The plumber?'

'That's right.'

'Fanny foresaw problems down the line for you. With Mike. So she ensured the house would remain yours and she rented the surrounding fields. The money from that has accrued nicely.'

In disbelief, I start to read the paper he has handed me.

The Mid Witch

'You're not filthy rich. But you are a woman with means. Which brings me to a very important point.' I put down the paper, and he asks, 'What are you going to do about Michael Turner?'

'Divorce. Not much point in trying to stick together now the kids have left home.'

'Exactly. Ms Lilith Blackwood, may I provide the necessary legal papers?'

'Yes.' I take a deep breath, and Ink gets up from her snooze and stretches.

'Good. Come with me, my dear, and we'll get everything sorted. And if you have questions, just pop back.'

Walter takes me into another office and hands the proceedings to a young man called Derick. An hour later, when I step onto the street, everything has changed, including the weather. The sun shines on the wet pavements as Ink and I head for the pet shop in Barrington to buy her a coat and organise a dog food delivery. I am no longer overdrawn at the bank. All my outstanding bills are paid, and I am free. The money from the field rental is a considerable sum, but one thing I know about money is that it never lasts. If I want to stay at the cottage, I need to earn more money. A bit of nude modelling is not enough. I'm not getting any younger, and without a pension, I need something to fund my impending old age. A way to save. A way to avoid becoming a financial burden to my kids.

On the bus, someone has left the free magazine *Alling-*

shire County on the seat. I flick through it, not taking much notice until I come to an article about a woman who has transformed her home into a stylish bed and breakfast establishment. I look her up on my phone. The prices she charges are amazing. 'This could be us, Ink. North Star Cottage bed and breakfast.'

When I get off the bus, I walk along Church Lane in the fading light and go into the churchyard to my mother's grave. How could she know that one day I would need money and the security of the cottage? 'Thank you,' I say as I put the orange roses the students gave me beside her headstone.

Ink is snuffling about, and I wander after her. I like peaceful graveyards. I walk along the cobbled path, listening to the wind in the trees. Like my house, St Gutheridge and All Angels faces away from the lane toward the ancient road that is now a footpath. I amble past the church to the oldest part of the graveyard. Here, the inscriptions on the headstones are indiscernible, weatherworn and ivy-covered.

A stone wall separates the consecrated ground from the field. In the far corner, the wall curves out to encompass ancient headstones. It is as if they set these outside the churchyard, and then, for a reason I cannot guess, they brought them into the fold of the holy. I walk through the weeds to get a closer look. Here the dead are long forgotten. I try to read the epitaphs, running my fingers over the ridges. Dates and names filter through my touch as if I read braille. None bear the name Blackwood.

The Mid Witch

A headstone in the furthest curve of the wall sits askew, small and inconsequential. The half-light shows pointed lines carved into the stone. Even before I pull away the ivy, I know I have found her. The star on my doorstep is on this stone, and beneath is the name Bethany Blackwood. I scrape away lichen to find the date and am amazed at the family history I have uncovered. I sit on my heels and make a low whistle, and Ink comes over for a sniff. 'She was 66. That's a good innings for the time.' I have a dip of sadness for my mother, who died, by today's standards, quite young. Cancer took her at forty-five. Above, the trees rustle in the wind, and a few raindrops fall on me. A blackbird warns the other birds of Ink's presence in their sanctuary. It is nearly dark, and I should get back. But Ink is most interested in the gravestone and begins a concerted digging effort at the base.

'Come, Inky dog. Time to go.' Ink carries on, and I am glad no one else is here to see my hound digging up the graveyard. I hook my finger under her collar, but she scoots away from me and begins digging again. 'Ink! Come on!' I say. In a few moments, the hole she has made is big, and I am concerned. I tug her collar, and she tugs back. She's a big, muscular dog. It is hard to dissuade her when she sets her mind on something. Her head dips into the hole. She sniffs and puffs. Moves some soil with her nose and snorts loudly. I shove the soil back in place with my foot. 'Good girl. No more digging today. Come on. Let's go home,' I say, and she wags her tail and trots off. There is something unusual about this dog.

The cottage is pretty in the half light, nestled in the overgrown garden, and as Maud flies to greet us, relief washes over me. North Star Cottage is mine, and I can stay. I stand and cry and laugh as the silly bird struts up and down the garden gate.

Big spots of rain fall on the path, and Ink trots ahead of me to the door. Her new red coat is waterproof, but she would rather be out of the storm. As I hurry to catch her up, I fumble for my key. As usual, it eludes me. The rain quickens, and I curse. There is too much in this bag. I need a new one. One with a pocket on the side for my key, not this ridiculous black sack. Ink bops her nose on the red door. 'Hang on, love,' I say, my arm up to the elbow in Big Bag.

Ink bops again and wags her tail. The lock clicks, and the door opens. I follow her in and watch as the door closes behind me and the lock clicks shut.

I take off Ink's coat and my muddy boots, wash my hands at the kitchen sink and fill the kettle. Then I check the door. Yes, it is locked. How strange!

'So, that's how you get in and out when I'm not here.' Rain patters on the windows, and I sit in the dark kitchen and drink my tea.

My mother anticipated I would need North Star Cottage. A dark weight in my heart that was there for so long that it became a part of me has gone, and in its place is light.

The Mid Witch

I walk through the house room by room and give thanks. Somehow, I am tied to this place, and it to me. So many women in my family have lived here and passed it on.

From the upstairs window, I look across the woods and fields – all mine. I stand there for a long time, until the rain stops and the clouds part for a harvest moon. Huge and beautiful, it rises above the trees and bathes me in moonlight.

Chapter Ten

The following week, I keep an eye on my phone, hoping Phil will call. Or at least text. When he doesn't, I chastise myself for being an easy lay. Pretty much this is the story of my life and is probably why I'm alone. I give men what they want, and then they leave. Well, I gave one man what he wanted, and then he left. Slowly. I console myself that at least Phil fancied me. At my age, I should be flattered.

I begin re-organising and decorating the cottage so I can take in paying guests. The work is cathartic. For the first time in many years, I am doing something for myself. I sort out the upstairs bedrooms. Move furniture. Paint the walls in soft pinks and unscrew the Venetian blinds my husband favoured. At the far end of the garden is a pair of stables serving as a garden shed. Here are tea chests full of the old furnishings Mike disliked. The old lady stuff, he called it. I let him modernise the cottage but insisted on keeping my mother's things. Even he knew better than to argue with my grief.

Opening the tea chests and finding curtains and loose covers is like meeting long-lost friends. I don't remember saving so much. China and rugs, paintings, books and curtains. In one chest, protected by a layer of wood chippings, is a sphere about the size of a football. I'm not sure what it is made of. It could be glass, although sometimes it resembles metal. Even here, covered in dust, the surface is mercurial. I lift it carefully with both hands, and Ink comes into the stable to give it a sniff and wag her tail.

'I'd forgotten about this,' I say. Mike had taken it down from its place in the kitchen window without asking and put it out for the bins. When he'd gone to work, I'd retrieved it and packed it carefully away. 'Can't believe it's still in one piece.' I carry it to the kitchen and wash it in warm, soapy water. Memories flood back of my grandmother doing the same. I get my decorating steps so I can reach the hook on the window frame. The ball twists, and the light catches the multicoloured surface. When I was a child, I thought it was a magic bubble.

The engine of Theo's sports car announces her arrival long before she walks up the path in her high-heeled ankle boots. I wave from the end of the garden, where I am pegging flowery curtains on the washing line.

'Hello, darling!' she trills when she sees me. I throw the last curtain over the line and get it pegged while she waits on the path. Her smart ankle boots cannot negotiate my unmown lawn.

'How are you?' I ask, giving her a hug. Expensive perfume washes over me, and Ink slinks away in the grass. 'Come on in. I was about to make some tea. How's the book getting on?'

'Awful! My agent is very problematic. I might have to rethink the situation.'

'You've finished it, then?' She waves my question away. Of course she's finished it. Theo is one of life's high achievers.

'How is the house sale? Had any offers?'

'Well, exciting news actually.'

'Do tell, darling. I've been in the mood for some good stuff all day!'

'Sorted out the attic, as you know, and when I got the junk out from under the stairs, I found an old deed box. Anyway, long story short, turns out I own North Star, and

The Mid Witch

I've decided to stay and do bed and breakfast.' I pass her a mug of tea, and she laughs.

'Really? However will you cope? You're always in such a pickle, darling.'

'Well, you know, new start, and I'm getting organised. Been decorating.'

She takes her tea into the living room and stands there in the chaos. The things I took out of the cupboard under the stairs are still in piles on the floor. Junk and furniture fill the entire room, and the only thing that is clear is the old easy chair where Ink likes to curl up for a nap in the sun. I wonder where she is.

Theo is heading upstairs before I can stop her. I kick the under stairs cupboard shut so she doesn't see the gift she left for Jason. 'Show me what you've done so far,' she says, picking her way through the mess. She stands in the doorways of the freshly painted rooms. They are bright and pretty, and I can't wait to hang the curtains and pictures. I'm already imagining jugs of flowers from the garden and new bed linen.

'Are you sure, darling? Don't people want smart these days? I mean, this whole cottage thing is a bit old news. People want TVs and video games, and nobody likes pastels.' Then she sees my face and gives me a hug. 'Oh, I'm so sorry. I was speaking my mind. I don't mean to be brutal, darling. And, of course, you must do what you want. After all, that's what life's for.'

She lets me go and heads off down the stairs, smart little

boots mincing around the debris. She sits at the kitchen table and checks her phone. 'Give it a go. You can always sell later if you want to,' she says.

I switch the kettle on and make tea, standing next to the kitchen window. A dark shadow in the grass must be Ink. Dogs are sensitive. She has probably decided Theo is not a doggy person. Sensible hound.

I put mugs of tea on the table. Theo doesn't snack, so I don't bother with biscuits. Eating in front of slim people always makes me feel greedy.

'If you want my opinion,' she says, turning the mug around and frowning at the rose design, 'it will all work out if you consider a few things for success.'

Theodora Grimshaw is a successful, self-made woman, and I know I should heed her advice. Mentally, I stroke down the spikes of irritation and listen.

'First thing to consider is parking. Nobody likes leaving their cars on the road. And what about breakfast? Where are they going to eat breakfast?' Her eyes swoop about the kitchen. The cottage doesn't have a dining room.

'But what worries me most is safety. You here on your own. There are an awful lot of weirdos about. Did you hear about that woman in Cornwall?' She then regales me about a woman who, like me, started a bed and breakfast in her 'empty nest' and was murdered. After this snippet of information, she chats about her agent and a wine-tasting trip she plans to take next year, then gets up and puts her mug in

The Mid Witch

the sink. It clinks as it settles on top of all the other washing-up.

'Wasn't that your mother's?' she says, stabbing the glass ball with a red-painted fingernail. It spins about wildly, and I put my hand out to steady it before it hits the window.

'Oh, I think it goes back generations.'

'You know what it is?'

'Not really. I found it and remembered it always hung there, and grandma used to wash it.' She used herb-soaked, moon-blest water, but I don't add this. Grandma Gwen had lots of odd habits.

'Well, *she* always was superstitious. It's a witch ball. Meant to keep away evil spirits. Complete nonsense, of course. But it's probably an antique. Maybe you should sell it?' She laughs, and I follow her back to the car.

Theo gives me a hug. 'Now look, if you do decide to go ahead, give me a call. I could put you in touch with all sorts of useful people. I know a brilliant fellow, can't remember his name, who could take out this' – she points at the yew tree that grows beside my garden gate – 'and make you a nice, neat little car park and landscape the garden. And then there's Midori, the interior designer.'

Theo gets into her car and ties a scarf around her head as the car roof folds back and hides itself like a piece of science fiction. As she gets her sunglasses from their leather case and checks herself in the mirror, a flutter of wings in the oak tree above catches my attention. Maud is there in her black-and-white perfection, stalking up and down and making a clattering sound as magpies do.

'Lovely to see you, darling.' She reaches out and pats my leg. 'You've lost weight! I never asked: how's your little job at the Uni?'

While I explain it was only part-time, she pulls her handbag onto her lap and finds a business card. 'I meant to give you this. And... this!' I take the card and a discount voucher. 'She's marvellous. Can thoroughly recommend.' She tosses her bag onto the passenger seat, and a large white blob falls from the bird above and lands in it. Theo doesn't notice. 'Make sure you go. That voucher only lasts a month. Do you good to get it cut and coloured.'

'I'm growing it,' I say defensively.

Theo laughs. 'Nonsense. You can't have long, grey hair, darling. You'll look like a witch.'

She pats my leg again and starts the car. 'Lovely to see you. Call if you need a hand with anything,' she says over the roar of the engine. As she pulls into the lane, another white streak of bird shit descends and lands softly on the back of her headscarf.

I walk along the garden path with the magpie on my shoulder. On the business card, artistically scribed over a lock of hair, is 'Charlie's Hair Design'.

Ink is sitting on the doorstep. 'Do you think I look like a witch?' I say. She wags her tail at the sound of her name. Silly dog. I make tea and sit on the doorstep star in the October

The Mid Witch

sun, and Maud's beady eye gleams as she eats the raisins I have thrown on the path for her. I text Jason about the gift Theo left him and feel guilty I forgot about it after I put it away in the tidied under stairs cupboard. Then I take a deep breath.

Something in me has changed. Theo's derision usually leaves me a jabbering wreck. Today I am stoic, unburdened by her negativity. This is more than feeling less weepy because of the HRT. This is something new.

In the kitchen, I wash the dishes as the sun goes down, and then I get the *Book of Shadows* and sit with Ink in the easy chair and read. Some words of Theo's have remained with me. It's time to make a new start and learn new things. She, of course, was trying to encourage me to gain new skills to make myself employable. A secretarial course, perhaps. But I have an odd feeling that the new skills I am about to learn are here, in the words of Bethany Blackwood. Ink snuggles nearer, and I pull the blanket over us both and snap my fingers in the moonlight just to see the sparks fly.

Chapter Eleven

I n the morning, I stand at my bedroom window and worry while Ink mooches about in the mist – she's let herself out again. Yesterday's laundry hangs forgotten and damp on the line. I went to bed thinking that Theo had not damaged my resolve to make a life for myself here, but a lifetime of

The Mid Witch

feeling inadequate in that woman's presence is not easily put aside. Car parks, dining rooms and my lack of organisation weigh heavily on my mind. Maybe I am incompetent.

In the kitchen, I make tea and check my phone. Still nothing from Phil. It's been over a week now, and it irritates me that I have a soft hurt in my chest. Dog walking, I decide, is the best course of action, so I get my jeans and boots on and my mother's old green gardening coat and tramp through the woods and fields. Autumn is my favourite season. The leaves are changing and red and orange hips light the hedgerows. The air is earthy, round hay bales stud the fields and crows pick through the stubble. We walk all the way to Horseshoe Cove and climb down the steep steps to the beach.

I can't remember when I came here last. Probably when the kids were small. The tide is out, and Ink digs in the sand. I wander around the tiny cove picking up rubbish that the sea has washed in. The gardening coat's pocket linings are worn through, making the whole coat one big pocket. Among the many items jangling about, I find a cloth bag and fill it with water bottles, lids, string and shards of coloured plastic that no longer have an identity.

The waves are small and gentle, and I dip my hands into the cold sea and breathe in the ozone. Climbing the steps with the bag of recycling, I am renewed. I must come here more often. If only to tidy the beach.

I return to North Star Cottage through the woods. Ink streaks ahead of me with her tail wagging. Jason is picking up windfalls under the apple tree. I rush to hug him, so pleased I almost cry. 'You should have said you were coming. How's the job?'

'Oh my god, mum, you've got a dog!' He pets her, and she does the whole skinny wriggle routine around his legs, her enthusiasm almost knocking him over.

'This is Ink. She's a greyhound.'

'She's brilliant!'

'She is.' Really brilliant. She can open locked doors.

We go into the kitchen, and he plonks the apples onto the draining board and then sits at the kitchen table in his old place. I fetch Theo's present from the cupboard. I'm always amazed at how remarkable my kids are when I haven't seen them for a while. I make a pot of tea and toast because that's all I have. 'You should have said. I would have met you from the bus.' And made your favourite cake.

'It's okay, I got dropped off.' He opens the present, which is a set of six gold-rimmed champagne flutes. He lifts one from the box.

'Very chic,' I say. Theo enjoys giving lavish, impractical gifts to my children.

Jason slides the glass back into its compartment. He's quiet, which is unusual. There must be something on his mind. I have the feeling he is not here to collect Theo's gift. Different scenarios race through my imagination. He's got a job abroad. Got somebody pregnant. Lost his job. He's hardly

The Mid Witch

touched his toast. I pour more tea into his mug. 'What's up, love?'

'Something I need to tell you.' He looks worried now, and my imagination is in overdrive. Please don't let him be ill. I wait.

'Since I've been away. You know, at Uni and stuff. Well, and work. London. I've been coming to terms with some stuff. I hope this won't shock you. Mum, I'm gay.'

I'm so relieved I grab his hand. 'God, I thought you were going to tell me you had cancer or something.'

He laughs with relief.

'It's fine, love. Just be yourself.' He puts some sugar in his tea. Perhaps encouraged by the atmosphere of confession, I blurt out, 'Got something to tell you.' His eyes, blue like his dad's, meet mine. 'I think I might be a witch.'

'That's funny, mum!'

I laugh with him, mostly because I might be losing my mind. Then I clear the plates to hide my embarrassment.

'Have you told dad?'

He's quiet again.

'Want me to tell him?'

'Pathetic, isn't it? Do you think he'll go nuts?'

Mike has a history of overreacting when things don't turn out as he planned. But I haven't seen that side of him for many years. We are all of us older. Wiser. Less given to outbursts of emotion.

'I don't know, love.' That's the honest truth. I have no idea. 'You see more of him than I do.' And his girlfriend.

'Only recently. Now we're building a relationship, and I've got to tell him this.'

'Better to be honest. Otherwise, what's the point?'

'He's mad at you. Says you're stopping him selling the house. Wanted me to have a chat – make you see sense.'

'Grandma left it to me. So I thought I'd keep it and do bed and breakfast.'

'That was his argument. That you can't afford it on your own, and he's…'

'He's making a new start with the hairdresser. It's fine, love. We're sorting out a divorce. Should have done it ages ago.'

'It's a great idea!'

'Divorce?'

'No. Bed and breakfast. That why you're decorating?' Ink comes and puts her head on his knee, and he pets her. I think my dog just likes men. 'Nice to have a dog. I worry about you here on your own.'

I look out at the garden and the apple tree where Maud sits. 'I'm used to being on my own here. I'm fine. Come on, I'll show you the guest rooms.'

Jason is in favour of 'shabby country style' and helps me move furniture and hang curtains and pictures. He loves rooting through the tea crates for odds and ends, and by the end of the day, I have two rooms ready. 'This is great. I'll bring my camera tomorrow and take some pictures. You're gonna need a website, mum.' He's mucking about with his phone on and off all day, and I wonder if it's a boyfriend he keeps texting but I don't like to ask. Then, as suddenly as he arrived, he's gone, running down the path as a car comes to collect him. 'See you tomorrow.'

The next day, he arrives bright and early and stays all day. He photographs the rooms and puts them on a website he made for me the night before. Then he sets up various sites where I can advertise and shows me how it all hangs together.

'Trouble is, I'm not ready. I mean, the rooms are great, but the rest of the place...'

'Which is why,' he says, 'I've filled in your calendar for the next month to give you a chance to get sorted.'

'Theo said I need a dining room.'

'No. People love the whole country kitchen eat-together-around-the-table vibe. You wait, those townies are going to lap it up. Maybe you should get some hens?'

'And a cow.'

'Couple of pigs.'

We laugh away, but I'd love some hens one day. Mike was always against animals of any kind. I am filled with joy because I can do as I please and make my own decisions.

We clear the sitting room ready for me to decorate next week, and Jason helps me choose white bed linen and towels for the guest rooms online. When he disappears again, I have a grip on the situation. All I needed was a bit of old-fashioned help.

When I get back from my morning dog walk with Ink the next day, the postwoman is waiting. 'Something to sign for,' she says, giving Ink a good ear scratch. We have a quick chat about the weather, and I take the large envelope into the kitchen to open. Divorce papers. I spread them on the table and sigh. I should have done this years ago. Everything needs a counter signature, so I text Cressida and ask if she would like to come over and do the honours.

By eleven o'clock, Cressida is sitting in my kitchen drinking tea and eating the cake I made for Jason. 'I love your place. It's like...' She trails off, and I laugh.

'What?'

'I was going to say it's like going back in time or something.'

'It is really old, I think. My family has lived here for generations.' My mind wanders to Bethany Blackwood's gravestone. She must have lived here, too.

I get the divorce papers out and find a pen. 'This is it then,' she says, signing after me.

'Yep. Time to move on.'

'How did you find out he was having an affair with the hairdresser woman? What she called again, Bobby?'

'Charlie.'

'Did he keep going off for a restyle and you got suspicious when he started having highlights and a perm?'

The Mid Witch

That's what I love about Cressida. She makes me talk about stuff I normally keep bottled up. Maybe everyone should get naked with new friends – break down a few barriers.

'Oh, no. Charlie is not the catalyst. Mike and I have been splitting up for years. We might make history as the longest break-up. Money was tight. I was raising our toddlers, and my mother became ill, so I spent a lot of time here looking after her. Mike got a contract with a building company in Germany and went away. First for three months, then for six. I was too busy taking care of the family, I guess.' Cressida pours us more tea from the pot and straightens the knitted tea cosy. 'We moved in here permanently, and he was home for a few months, and it was fine, and then...'

'Off he fucks again!'

Cressida's outbursts always make me smile.

'Yeah, it went on for years. He'd be back a few months and then off again. I was too trusting to see what was actually going on. Even when the evidence was under my nose.'

'He was screwing around then?'

'Oh yeah. Texts on his phone. Photographs of him with other women. I ignored it all. I really believed that one day he would see the light and notice me, the good and faithful wife, and we'd have a fairy tale ending.'

'Sounds like a complete dick, if you ask me. And what about you and finding love, or are you still secretly in love with Mike the bastard?'

'Recently, I'm not in love with him. No, I think that flame has finally gone out. But for most of the years, I loved him, yes.'

'Thirty fucking years!'

'Too long?'

'Much too long. Which reminds me, Randy Landy cornered me in the corridor.'

'Randy Landy?'

'Phil Landy. Fine arts. Skinny tall bloke with a ponytail.'

'What did he want?'

'Asking for your number and spouting some shit about you writing it on a bit of paper, which he lost. Of course I didn't give it to him.' Cressida is full of fun and expletives, but she is perceptive and notices something in my expression. 'Oh my god, you do fancy him!'

I am blushing, which is ridiculous at my age.

'Don't worry! I'm at Uni tomorrow for a forty-five-minute drawing class. I'll make sure he gets your number, and before you know it, Randy Landy will have his hands in your pants.'

I cover my face with my hands and laugh.

'He's already had his hands in your pants!'

'Worse!' I croak.

'Oh no! He's shagged you senseless in his store cupboard, hasn't called and now you feel like a jilted teenager. What a cunt.'

'Oh god. He's the University Lothario?'

'Yes, child. Randy Landy. Clue in the nickname.'

The Mid Witch

'I never heard it until now.'

Cressida shakes her head and looks remorseful. 'I should have warned you not to go into that cupboard. He's a notorious shagger.'

I cut us both another slice of chocolate cake. 'Did you?'

More infectious, loud laughter. 'Me? *No way.*'

As usual, I've been a complete idiot and made a fool of myself. Cressida reaches across the table and pats my hand. 'I'm gay.' This makes me feel a lot better. 'He did make a pass at me, though, when I first arrived. So, how was it?'

'The sex?'

'Of course the sex! I've heard he's got all sorts in that cupboard to please a woman. Toys, candles, soft fur blankets...?'

'He was a bit organised!'

'Tell me!'

'Lubrication. Kitchen roll!'

Cressida is weeping. 'Excellent. So, are you going to shag him again?'

I hesitate, and Cressida is in tucks. 'You are! To be fair, everyone says he's an outstanding fuck with a very long cock, by all accounts.'

'It was pretty good. I just wish...'

'Now, come on. Don't be having a heap of rubbish notions about romantic claptrap and love. You fancied each other. You had a nice time. You'd both like to do it again. So what? Enjoy! If you ask me, this is exactly what you need. A bit of casual, no-ties sex. Now, show me your guest rooms and then we'll drive you to your ex so you can give him his goodbye papers. I'll even drop you off at Uni if you like,' she says with a wink.

'No. Not Uni. But I'd love a lift to Market Forrington. I can leave these at Mike's work.'

'Which is?'

'The Water Works.'

'Wow, that's his – the fancy bathroom place?'

I leave Ink in the cottage, sleeping in the easy chair. No point worrying now I know she can open doors. 'I love your garden,' Cressida says as we walk to the car. My lawn is hay with a few flattened patches where the dog likes to lie. 'Always nice to let nature have her say.'

She puts the bag of windfalls I have given her in the boot, and we get in. 'Did Uni call you about the Enterprise Event?'

'No.'

'They're having a big do to launch the project. You know the whole, "We're not just teaching degrees, we're teaching enterprise"?'

'I've seen the posters.'

'Well, next week is the launch party. You know the sort of thing. Talks by local businesses and lecturers. A bit of entertainment from the drama and music departments. All very uplifting. Anyway, they need staff. Front of house. Serving refreshments, pointing to the loo, handing out leaflets. Good pay – double time. You in?'

'Yeah, sounds good. Could do with a bit of extra cash.'

'I'll let them know. They probably overlooked you because you're new.'

Market Forrington is busy, and Cressida drives around for a parking space and pulls in just as another car pulls out. Horns beep, and a young man in a massive four-wheel-drive shouts abuse as she steals his space. Cressida ignores him and reverse parks with a serene smile. 'Face it, honey, I'm a fat woman in a compact car, and I'm so much more nippy than you!' She unclicks her seat belt and grins at me. 'Sometimes you've got to get your agile on! Right. Now it's your turn.' She's parked across the road from Charlie's Hair Design. 'Is that her?' she asks.

In the window, Call Me Charlie is saying goodbye to a customer. She is slim and pretty in skinny jeans and a fitted one-sleeved top. 'Yes, that's her.' I wonder if her other arm is cold.

Cressida picks the envelope out of Big Bag and presses it into my hand. 'Right. Go in there and tell her to give your husband these divorce papers.'

I am about to explain that I am going to walk to the end of the street to Mike's showroom and leave them at his office. But Cressida hands me a lipstick from her bag. 'Put this on,' she says, flipping down the mirror on the back of the sunvisor. 'Some tasks must be performed in' – she looks at the lipstick – 'shade 592, devil's kiss red.'

I apply it, blot my lips on a tissue and grin. Am I really going to do this?

I am.

I get out of the car and march across the road and into the hair salon. The salon is big and full of the buzz of hairdryers and gossip. A trendy young apprentice with mauve hair calls from the sink, where he is shampooing a woman. 'Someone will be with you in a minute!'

Call Me Charlie is helping her next customer into a gown. She settles her client into a chair and comes back to speak to me. 'Do you have an appointment?'

'No, I...'

She goes to the desk and opens the appointment book.

'How can I help?' She is smiling. Waiting for me to speak. She doesn't even recognise me. 'Who normally does your hair?' she asks pleasantly.

Middle age comes with invisibility. I am unmemorable. Another grey-headed, wrinkled face in a sea of the same. I wait. Surely the penny will drop.

Nothing.

I hand her the envelope. 'Could you give Mike these divorce papers?' I say and leave.

Chapter Twelve

I spend the week decorating the sitting room. I even send a message to Mike and ask if he wants the grey, low-backed sofas and matching curtains. Of course he doesn't reply, so I put them on a local, free, buyer-collects website. I even tackle the garden. Pull some weeds and trim a few things. The lawn is beyond the lawn mower; a combine harvester would be more use. Gardening used to be my relaxing activity, and it's funny how everything is out of hand. Even if I had a month, I couldn't get it tidy. 'I might need to employ someone to help,' I say to Ink. 'Just to get me back to square one.'

The new white bed linen arrives, and I launder it and dress the beds. Jason was right about not using my mother's old flowery sheets. The rooms are sweet and smart now. I send him a picture. I expect him to reply with a smiley face, but he sends a picture of himself and another guy walking in a London park. The caption reads 'lovely autumn day'. He looks happy, and I'm relieved. At some point, I will have to get hold of Mike and speak to him. Better he shouts at me than at Jason. Hopefully, Call Me Charlie has a nice broad mind that she has impressed upon him. This is doubtful. Mike can be very magnanimous until something involves his own family.

Friday is the University Enterprise Event. The email stipulates wearing all black and arriving early for job allocation. I don't want to buy anything, so I unearth a black velvet dress that was Belinda's. Do all teenagers go through a gothic phase? It has long sleeves and a scooped neckline. I am surprised I can fit into it. Dog walking and decorating have done wonders. I'm not skinny, but I'm definitely not as fat. The dress is long, almost to my ankles, and I'm sure everyone

The Mid Witch

is wearing short skirts right now. It is very out of date. But then, I'm out of date, so who cares? My hair is wild, so I screw it into a bun and wait in the lane for Cressida to collect me.

Cressida pulls up, and I get in. She's stunning. Her hair is tied in an elaborate black scarf, and her dress is a sea of black taffeta and lace. Next to her, I feel like a weed.

'Right!' she says as she drives off. 'Let's earn some cash and drink cheap wine! Nice boots!'

'Belinda's. And the dress.' The boots are flat lace-ups, also left over from Belinda's gothic phase. I think she only wore them for a week. Probably because they take about an hour to fasten. Teenagers are naturally lazy. Mike must have been around because I remember having a row with him about the cost.

'Looking good. Much better choice than me. My feet will be in shreds by the end of the night, but you know what I thought?'

'Fuck it!' we say together.

Cressida is wearing high gold court shoes with vicious points.

When we get to Uni, Cressida parks and has a look at me. She pulls my hair loose and makes me apply the devil lipstick.

The event is in the newly built Enterprise Hall, which is a smaller space than the theatre where they hold the graduation ceremonies. Most of the helpers for the event are students, and an amiable woman called Jackie coordinates everything. Her pleasant manner has us all working away enthusiastically, lining up wine glasses on cloth-covered tables and setting out chairs. There are leaflets and tubs of flowers for the stage. Banners to hang. Cushions for the seats. And so much more. In a couple of hours, she gathers us all together, tells us what our roles will be for the evening and then announces we have twenty minutes to ourselves and that the staff canteen is open in the basement. I've lost Cressida, who is helping in the shop and art gallery area, and I search in Big Bag for my phone to see if she's free.

'Cressida said you were in here. Nice dress.' It's Phil.

'Nice suit,' I say, although it looks strange, as if the clothes are wearing him. I'm not sure if it is completely out of date or high fashion. Are black velvet suits and frilly shirts back in?

'I've been trying to get hold of you.'

'Yeah?' I hope I sound casual. 'What are you doing here?'

'Art gallery. All part of University Star Ship Enterprise. Don't know what's wrong with art students these days. They seem to think they need to earn a living. What's wrong with art for art's sake and total poverty?' We laugh, and he grabs my hand and leads me into the corridor and up a staircase to an empty classroom. We go in, he shuts the door and I fully expect him to explain losing my number. But no. Phil pins me against the door and kisses me. That kiss. He knows what he's doing with that kiss, and soon he is grabbing my breast and thumbing my nipple through the velvet dress.

The Mid Witch

'How long have you got?' he breathes into my neck. His hard, long cock is pressed against my thigh.

I don't wear a watch, and Big Bag has swallowed my phone. 'Twenty minutes. Fifteen?'

He pulls back, and there's a massive grin on his face. 'Fancy a quickie?'

I laugh because this is ridiculous. I'm a middle-aged woman about to have sex in a classroom where anyone could walk in.

'A quickie?'

'Fast sex.' His eyes twinkle, and I can't wipe the grin off my face. He nods at the clock on the wall. 'We need to be back at seven thirty?'

'Yeah.'

Phil props a chair under the doorknob to keep out intruders. He's such an expert at this. Then he unbuttons his velvet jacket and hangs it on the back of another chair. The fitted frilly shirt has flouncy cuffs. I can't help laughing.

'What? You don't like vintage?'

I grab a handful of the shirt frills and pull him close. We kiss while he pulls down my knickers. Oh god, I have a panty liner on as a precaution in case I sneeze and wet myself. And my knickers are huge tummy suckers. I pull away and deal with them myself, hooking them over the lace-up boots. He turns knicker-free me around and bends me over a desk. One hand fingers my pubic hair. With the other, he unzips himself. But I know I'm not wet enough. I haul Big Bag nearer and find a tube of sun cream. Not ideal. God knows how long it's been in there. A strong smell of synthetic strawberries fills the air as Phil lubricates himself. Then, with a quick angle change of my hips, he's inside, hard and long, and I'm gasping as he pumps me. From behind, his cock hits just the right spot, and I moan and hoot like a wild creature, long beyond caring if anyone hears us. He doesn't stop. Five minutes of frantic thrusting, and then he's coming with a long 'ahhhhh'. It really is rather musical.

We stay locked together while he gets his breath back. I rummage in Big Bag for some tissues and find a small, fiddly packet. When I get them open with my teeth, I hand Phil some and we tidy ourselves up.

My heart is racing and my vagina is clenched, ready to come. That's the thing with a quick fix. Only one of you gets fixed. I'll have to sort myself out later. I reach for the big knickers to get them re-instated while Phil washes at the sink at the back of the room. As he dries himself on a blue paper towel, he turns to me. 'Leave them off,' he says as I hop about on one leg and nearly lose my balance. I'd like to stuff them into Big Bag and be free. But that is a young woman's privilege. Middle age comes with the fear of the piddle sneeze. The laugh piddle. The cough piddle.

As I wrestle with my knickers, Phil returns. Pulls me close. Looks into my eyes. 'We have a whole five minutes,' he says, guiding me to the wall and pushing me against it. I can't argue. He's kissing me and has a hand up my dress. 'Put one foot on here,' he says, pulling a chair nearer.

'We should get going...'

Phil kisses my mouth, moves down to my nipple and breathes his hot breath through the velvet. His fingers, which were rummaging about aimlessly, find my clitoris. He pats with his fingertips and rubs lightly and then firmly. The pace increases until I am gripping his shoulders. He scrapes his teeth over my nipple, and I come. My head drops back and I let out a gasp. He doesn't let me go. Keeps me against the wall and plunges two fingers inside me. 'God, I'd fuck you again if we had time.' He moves his hand quicker, and I flick my pelvis in rhythm until a throbbing vaginal climax takes me.

My legs are weak. I sit on the chair and fight the pants back over the boots. Phil is washing his hands at the sink. I grab the rest of the tissues and do what I can to clean myself up and wash my hands. Phil is buttoning his suit, and I wish there was a mirror.

I put Big Bag over my shoulder.

'Do you want this?' It's the tube of strawberry sun cream.

'God, no. It stinks.'

He laughs and tosses it into the bin as we leave the classroom.

The Enterprise Hall is a hive of last-minute activity when we return. We both head off to our duties. Cressida finds me pouring cheap wine into glasses in the hospitality area. She grabs herself a bottle and joins in. 'Phil was like a dog looking for a bone when I told him you were here. Did he find you and apologise for being a total cunt?' She breaks off and then laughs so raucously I have to shush her. 'He found you. And by the looks of that comely blush on your cheeks, he took you back to his love cupboard and shagged you senseless!'

'No,' I say.

She gives me a disbelieving look.

'No, we went upstairs. Empty classroom.'

'Improvisation! I like it. And?'

'Yep. We had a big fast shag.'

'Was he any good? Did he reach the parts?'

'God, yes.' My fanny is still vibrating.

'Good man, Phil.' More raucous laughter.

Cressida and I help organise canapes and cheese in the kitchen for the interval. Then we stand at the back of the hall and listen to the speeches.

In the interval, we waft about with trays of nibbles. The general theme of the evening is to get local businesses to support the Uni in their entrepreneurial endeavours by providing work placements, advice and funds. The students are out in force, confidently chatting with the great and the good and showing off their talents. How nice to have all that education and potential ahead of you. I take my tray over to a group of girls, and they fall upon the morsels. They are not much younger than my own kids.

'What are you studying?' I ask one girl as she makes a little stack of crackers in one hand. Her eyes are on the room.

The Mid Witch

They must get asked that so much. I try again, slightly louder, looking right at her. 'Do you think this has been useful? This evening?'

'Oh my god!' she says to her companion. 'Is that Randy Landy?'

The other girls follow her gaze. 'In his vampire suit!' they laugh. The girl furthest from me reaches over and takes a handful of garnish without looking at me. A group of students walk past, and garnish girl nibbles a bit of parsley and says, 'Who's wearing stinking strawberry perfume?'

'Probably one of the first years.'

I, the invisible woman, take my canapés elsewhere. With the music department playing easy listening, it's all very civilised. Until I see Mike. He is chatting to Grant Fucking Rutherford. They are both wearing smart suits and seem to be getting along, which figures. Unlike Grant, my soon to be ex-husband never looks quite right in formal clothes. This a trait he shares with Phil. Phil looks better in his jeans and t-shirt. And Mike? Mike looks better in plumber's overalls. But since he opened the showroom, he doesn't get his hands dirty. Mike the plumber has become Mitch the businessman.

I watch him chatting animatedly with the estate agent. He's had his hair dyed a subtle sandy blonde that matches his neatly trimmed beard, and that little spot on the back of his head where his hair is thinning has gone. Charlie's Hair Design has worked ceaselessly. From his tanned skin to his fashionable, tight-fitting suit, Mike looks ten years younger – but in an odd way.

As I carry my tray through the crowd, I stay as far away from Mike and Grant as possible while looking for Call Me Charlie. When everyone filters back into the hall for the last part of the event, I keep busy in the kitchen.

Cressida comes in, sits on a worktop and takes off the gold shoes. 'Fuck, I think I've strangled my feet.'

I laugh as I stack glasses in the dishwasher. It's simple work when everything is the same size.

'Do you think anyone would mind if I ran my feet under the tap?' It's a rhetorical question. I know Cressida well enough to realise that she is going to do this. She slides along the worktop to the nearest sink and turns on the tap. 'Oh my god. That's so good.'

I start the machine and pass Cressida a wad of kitchen paper to dry her feet. 'Remind me to burn these devil shoes. It's the only way to be free of their spell.'

'Did you watch the last bit?'

'No. Ended up vacuuming the art gallery. Did you go in?'

'No.'

'That painting of you is in there. The one where Ink has her head on your knee. Looks fab now it's all framed up.'

My blood runs cold. Cressida notices I've gone pale. 'What's up?'

'My husband – ex-husband – is here.'

'Will he care?'

'No. But I feel embarrassed.'

'Oh, I shouldn't worry. Not everyone went in.'

'Art galleries were never his thing.'

Jackie finds us and sends us to the foyer to hand out leaflets. There are lots of people milling about talking, and I tuck myself behind a free-standing notice board in the hope Mike doesn't see me.

He does.

He strides across, grabs my arm and pulls me away. I yank myself free.

'Come with me!' he says.

'No!'

'You want to do this in front of everyone? Fine!'

Behind him, several people stare. The leaflets are all over the floor. I follow him back into the Enterprise Hall which is empty now. As soon as the door closes, he rounds on me. 'Tell me what you were thinking.' His voice has that strange calm quality it gets before he's about to blow.

I open my mouth to speak, even though I know that nothing I say will be heard.

'How do you think I feel? A respectable businessman at a prestigious event?' He points in the direction of the art gallery. 'I know what this is. This is your way of getting back at me. Just because I stopped the payments, my wife has to pose nude. In front of spotty youths.'

His face doesn't move much. I think he's had Botox.

'Can you imagine how fucking embarrassed I am?

Walking around that exhibition with the Business Guild, and then I'm confronted with you. In high fucking detail: grey pubic hair, stretch marks and droopy tits! My overweight, old wife in her birthday suit, clearly labelled Lilly Turner!'

I've had many a verbal lashing from Mike over the years. When he was spoiling to leave, he would have one of his outbursts and fly off in a storm of abuse. His going was always my fault.

'Come on. Get your things. We're leaving.'

Shocked and embarrassed, I return to the kitchen, retrieve Big Bag and tell Cressida I have a lift home. She is chatting to a woman and gives me a wink, no doubt believing I am off for another tryst with Randy Landy.

Mike is waiting in the foyer. We walk to his car in the rain. He has his jacket over his arm. I bet he wouldn't let Call Me Charlie get wet. The last time I sat in a vehicle with him, he drove a plumber's van. Now he has a smart two-seater sports car. Mike drives in silence until we've left the University campus. 'It's got to stop,' he says.

'What?'

'All your nonsense. Walking into the salon the other day with divorce papers. Charlie was so embarrassed and upset. You never used to be this bitchy.'

I sit there and take it. Like I always do. Mike is angry and disappointed, and it's all my fault.

'Why are you making an exhibition of yourself?' He looks at me as we wait at the traffic lights. The windscreen wipers

The Mid Witch

swish. I'm silent like a naughty child, and behind my eyes, tears prick. I don't want to cry. I take a deep breath and rub the tips of my fingers, hoping to see a spark. But the sparks only come in North Star Cottage. Another reason I believe it is my imagination. A bit of nonsense cooked up by a lonely middle-aged woman.

'And why the fuck' – he shakes his head in disbelief – 'are you dressed like a witch?'

We're on the dark country roads outside Barrington. I wish I'd had the sense to tell him to drop me off at the station.

'Look,' he says, trying to sound calm. His hands grip the steering wheel. No disguising those big plumber's hands.

'I'll sort out an allowance for you until we get the cottage sold. How about that?'

'I'm not selling.'

'Lilly, enough!' he shouts.

'Yes. Enough. I'm not selling!'

'You've got to face reality and realise you can't afford to live there, and I can't keep supporting you.'

'The cottage is mine, and I'm going to do bed and breakfast. And anyway, I'm not your problem – because we're getting divorced.' Mike pulls the car over and screeches it to a halt. A car drives past. The road is dark and quiet when it has gone. Rain patters on the windshield.

'You think you can live there on your own in the middle of bloody nowhere with your mad dog, and people will pay? Fucking pay to come and sleep in that mess? All I'm trying to do is make everything alright for you so you can have a nice tidy little flat and be safe with a bit of financial security, but no. You have to dig out some scrap of paper your weird mother made me sign and FUCK EVERYTHING UP.'

'You can shout all you like, but I'm still not selling.'

He presses a button on his fancy car, and the passenger door opens. 'Right! I've had enough. You want to be independent? Get out!'

I sit there like a frightened kid, and he shouts again. 'OUT!'

I get out of the car with Big Bag and stand in the rain as he drives off. I'm not entirely sure where I am. Usually, I take the train to Barrington. I walk in the direction we were heading, fully expecting him to circle back and pick me up.

The rain quickens, and it's cold. Sheltering under a tree, I dig out one of my ponchos. No point getting soaked while Mike comes to his senses.

The orangutan keeps off the wet but not the cold. I wait under the tree for the rain to stop and Mike to return. I make up things to say to him when he gets here, the bastard. It's about time I told him that his support has barely kept me. When the kids were small, I had to scrimp and save, and whenever I broached the subject of getting a full-time job, he shut me down. I wait for ages, and when I realise he's not coming, I decide to call someone. Cressida or Belinda or Theo. Belinda is the nearest. My phone is dead. I usually charge it on the train with a little cable that Jason bought me.

The Mid Witch

Walking, then. Maybe there will be a bus stop. At least I have the proper footwear for the weather. My anger dissipates.

I walk and walk, lonely and hungry. My pussy itches from that damn sun lotion. I want a bath. I miss my dog, and I'm starving – and, yes, out at night in the dark on my own, I'm scared.

It's late, and there is no traffic. I'd feel safer walking away from the road, but without a torch and with no pavement, I have no choice. I plod on, watching where I am going as best I can. No streetlights or moon to help. On either side, dark shapes of trees and hedges loom. The rain is relentless.

A car approaches slowly in the downpour. I step off the road and wait under a tree. I am not sure what is worse – being out here on my own or being approached by potential strangers. When the car has gone, I carry on. I can survive the rain and the dark and the extremely long walk home, but I won't put myself in any more danger.

After a while, I am hardly thinking. I am just walking. Then something moves ahead. There's a dark shape trotting toward me.

A dog. It's Ink!

'Oh, my darling, why aren't you home, safe and dry?' She's shivering, and so am I. We get off the road and shelter under a huge oak tree. I pull the poncho over my head and get Ink beneath it with me. She snuggles up, and I cling to her for warmth. 'I don't know how you got here, silly dog. But I'm glad you came.' I'd have a good cry if I had the strength. This is all so unreal.

Her warmth soothes me, and with her near, I feel much safer. 'We'll wait here until morning,' I whisper in her ear as we both fall asleep.

The whoosh of traffic on the wet road wakes me. It is barely light, and when we get up, I am wobbly and tired. The rain has stopped, and we begin our walk again.

Eventually, we find a bus stop.

Chapter Thirteen

An hour later, we are back at the cottage. At last.
After I feed Ink and Maud and eat a bowl of cereal, I take a hot bath to get warm and free myself of the itchy strawberry sun lotion. Then I get into bed. Ink joins me, and we sleep all morning.

When I am up again and dressed, I check Ink's paws. They are fine – unlike those of a dog who walked twenty miles to meet me. I cannot comprehend how she got there. My only thought is that something terrible would have happened to me without her. I could have fallen. Been run over by a car. Got pneumonia without her warmth. I give her a hug, and she leans into me. 'I love you,' I whisper into her sleek neck.

She wags her skinny tail twice as if to say, 'I know.'

In the afternoon, Cressida calls. She listens without interrupting as I tell her my sorry tale. Well, a version of it. Most of Mike's vitriol is too painful to repeat, and I don't mention the dog. Ink is not a normal dog, and instinct makes me keep her abilities secret.

'What a complete and utter bastard,' she says when I finish. Even my sanitised version is still awful.

'I hope you kick him in the nuts the next time you see him.'

'Only if you lend me your gold shoes.'

'Making him wear them would be a better punishment. I think I've bruised my toes.'

'Anyway, one thing I'm sure of is that Mike and I are definitely finished. I've had enough. No more procrastinating. Divorce is the only answer.'

'You've got to move on. Stop making excuses for him and start thinking about yourself. You're a beautiful woman, Lilly. It's time you started believing that.'

The Mid Witch

She offers to come over after life drawing, but I put her off. All I want to do is sleep. I'm shattered. Emotionally and physically. I cook some pasta, eat and then make a hot water bottle. The cottage is cold, and I don't want to put the heating on because of the cost. Ink gets into bed and waits there while I take a shower. That strawberry sun cream is still itching. I smear myself with aloe gel, which is very soothing, and realise I have not taken my HRT for two days. I've also forgotten to change the patch. No wonder I feel like crap.

The following week, I am vaguely unwell and suspect I have caught a cold, which is not surprising. I am still itchy down below, and I take some antihistamines. I must have an allergy to the sun cream. Also unsurprising. Another unsurprising thing is that Phil does not call. He didn't ask for my number again, but if he really wanted to contact me, he could ask Cressida for it.

I keep busy and finish decorating the sitting room. A young couple who are very grateful collect the grey, low-backed sofas and blinds. Best of all, I get the chimneys swept and the solid fuel range cooker in the kitchen serviced. Then I do something else. I employ an odd-job man for three days. This is expensive, but I need help and I don't want to bother Jason or Belinda. They're already rushed off their feet with their own lives. Any-Job-Steve – it says so on his van – is a real treasure. He has power tools and knows how to use them. I'm not sure if he's older than me or weather beaten. Either way, I don't want any accidents, and I caution him about the large round stone in the centre of the lawn before he tackles the grass with a mini tractor.

Once the lawn is reduced to manageable stubble, I show him my fallen tree. Any-Job-Steve has a chainsaw and soon chops it into logs and stacks it all in the stable I use as a log store. He even brings the seasoned wood to the front to use first. Steve cuts hedges with another device, cleans gutters, blows leaves into a pile and gets the compost heap sorted. Slung under a hedge, he finds a stone basin.

'This is a lovely thing,' he says, dragging it out.

'It used to live on top of the stones on the lawn. Can't think why it got moved. Or when?'

'Make a nice feature planter,' he says. It would.

We haul it onto a sack and drag it into place. It's solid stone and is about a metre wide. When we get it positioned, we have to stop for a cup of tea. I am exhausted and leave Any-Job-Steve to get on without me, though I can normally work in the garden all day. I pick a bunch of late dahlias and put them in a big blue jug on the kitchen table to cheer myself up.

By the end of the week, the cottage is transformed. For Ink's sake, I keep the fire in the range burning. Greyhounds love warmth, and a pile of blankets beside my mother's old cooker is now her favourite place. But I am still poorly, and I make an appointment with the doctor.

Chapter Fourteen

These days, there is never any chance of seeing your own doctor. When I am called from the waiting room, Dr Neilson is a man roughly my age. I tell him more or less what has recently happened to me, about getting caught in the rain and using an old tube of sun cream for sexual lubricant.

'So, you think you might be allergic to strawberries?' he asks after I've chatted for what seems like hours.

'Well, not real strawberries. I don't think it had real strawberries in it. It was a tube of cream in my bag. Might've been in there for years.'

'Indeed,' he says, looking away from his computer screen for the first time.

'And, er, Dill, is he your regular sexual partner?' He's moving his mouse and looking at his screen again.

'Phil. I suppose so.'

'How many sexual partners have you had in the last three months?'

'He's the only one in the last three years.'

'Indeed. And what about Dill?'

'Phil. I don't know.' God only knows. Randy Landy is probably bonking someone in his love cupboard right now.

'Mmmn well, let's take a quick look at you and then send you for some bloods.'

I suffer the embarrassment of having my privates examined. I lie there with my feet in the stirrups and try to act nonchalant. A nurse holds a lamp for him, and he takes a swab. When he's finished, he stands with his hand on my knee. No doubt he thinks he's being casual and friendly and that his hand on my knee will make me feel at ease. He chats away about blood tests and the swab and something else. All I can think of is that I am lying on my back with my legs in the air with a cold draft blowing on my fanny. When men have their testicles examined, do female doctors stand there explaining the next part of the procedure while they have their pants off? I think not.

When he goes, I get myself together. Untangle myself from the bed of shame and get dressed. What I should do is tell him that his casual manner is inappropriate. That my dignity should be considered. Of course, I say nothing. Like most women, I am hard-wired to put up with stuff. I provide a urine sample and have blood taken. Then I sit in the waiting room to be called back. This takes forty-five minutes.

'Ahh, yes. Well, the blood sample will take a few days to process. And we'll notify you if there is a problem. In the meantime, this prescription will clear up the STD. You'll need to notify Dill about the, er, situation you're in.' As he speaks, his eyes are on his computer screen, and he moves the mouse now and again. What is he doing? There can't be that much information about me. Is he playing patience?

'Or we could get in touch with Dill for you?'

'No. I'll tell him.' I don't even have his number.

'Jolly good.' He hands me a prescription.

'Thank you,' I say.

His eyes are on the screen again.

'Condom. Tell Dill to use a condom,' he says to my departing back.

I take the prescription to the big chemist in Marswickham

so that I don't have to suffer any judgment from the small chemist where I get my HRT. The girl at the counter is oblivious to my predicament when she hands over the white paper bag after thirty minutes. After that, I walk to the train station. This has all taken much longer than I expected. I thought I'd got a rash from some out-of-date sun lotion. The reality is I have a sexually transmitted disease.

On the train, I swallow a pill with some water and hope that Ink is okay. That's the trouble with a dog that can open doors. You never know if she will follow you if you're gone more than a few hours. Now I must go to the University and tell Phil he's a nasty, contagious rat. Happy days.

Barrington University is buzzing when I get there. I walk to the fine art building among throngs of students. On the way, I pass the new Enterprise Hall. Despite the many people milling about in the October sunshine, I feel bold and go inside, then cross the large airy foyer into the art gallery.

Soft music plays as I walk slowly and look at the artwork. There are glass cabinets with jewellery and pottery, sculptures and textiles. The paintings are many and varied, and in the room's heart is me. The painting has a tasteful frame and seems bigger. Something inside me is happy. It is a beautiful work of art, and I am glad I am a part of it. The artist has changed nothing about me. I look the same: middle-aged and chubby with grey hair, overgrown pubes, stretch marks, thread veins and cellulite. It's a picture of a real woman. Ink looks gorgeous in contrast – all sleek black fur and toned muscle. On the wall is a note about the artist.

Nicole Butler is a third-year fine art student who specialises in portraits.

Lilly Turner and her Dog is sold, but you can find more of Ms Butler's art on her website.

Sold.

I cannot believe that someone wants this picture, although I don't mind it. Which is strange. Becoming comfortable with myself is new. Must be an age thing. Maybe the buyer likes dogs! Then I realise that Mike, out of sheer embarrassment, must have bought it before discovering he could not take it until the exhibition ends in six weeks.

The price is on a tiny sticker. The shock of the expense makes me sit for a moment on the flat black leather couch in the centre of the room. What a waste of money. For something he will destroy. Then again, maybe the expense will make him hang it in his smart flat. When his women ask about the ex-wife, he can point at Ink and I. Might save time.

Phil's room is empty. This is a great relief. A circle of easels surrounds the dais where a large, complicated still-life rests. I find a pad and a pen on his desk and sit on the chair to compose my note. Not a simple task.

'Dear Phil,' I begin, because you've got to start somewhere. Then I hear a noise. Oh my god, there's somebody in the cupboard. Why the fuck doesn't he lock the classroom door? Did he lock the door when we were 'at it'? I can't remember. Maybe I should leave and post a letter c/o the University? Maybe he's just in there having a tidy-up. Then I hear it: 'Ahhhhh'. Phil's musical come sound.

No wonder this guy never texts. He's too busy. I write a curt note: 'You have an STD. Please go to the doctor and tell all your sexual partners.' I underline the 'all' and debate whether to leave it unsigned to see if he contacts me.

The door opens.

Phil, with an armful of sketch pads, steps nimbly around the door and closes it with a flick of his foot before I can see who is in there.

'This is a lovely surprise,' he says.

'Really?'

'Yes, really. Want to get some lunch?'

The cupboard is quiet. Perhaps I'm being too harsh and the poor bloke was having a wank. 'I was just leaving you a note.'

'Look, I've been meaning to contact you. Maybe we could—'

'It's fine, Phil.' Still no sound from the cupboard. 'I haven't come to hound you. I needed to tell you this.' I hand him the note.

He's all smiles. 'What about next Wednesday? I finish early and we...'

'Read the note, Phil. It's important.'

He looks at the note, and his eyebrows raise.

'Make sure you tell whoever's in there. Get yourself to a clinic and get some condoms.'

To his credit, he has the sense to look ashamed.

He follows me to the door. 'Maybe we could meet for lunch?'

'It's fine, Phil. You don't have to take me to lunch because you've given me an STD.'

Outside, I keep a brisk walk all the way to the station and don't look back. I don't want to know who's in Phil's love cupboard. All I want is to get home to the cottage and Ink.

I'm exhausted and treat myself to a taxi from the station. When I get out, Mike's van is in the lane. Or one of his vans. I often see them about with their 'The Water Works' logo, all grey and blue.

The last thing I need is an argument.

Ink is not here to greet me, but at least Maud is in the apple tree. White lilies are in the kitchen sink, their cloying scent filling the warm room.

Mike is coming down the stairs with a rhythmic step. Into the kitchen he bounds, wearing expensive grey tracksuit bottoms and a white t-shirt. His hair is damp from the shower and his feet are bare on the old quarry tiles.

'Where've you been? I was getting worried,' he says, as if we live together.

'Where's Ink?'

'Who?'

'The dog. Where's my dog?'

'In the garden.'

I chuck Big Bag on the table and go outside, then call her name and whistle.

'Look. I'm sorry, but I shut it in the stable. I went to get some wood – you know, keep the home fires burning – and I shut it in there. It'll be fine.'

'No. It's not fine. She's a greyhound. They really feel the cold.' I check the stable, but she's not there.

Mike stands barefoot on the path. 'Garden's looking better.'

I walk past him into the cottage to get my wellington boots from the under stairs cupboard. Mike follows. She's probably gone into the woods or is wandering along Church Lane. In the sitting room, Ink is in the easy chair, snoozing.

'How did that happen?' says Mike.

Ink rolls on her back, and I give her tummy a rub and wrap her blanket around her. 'Good dog, Ink.'

In the kitchen, Mike opens a bottle of wine. It's a screw top – cheap then. He's set the table for dinner. He must have made his cottage pie.

'Look,' he says, sniffing the wine. 'The other night…'

I sit down. Maybe he came back and tried to find me but I was hiding behind a tree. Perhaps his car broke down.

'It was all a bit of a shock. Seeing you at the Uni. And that painting. Then I had a think, and I realised why I was so upset.' He hands me a glass of wine.

What I want is a cup of tea.

The Mid Witch

'I still care about you,' he says.

The words hang between us. I look at him, all clean with his highlights and spray tan. He smells of something expensive – a gift from Call Me Charlie, maybe.

'Get a shower, and we'll talk. Dinner in fifteen,' he says.

I do as I'm told and come down in my old dressing gown. I don't have any new clothes for relaxing in. My relaxing is usually a solitary occupation.

He's thrown away the late dahlias from the table and put the lilies in their jug. They stink. I've always hated them – and white ones in particular. Annoying to be named after a flower you dislike. Then I remember my name is Lilith.

He dishes up the cottage pie, all smiles. Do I want more broccoli? Bread? Wine? This is Mike at his most charming.

I get up and feed the dog. Mike fidgets, trying to keep his patience. His cooking needs to be treated with respect. Ink comes into the kitchen and eats her biscuits and meat noisily, then laps water. I eat a few mouthfuls of Mike's signature dish, then leap up when Ink stands by the kitchen door. It's best Mike doesn't find out she can open doors. Two minutes later, I jump up to let her back in, then pull her pile of blankets in front of the range cooker so she can lie where it's warm. The dog gives me a quizzical look.

'I think getting the range working was a great idea. Especially with the price of fuel.'

'Yeah. Keeps the kitchen warm. Ink likes it.'

We eat in silence. Ink wanders about the kitchen, sniffing Mike's shoes on the doormat and re-licking her food bowl.

'I've been thinking,' he says, putting together his knife and fork. Here it comes: Mike's prepared speech. Or, to put it another way, how Mike sees the world now.

I get myself a glass of water and sit back down. The last thing I want is alcohol.

'I get it about the house. Been in your family for years and all that history and stuff.'

Ink is harrumphing by the range. She's dug her blankets into a heap, and now they are uncomfortable. 'Let's get you sorted,' I say as I organise her bed the way she likes it and then cover her with a soft fleece when she curls up.

When I sit again, Mike has folded his arms. He never could just chat while you did stuff. When he speaks, he expects your total attention. Some people are like that. They can't bear half-measures. It was difficult when the kids were small. They constantly distracted me.

I compose myself and look right at him, and he begins again.

'I understand you want to keep the cottage, and I think the bed and breakfast idea is great. Be something for you to do. Jason showed me the website he's made. It's got potential. It really has. And people love this whole country shabby look these days. Might need to think about parking, though.'

Mike has plans for the bed and breakfast venture. This encompasses putting in a driveway, a garage and an outhouse

The Mid Witch

for a utility area with a washing machine and a big freezer. When he's finished talking about his vision, he reaches over the table and takes my hand in both of his. Looks into my eyes. Mike the businessman morphs seamlessly into Mike the lover.

I slide my hand free and clear the plates, then start filling the sink with water. He comes behind me and puts his arms around my waist. Nuzzles my neck. Mumbles into my hair, 'We could get a dishwasher. That would help.'

Mike has always taken my silence as agreement. This is probably my fault as I am not good at speaking my mind. Any interaction on my part is met with derision. Over our long on–off marriage, I have tried not to rock the boat when he's around. Because deep in my heart is the belief that this time I will get it right and Mike will stay and we will find our happily ever after.

His hands slip into the folds of my dressing gown and under the hem of my big t-shirt. Before he gets too far, I clamp my hands over his. 'What's up?' he murmurs.

What's up! I've got an STD. The only time I have ever been unfaithful to you in thirty years, and now I have the clap. Honestly, you couldn't make this stuff up.

'Sorry. Bad timing. Period.'

He steps back. 'Can I get you anything? Hot water bottle or something?'

Mike has never asked such a thing, and I can only think this is Call Me Charlie's influence. I've not had a period for two years. Mike has no idea what's going on with my body these days. Then again, he never did.

'I'll go on up then,' he says.

The sink is full of washing up. Mike's cooking always generates a lot of work. I scrape the plates into the bin on top of the dahlias, whose petals were falling yet would have been beautiful to me for a few more days.

When I've sorted the kitchen, I go upstairs. Mike is in what was our room, which I have readied for guests. I stand in the doorway and watch him snoring contentedly in the new white sheets. Then I get ready for bed, creep downstairs and spend the night on the easy chair with Ink.

In the morning, Mike brings me a mug of tea. 'Couldn't sleep, love?' he asks.

'Just restless. Didn't want to wake you,' I say, although the truth is I am sleeping very well because of the HRT I take at night. It's an added bonus.

Mike mows the lawn and fills the log basket in the kitchen before he goes to work. Then he kisses my cheek and trots along the path with a spring in his step. Happy Mike.

I wonder how long this will last.

Chapter Fifteen

When he's gone, I sit on the doorstep star with Ink, and we watch Maud eat the bird food I've tossed on the path. It's late October, and the sun is shining. I make toast, take my antibiotics and wander around the garden in wellies and a dressing gown with my mug of tea.

Leaves are falling in the breeze, and the damp garden smells delightful to me and the dog. I go through the gate into the woods and crunch along, admiring toadstools and the colours of autumn. I pick up sticks for kindling and carry them back to the stable. My phone beeps as I stack them on top of the pile next to the newly cut logs. It's Jason. I feel guilty that I haven't told Mike about him being gay. There hasn't been a right time. Then again, picking the right time to tell Mike anything is always tricky.

'Mum!'

'Hi, love.'

'What time do you want us on Sunday?'

This is news to me. Since the HRT, I am less forgetful. Then again, maybe not.

'I don't mind.'

'Thing is, I thought I'd bring Jonathon. But he's got some stuff he's got to do Sunday morning, so we couldn't get there until two.'

'That's fine, love,' I say. Did I ask him for lunch?

'I thought now is as good a time as any for you to meet him. You told dad, right?'

'Yeah. He's fine,' I lie.

'Great. I've talked to Belinda. She's cool. And it's going to be great to all get together. Do some family stuff. I don't mind if you lot need to eat earlier. I know it's tricky with the twins.'

'Oh, I'm sure we can give them a snack to keep them going.' So Belinda's coming too.

'Oh, and Jonathon can't eat dairy. Is that okay?' He sounds so happy.

'No problem. No dairy.'

'Okay, see you Sunday.' And he's gone.

As soon as he hangs up, there's a text from Belinda: 'Had a long chat with dad. Such great news. What time Sunday?' No doubt the good news is that Mike and I have got back together. He's had a ring round and given his version of events. When the kids were small, he arrived and then – after the row – went. Belinda and Jason always accepted him back without question. Even when they were moody teenagers. Sometimes they asked when he was coming home and I got very good at making excuses for him. I didn't want a family where the children felt the need to take sides. More importantly, I didn't want my children to be fatherless. I developed thick skin and a neutral stance.

I spend the day gardening and then make macaroni cheese. I don't even know if Mike plans to come home for tea, and I can't be bothered to send him a message that he will ignore. While it's in the oven, I shower and put on a clean pair of jeans. Since Cressida has been making me put on lipstick, I feel I look flat without it, so I go into the ensuite bathroom to search in the cabinet.

Mike has made the bed and drawn the curtains. The bathroom is tidy. His towel – one of the new white ones I have purchased for guests – is on the heated rail. I open the cabinet and jump back with a horrified squeak. Ink comes bounding up the stairs to see what the matter is.

On the shelf is a lump of fur. I think it is a mouse or something. I pick it up. It's a small hairpiece for Mike's bald patch, and I laugh and can't stop. As I put it back, Ink snatches it away.

'Bad dog!'

I chase after her down the stairs. She skips around the garden, shaking it and tossing it into the air. She's delighted, tail wagging.

'Ink, come on! Give!'

She takes no notice and zooms off every time I get close.

Trying to catch a greyhound murdering a toupee is hopeless, so I go inside, find Ink's box of dog biscuit treats and give it a shake. She's back in the kitchen in a moment with an expectant look. Mike's hairpiece hangs from her snoot like a hipster's highlighted beard. We swap biscuit for beard, and I take Mike's accessory back to the bathroom cabinet and set it on its little stand, where it looks bedraggled next to his fancy cosmetics and high-tech electric toothbrush. Oh dear.

Mike is late for dinner. I put some tinfoil over the mac and cheese to stop it from burning and wait. When he arrives, he's all charm. 'How are you feeling?' he asks as he washes his hands at the kitchen sink. For a minute I can't think what he means, and then I remember I am supposed to be having a period.

'Not too bad,' I say, getting the dish out of the oven. As

The Mid Witch

Mike sits, I peek at the back of his head. He has a fine head of hair for a man his age, and unless you look closely, you can't tell the fake from the homegrown. Good job, Call Me Charlie. Although I suppose he's looking for a new hairdresser now. Or maybe not.

He chats about his busy day, which was tricky because his staff and customers are a real nuisance. After we've eaten, he goes to his van and begins unloading his stuff. He lugs it through the gate and along the cobbled path. 'Have to think about getting some tarmac down until we can get the drive in. People want to drag their wheely suitcases along,' he informs me.

He has more belongings than normal. This is an improvement, I suppose. Usually, he arrives with only a few suitcases of clothes. Today there are boxes containing kitchen paraphernalia: a white dinner set, a collection of fancy knives, a high-tech corkscrew and some cookbooks. There are also towels and bedding in manly shades of grey. And clothes. A lot of clothes. I think of the stocked bathroom cabinet from this morning. He used to have a wash bag that he never unpacked. Perhaps he is staying this time.

He dumps most of it in the sitting room, which I am still decorating. In the kitchen, he turns me around from the sink and kisses me. Normally when this happens – this first kiss after he's 'been away' – it is like a drink of water after a long thirst. This evening I am not melting into his arms, longing for human contact. Desperate to be loved. His lips are oddly hard

– must be the Botox – and he smells perfumed but not in a good way. Instead of pulling him closer, I have the urge to run my hands through his hair!

'Is it nearly over?' he mumbles into my neck. I can't think what he's on about. What's nearly over? Our marriage? The menopause? The STD?

'It's been too long, Lil,' he says, sliding his hands inside my t-shirt.

Oh, I keep forgetting about the fake period. I pull away. 'No. Sorry.' It may last some time. 'I'm going to take Ink for a walk. Want to come along?'

Mike sits at the kitchen table. 'What, in the dark? I'll pass.'

Outside, the moon rises above the trees. I sit opposite him and take a deep breath. 'Jason called,' I say.

'Oh yeah. Meant to have said. Asked the kids over on Sunday.'

'Be good to ask me first?'

'Why? Are you busy?'

'No, I'm not busy. But, you know, be nice to know what's going on.'

'Thought I'd told you.'

'He said he's bringing someone. A guy.'

'I'll cook,' he says, all defensive, as if I have a problem with making a big lunch.

'It's fine. I don't mind cooking. Be nice to see everyone. No, what I'm trying to tell you is Jason is gay.'

The Mid Witch

'What makes you think that?'

'He told me. He's bringing his date on Sunday, and his name is Jonathon.'

To his credit, he doesn't rant and rave like a Victorian patriarch, as I thought he would. He's calm. Possibly shocked. I fetch Ink's collar and lead from the hook on the back of the door. As soon as she hears it, she appears in the kitchen and sits while I fasten it as if I trained her to do it. Not for the first time, I wonder who had her before me. Apart from toupee theft, she has lovely manners.

I pat Mike's shoulder as we leave. 'It's fine, love. He's still our boy. And I'm sure Jonathon is lovely.'

'This is all my fault,' he says, turning in his chair to look at me. 'I've been an absent father. A poor role model.' Mike rubs his eyes with the back of his hand. I pass him a tissue from the garden coat pocket and wait while he blows his nose. Then I gather him to me so his head rests on me where I stand.

'Gay or not gay... it just is. It's not a fault thing. It's a fact of life. And it's good he feels comfortable with himself and he can tell us.'

I hold him close, and he holds me around my legs. 'It's okay,' I say softly. 'Nothing's changed. Jason is still the same. We just know something more about him now. He sounded really happy when I spoke to him.'

'I've made so many mistakes,' Mike says, pulling back. His blue eyes are filling with tears.

It's unlike Mike to show any remorse. Perhaps he's changing – maturing. I hold his face in my hands.

'It's okay. Jason is happy, and that's the main thing. The only thing, really.'

Mike's eyes never were easy to read. But a moment ago, they had definitely looked sad. Now there is something else that I cannot understand. Abruptly, he gets up, pushes past me and heads upstairs.

Ink and I walk along Church Lane in the moonlight.

Chapter Sixteen

The week is busy. I go to the University twice for modelling, although I don't tell Mike. I am surprised on two accounts: firstly, that I'm doing something Mike disapproves of, and secondly, that I don't care if I bump into Randy Landy. This is highly likely even though I am working in the other teacher's class. Mike leaves early, returns late and makes no more sexual advances toward me. I don't care. Really, I don't. Normally, Mike's reappearance has me spinning because I try to please him by making an effort with homemaking and how I look.

As I hang his clothes in the wardrobe and fold his t-shirts into the drawer, I know this time will be different. The slow crawl of the menopause has shifted a part of my brain. Maybe this marker into the last phase of one's life is a wake-up call. This is it. Time is running out, and I must do as I want. Say what I think. Be myself. If Mike is going to stay this time, there will need to be changes. I need answers. As soon as I can get Mike to have a conversation, I'm going to lay some ground rules for this marriage.

The rain has eased on Friday, and I walk with Ink into Foxbeck village. I have done the grocery shop online, so I'm all ready for the big family roast on Sunday, but I would like a small gift for the twins.

Janice, the shop owner, is putting up a Christmas tree in the window when I arrive, and everything is in disarray. 'Oh, Lilly, hi. How are you?' She went to school with Belinda.

Ink is wagging her tail madly, and Janice gives her head a pat. 'Love this dog. Is she a greyhound?'

The tree is decorated on one side, and I help her manoeuvre it into the window. 'It's the only way, or else you can't get at it when it's in place.' We shuffle it as carefully as we can while all the decorations jiggle and shake.

The Mid Witch

'I know you think it's too early.'

Secretly I do. We've not had Halloween yet.

'But it's a big job, decorating the shop and getting out the seasonal stock. People don't realise.'

She stands back to look at the huge tree now stuffed into the bay window. 'This is a bad idea. It's going to drop needles everywhere and be bald by December.'

'What about putting it into a bucket so it can be watered? I've heard that's supposed to help.'

Janice straightens her back. She's tall. My Belinda is short, like me, and the two of them always looked quite comical. The tallest and the shortest kids in the school.

'Yes! That's the answer. Can you watch the shop while I find one out the back?'

I stand there holding the tree while Ink, lead trailing behind her, gives the little shop a good sniff. From the window, I can see the village green and a few people coming out of the pub. They stand and chat.

'The thing is,' says Janice, dashing back in, 'got to get the tree up early or you miss the moment. These days everyone shops early. I'm going to the shed. Be five minutes. You okay?'

'Yeah, fine.' I push in between the branches so I can rest the tree on my shoulder. This might take a while.

The people on the village green have gone. There is no one about, and I wonder how these local shops survive. Then the bell over the door tinkles and a customer comes in. They browse on one side of the shop, and I can't see who it is from the window. I should say something so I don't startle them when they walk past the tree. I peer through the branches. Oh my god. It's Call Me Charlie. I keep very still. The last thing I need is a confrontation with Mike's ex. Then again, what is she doing in Foxbeck? Has she come to find Mike?

Theo would call her appearance very 'up together'. Long grey coat. Nice leather boots. Scarf draped artfully about her neck in shades of green. Expensive shoulder bag. And, of course, her hair – bobbed and blonde – is immaculate. Even in the overcoat, she looks slim. She picks up a snow globe and gives it a shake.

Ink is walking quietly along with her head held high, sniffing. I hope Call Me Charlie likes dogs. Ink is big, and although I find her beautiful, she might frighten non-dog lovers. I should call her to me, but I'd rather stay hidden.

'How much are these?' asks Call Me Charlie when Janice reappears, carrying a large silver bucket.

Janice laughs. 'You know, I have no idea. They're new. Hang on, let me go poke my computer. Sorry about the mess.'

Call Me Charlie goes to the counter at the back of the shop. I keep still. She won't see me here. People hardly notice small, middle-aged women holding Christmas trees. Then Ink places her long snoot ever so delicately in the shoulder bag. I hope she is just giving it a good sniff. But no. Seconds later, Ink gently lifts an item from the bag and brings it to me, tail wagging. It's hard to see what it is through the tree branches. Carefully I put my foot on Ink's lead so she can't get up to any more mischief. Call Me Charlie and Janice have a pleasant chat, then the doorbell tinkles and she's gone. Phew!

'Well,' says Janice, beaming. 'That proves my point. People *do* want Christmas stuff early. She bought two snow globes.'

'Brilliant.' I take my foot off the lead, and Ink wanders off.

We get the tree wrangled into the bucket without any decorations falling off, and then Janice goes in search of the perfect gift for twin seven-year-olds. Ink is sitting very straight, skinny tail thumping the floor, with the pilfered item in her mouth. I'd hoped she'd pinched some food – a sandwich or a packet of crisps. Instead, the item is pink and plastic. Must be a large hairbrush. Thank god. If Ink had taken her wallet or phone, I would be honour bound to chase after her and return it. I'm pretty sure she's got plenty of hairbrushes.

'Give,' I whisper. Ink obediently drops it.

My plan is to leave the brush there and let Janice return it when Call Me Charlie calls again.

'These are very nice. Only came in yesterday. Should keep them busy.' Janice holds up two activity packs.

'Busy is good,' I say, looking at the floor.

'They each have a colouring book, six felt tips, a storybook, a toy and a tub of modelling putty. Oh, and stickers.'

It's hard to concentrate on what she's telling me. I can't take my eyes off the enormous hot pink dildo that Ink has deposited at my feet. She has her front paws on the floor and her bum in the air, her skinny tail like a hook. The hook of happiness. It's clear this dog would like to play fetch the dildo.

'... I've got dinosaurs, volcanoes, ponies, kittens or puppies...'

I grab the dildo – which is surprisingly heavy – and shove it into Big Bag.

'... mini-beasts and farm animals.'

'Gosh, not sure,' I say, clamping my hand on Big Bag to keep it shut before Ink gets her snoot in there.

'Oh look at her, wagging her tail. She's such a cheerful dog. Would she like a biscuit?'

Janice brings out a large jar from under the counter, and Ink sits like a blameless angel for the treat with one paw raised. Kleptomaniac? Me?

'Dinosaurs and mini-beasts. Better keep it educational or I'll be in trouble.'

Outside, I take a deep breath of crisp autumn air and relax. That was a narrow escape. We head for home.

'Mrs Turner!'

It's Call Me Charlie coming out of the post office. Oh no. I don't want a scene. Not here where I live. I can sense the cottage curtains twitching. These sleepy villages may look quiet, but they have ears.

'Mrs Turner!' She catches up with me as I'm rooted to the spot. Clearly, she is embarrassed. Does she know I have her dildo? Ink pulls on the lead, and I take a step so she can get on the grass. We both watch her take a long pee.

'Look. The thing is, I owe you an apology, plain and simple. No matter what you might think, I don't go out with married men. It's one of my rules.' I listen. Of all the things I thought she was going to say, this is not one of them. 'When you came in with the divorce papers... it shocked me.'

'You thought he was divorced?' The bastard.

'Mitch said you had an open marriage. Then you turned up that day, and I realised that was not the case. When I confronted him...' She shakes her head, and her hair moves like it's in a shampoo ad.

'What did he say?' I'm curious: does Mitch get as angry as Mike?

'He said you were getting divorced. Said it had all been over for years, anyway.'

I nod, fascinated by her. I've never come face to face with any of his lovers. Probably just as well, if they were all as young and good-looking as this one. 'Anyway. I kicked him out... You probably heard?'

'You were living together?'

'Not officially, no. But you know how it goes. Little by little, you spend more time together, and before you know it, your flat's full of his stuff.'

No, Charlie, I don't know. I've been married since I was nineteen. I don't say anything. I stand there like a fool, and she goes on trying to explain.

'Anyway, after the divorce papers, he started getting serious. One minute it's a casual, open relationship thing you're having with an older guy, and the next, he's getting heavy and wants exclusivity.'

'It's fine. He always was a lying shit,' I say.

She smiles and shakes her hair again. 'Aren't they all?' My god, she's so pretty. I imagine all men fall at her feet. No wonder she doesn't want an exclusive relationship. If only I could introduce her to Randy Landy.

Neither of us is sure what to do next. So we sort of roll our eyes to heaven in an 'aren't men awful' gesture and go our separate ways.

Halfway along Church Lane, I can't resist lifting out the dildo. Is this for her own personal use? Or did she buy it for a colleague? I've never held one before except in my late twenties when a friend had an Ann Summers Party. No one bought anything, but we laughed a lot.

Ink is excited about seeing her 'toy' again, so I unclip her lead and chuck it for her. We play fetch the dildo all the way home. If nothing else, it keeps her from rushing into the graveyard and trying to dig up my ancestor. When we reach the cottage, I throw it one last time. Ink has lost interest and waits for me to unlatch the garden gate. The dildo is un-retrieved somewhere in the ditch. A lost cock in the countryside.

Chapter Seventeen

I intend to have a chat with Mike about our marriage as soon as the opportunity arises. But family moments are precious, and I don't want to rock the boat before Sunday. Apart from Jason's graduation, it has been ten years since we were all together. On Saturday, Mike goes to the warehouse to chase up an order he needs for the following week, and I have a big clear up, starting with the kitchen table. There is always a pile of stuff at one end. The table is large, and it is too easy to push everything aside when space for eating is required. Tomorrow we will need all the space.

I sort the junk. Put the newspapers in a pile to light the fires. Hang dog leads, coats and shopping bags in their rightful place. Put my notebooks and biscuit packets away. At the bottom of the pile, I find the shadow book. Since Mike's return, I have not looked at it. In fact, the whole witchy business is far from my mind. Now I have some company, the strange feeling within me has gone. Last night I even slept the night with Mike. No sex, but we had a nice cuddle in the dark. Even though the sky was clear and the garden flooded with moonlight, I stayed next to him after he turned over, listening to his soft snore. How nice it would be to make this work. As we reach this mid-point in our lives and old age looms, I imagine companionable moments around the fire and walking the dog. Our children breezing in for a quick visit because they were passing. Cake and cups of tea and cosy family Christmases with the grandchildren.

The old leather suitcase is at the back of the under stairs cupboard. I set the shadow book on the arm of the easy chair so I can put it away later. Mike will be home for lunch, apparently, so I make us some sandwiches. He doesn't come home, but he texts with an excuse, which I take as progress. He's going to be late. Never mind. When I've done all my jobs and

The Mid Witch

made a big apple crumble for tomorrow, Ink and I settle in the easy chair. I'm tired after a restless night.

The dog is soon asleep, her feet twitching in time with her dream. But I lie awake thinking about tomorrow. The occasion has taken on the proportions of Christmas day, and I wonder if I should peel the veg tonight or make an extra pudding. Should I wrap the twins' gifts? Mow the lawn? Does Mike still fancy me after shagging the beautiful Call Me Charlie? The shadow book is on the chair arm. Maybe reading will settle my brain for sleep. Maybe what I need is a love potion?

The book, with its flimsy, handwritten pages, is difficult to navigate. There is no index, and each entry is random. I can find nothing again, even if I mark the place with a scrap of paper. 'Show me a useful love potion,' I say as I open the book. The pages flip as if blown by a breeze and then stop. Here is a drawn heart entwined with ivy. The title is Attraction and Success.

Although the list of ingredients is long, most of what's needed grows in the garden. I don't have any honeycomb but I have a jar of honey, and I can't think what difference this will make. The spell requires 'candle red, white and coloured'. I'm not sure if this means one or many candles. I rootle about in the kitchen junk drawer, which is full of odds and ends that might be useful, and find two packets of birthday cake candles. One packet is multicoloured and the other is metallic.

At the end of October, the nights are drawing in fast, so I pick my herbs in the fading light and spend a happy hour grinding them with honey and moon-blest water from the birdbath. The instructions state I should place the potion and candles on oak wood and burn everything beneath the moonlight while chanting. Here I am most confused. The shadow book is full of incantations in another language. The old English is tricky enough. I copy out the words to see if they make more sense. They are just as unpronounceable.

The stone basin that Any-Job-Steve helped me haul into the centre of the lawn still needs filling with soil and spring bulbs. I'm glad it's empty for now because it will make a nice safe place to start a fire. After I clear up the kitchen, I line the fire pit with newspaper, kindling and oak logs and tip on the herby concoction. Next, I squirt the honey. The candle instruction is most confusing, and I'm sure that these birthday candles are too small. I decide to use them all to compensate and stick them into the thick herb paste. I can never find the matches, but I don't care. The full moon is bright as I light the candles with sparks I snap from my fingers. Ink and I squat on the frosty grass as I look at the words on the scrap of paper. Since I do not know how to say them, I toss them into the flames for good measure. I am sure this is all nonsense, yet I am strangely soothed by the procedure.

The candles, multicoloured and metallic, are pretty. I run back to the cottage and return with a picnic blanket and rugs, and Ink and I wrap up and watch the flames. Soon the candles burn away and the true fire begins. Bright orange and blue flames flicker, and the air is herb scented. I breathe it in and Ink sighs. Around me, the frosty garden glitters and the moon fills me with joy. I put my arm around Ink and remember sitting here, just like this, on a rug on a cold winter night when I was a small child with my arms around Rufus. Grandma Gwen lit the fire, and we sat together and watched the flames. There were herbs on that fire as well. Sweet and pungent, different to mine. I slept, and when I woke much later, there were others gathered. Adults softly murmuring like wind in the top branches of winter trees.

'Bloody hell! Lilly!'

Startled, I jump up. It's Theo.

'This! This creature frightened the life out of me!'

Ink, still draped in a blanket, is standing on the path, blocking her way. I whistle softly, and she comes to my side with a huff.

'What on earth are you doing out here on such a night?'

I look at the sky, all stars and a giant moon. It's a beautiful night.

Ink and I follow her into the kitchen, where she turns on the light. For once, the place is tidy. The kitchen table is empty, and Mike's horrid white lilies are in the middle. Theo picks up the vase and gives them some water from the kitchen tap. 'I bumped into Mike this morning. Such good news.'

I must look blank.

'About you getting back together at last!'

I fill the kettle while she rearranges the flowers.

'You don't look very happy about it, darling.'

I sit, and Ink lies by the range, still in her blanket, and puts her head on my foot.

'Oh, you know Mike. I'm sure he'll bugger off again the first time any woman bats her eyelashes at him.'

Theo makes tea. 'He seemed very... happy.'

Probably bonking someone already. 'Really?'

'Yes. Well, even blokes like Mike settle down in the end. Most people come to their senses when they get a little older. I'm sure that girl he was seeing... that hairdresser... Charlotte! Now I know why Mike is looking good for his age. But you know, she must have made him feel a bit...'

'Tired?'

Theo throws back her head and laughs. 'Exhausted, I should think. Have you seen her?'

'Yes. I've seen her.'

'Well! I think these men like it all to start with and then... then they miss the comforts of home. They want the reassurance of the familiar.'

Yep, that's me. I'm like a pair of well-worn slippers. Good old comfortable Lilly.

'Perfect timing, of course.'

I stare into my tea and let her ramble on.

'You'll be all snug for a family Christmas.'

The witch ball hanging in the window has taken on the

glow from the fire outside. The flames flicker on the surface as if it, too, burns.

'I'm sure you can remind him of the comforts of home. I bet little miss hair salon never cooked him supper,' she says, glancing around the kitchen, which is clearly foodless.

'Mike said he'd bring fish and chips,' I lie. I have cooked all week, and he hasn't turned up for any meal. Mike is already slipping away.

'Well, that's cosy too.' She stands and swings on her cashmere poncho without disturbing a hair on her head. 'And all the decorating won't go to waste.'

I'm about to tell her that Mike is happy about the bed and breakfast and that I have a booking for November, but I am not quick enough. She is on a roll.

'Mike's right. I think selling the cottage in the spring is much better. Cosy Christmas here and then a lovely new start for you both in the new year. And nobody enjoys moving house in the winter.'

Theo steps carefully over the doorstep star and points a manicured nail at the fire pit. 'Shouldn't you put that out? Smells awful.'

She minces along the cobbled path, and I follow. 'Oh, I nearly forgot.' She delves into her bag and brings out two little gifts wrapped up with bows. 'Little something for Amy and Sophie. Mike said you were having a big family lunch.'

We air kiss, and off she goes.

The lilies look refreshed after Theo's attentions, and the

kitchen smells like a funeral parlour. I turn out the light, grab a log from the log basket and go back to the fire. Perhaps Mike will join me here when he gets home?

I wake much later, cold now that the fire has gone out. A soft drizzle falls from a moonless sky. Ink is still next to me, her warm body keeping me safe. Dragging the blankets with us, we go back into the kitchen. Ink gives herself a shake. I am wet through and am reminded of the night Mike left me to walk home in the rain. That night hides in a dark place in my mind along with so many other bad memories. All of which I never speak truthfully about. I'd rather give a tidy version. Not upsetting the children was my priority. Guarding them from the reality of Mike's true self was my duty. Even now my children are adults, the habit continues. Tomorrow we will play happy families. Tomorrow I will perpetuate the myth that we are normal. Only now am I realising that I am trying to protect myself from the truth. I strip off in the kitchen, hang my wet clothes on the range, and add a few logs to keep it burning through the night. The kitchen clock reads 2.30am.

Upstairs, I check the bed and am unsurprised to find it empty. It has begun again. 'No Mike then,' I say to Ink. He will appear with a feasible excuse. Funny how he has never given me an STD. Vaguely, I wonder where he might be and with whom. The hairdresser or someone new? 'So much for the spell,' I say. Ink is already asleep on the bed.

Chapter Eighteen

In the night, I wander about as usual and end up sleeping in the easy chair. In the morning, Mike is bright and breezy. 'Sorry, got waylaid. Work shit. Didn't want to wake you.' He hands me a cup of tea and goes back to the kitchen.

'Toast?' he calls. I get up from the easy chair and sit at the kitchen table. Mike makes toast while regaling me with a delightful story involving broken-down delivery vans and a cracked bath for a very important customer. I'm not really listening as I know it's all a crock of shit, and if I say anything at all, the whole day will have an unpleasant atmosphere.

Mike is already dressed and spruced up. His cologne has the certain smell of a gift from another woman with subtle notes of guilt.

When I come downstairs again in my best dress, Mike has taken over the kitchen. He puts a glass of wine in my hand. It's only ten o'clock, and I need more tea. 'Everything is under control,' he says. 'Special treat. Just relax. I've got this.'

The chickens I was going to make a traditional roast with are in a large casserole dish, and he is tipping in a bottle of red wine. There is a strong smell of garlic – or is that the cologne? I have never known him cook anything more elaborate than a fry-up, beans on toast or the cottage pie. Ink is in front of the range, and Mike shoos her out of the way so he can open the door. 'That dog reeks!' he says as Ink gets up slowly and stretches.

'I don't think the dog smells.'

Mike is positioning the casserole. 'Long and slow, that's the secret,' he says, closing the door with a flourish.

'You'll need to keep an eye on the fire. Watch it doesn't get too low.'

He rubs his hands together. 'Right. Desert.' He delves into a bag of shopping on the draining board and lifts out a few bars of expensive chocolate.

'Don't forget Jonathon can't eat dairy.'

'Jonathon?'

'Jason's boyfriend.'

Mike reads the ingredients on the chocolate wrapper. 'The chicken will be fine. But this is no good.'

'I made a crumble that's dairy free.'

'Perfect. He can have the boring crumble, and the rest of us can have my speciality chocolate torte.'

I leave him to his culinary delights and take Ink for a nice long walk. We go through the woods and over the fields to the beach. The sea is raging and beautiful. Tall waves crash on the rocks and seagulls whirl in the wind. I sit for a while on the shingle, breathing in the cold, clean air and letting the rhythm of the sea soothe me. Ink snoops about, sniffing and paddling in the foam. Few know about this little cove. It is only accessible by footpath and almost always empty. Thank god.

We take the long way home through different fields and past the ruins of stone cottages that once belonged to smugglers. The path hooks past North Star, and on the higher ground, I can see the cottage nestled in the overgrown garden. A sliver of smoke rises from the chimney. Maud sits in the bare branches of the apple tree. This is mine. This house and these fields and this wood. All mine. I kneel and press my hands into the cold soil of the newly ploughed field. The earth breathes much like the sea, and I sit there like a crazy woman with my eyes closed until Ink comes and puts her wet nose on my cheek. Below, in the garden, two little girls are running around the lawn.

'They're here!' I rush down the path with Ink striding beside me. Brian and Belinda already have glasses of wine in their hands. Have I really been that long? 'Sorry. Walking the dog.' Why didn't Mike text?

Belinda gives me a dutiful kiss. 'Late for your own party, Mum.'

The twins shriek when Ink goes to sniff them. 'Can't we tie her up?' says Mike.

'No, she's fine.' I settle Ink by the range and put a blanket over her.

'Have to sit in here, I'm afraid. We're in the middle of decorating the sitting room,' says Mike.

I put the kettle on before Mike has the chance to give me more wine. I'm gasping for a cuppa now. 'Anyone want tea?' I ask.

'Are you going to change?' Mike whispers when everyone goes to look at the sitting room. He's eyeing my mud-spattered dress and snagged tights.

'Possibly.'

Everyone gathers around the table, and I give the twins their activity packs. It's nice. Belinda chats about school, and

The Mid Witch

Brian drinks his wine quietly. Mike is wearing a smart navy apron to protect his white shirt. He must have attended a cooking course. These days, a Lothario must offer more than shagging. I make tea and sit with the twins. When they get bored, we put our coats on and go outside. Ink comes along, and I show them how she will fetch a ball and then drop it at their feet to be thrown again. Ink is very gentle with Sophie and Amy. Soon they are patting and hugging her, and the big black dog and the two little girls are best friends.

Jason arrives with Jonathon earlier than expected, which is a relief because Mike is clearly worried about the meal. Jonathan is charming. He's good with the kids and asks lots of questions to get people talking. Best of all, they get along well. They look at each other constantly.

There is something about having a stranger that makes us all behave nicely. Mike leaves his phone alone and attempts to listen. Brian says a few sentences of his own. Belinda curbs her bossiness. I mostly do colouring-in with the kids.

Mike is very pleased with his new cooking skills. Turns out Jonathon is a bit of a cook too, and soon the two of them are discussing marinades and char grills. Who knew?

Theo's gift turns out to be false nails and makeup. Belinda is horrified. Amy and Sophie are thrilled and go to the bathroom for a 'glow-up'. This keeps them busy for hours. They come to show us the results, which are delightfully horrific. Sparkly eye shadow, bright pink lip gloss and long, gold false nails.

Sensibly Belinda has brought their pyjamas, and I run them a bath and have a happy time getting the make-up and talons off and the clean pyjamas on. Then we three get into Mike's bed with Ink, and I read them stories until they fall asleep.

It is late when everyone leaves. Brian and I carry the sleeping kids to the car, and we say our goodbyes quietly so as not to wake them. Mike and I wave them all off and walk up the path, arm in arm. It has been a lovely family day. Just what I needed.

Spending time with my granddaughters has left me in a good mood. I hum a silly song I was singing to them as I wash up. Mike collects the dirty dishes from the table. 'We must do this more often,' he says.

'Jonathon seems like a nice bloke,' I say.

Mike doesn't reply. He's been great all day, but I can tell he's still coming to terms with having a gay son. 'You sure it's not a phase he's going through?'

'No, love,' I say gently. 'Jason's gay, and it's fine.'

Mike nods slowly. In the kitchen, I run hot water into the sink.

He changes the subject. 'Bumped into Theodora.'

'Yeah, she popped in last night.' My pleasant mood dissipates. 'She says you're planning to sell the cottage after Christmas.'

'I'm sorry. I asked her not to say anything until I'd spoken

The Mid Witch

to you. It's only an idea. Maybe we should sell. Get our own place and make a new start.'

From behind, he puts his arms around my waist. Speaks into my neck, which makes my back tingle. 'We haven't got the kids to worry about. We could go anywhere we wanted. So long as I can get to the showroom without too much of a drive.' His arms tighten, and he presses himself closer. The length of his cock is hardening against my leg. It would be so easy to yield to his advances. Pretend everything is alright. I usually do.

The witch ball gently spins. Moonlight swirls across its surface, white and grey like clouds. Something inside me is shifting – like a tide or a gathering storm I cannot stop. I am troubled by strange impulses, and the only word that can vaguely explain the vibration inside me is defiance.

'I'm not selling North Star,' I say quietly, and our happy moment has gone. Mike lets me go and pulls away, his lip curled in disgust as if he'd held a corpse.

'I'm just trying to make everything all right,' he says, and I can see the effort it costs him to pretend he's calm.

I dry my hands on a tea towel and face him. 'Living somewhere else won't fix us, Mike. We have to do that ourselves. If you don't want to be with me here, I doubt you'll want to be with me in another house.'

Mike tilts his head ever so slightly on one side and raises his eyebrows and gives me his patronising stare. I wait. Will he shower me with a tirade of abuse or stomp off and sulk? It can go either way with Mike. He sighs loudly and heads to bed. I'm glad. It's late, and I'm tired.

The last thing I need is a row.

'What's this fucking dog doing in my bed!!' Ink trots past me. The kitchen door opens, and she huffs as she walks over the doorstep star and into the moonlit garden. It's my imagination, I know, but it sounded a lot like laughter.

Chapter Nineteen

Mike is riled, so I stay downstairs with Ink and we sleep in the easy chair. I don't even bother to go up and brush my teeth. The twins have worn the dog and me out. We sleep well and don't wake until I hear Mike in the kitchen. Ink has gone – she has probably let herself out for a pee – and I stand in the doorway, wrapped in a blanket. Mike leans over the kitchen sink, wiping tears from his face with a tea towel. My heart goes out to him. Apart from the other day, I have not seen him cry since we were young. Poor man. Shuffling over in my blanket, I put my arm around him.

'That fucking dog!' He shoves me away. His face is red and blotchy, and he blows his nose on the tea towel. 'That fucking dog has got to go!' At that moment, Ink noses through the back door and comes in from the garden. 'That dog.' He sneezes twice. Ink wags her tail and rubs against his grey track suit as if they are the best of friends. Mike shrinks away as fresh tears fall, and Ink gives herself a good shake.

Uncontrollable sneezing grips him. All he can do is point at the dog and utter, 'Allergy!'

'Look,' I say, trying not to smile. 'It might not be the dog. It could be...' I search for something else that might have caused Mike's predicament. 'It could be these,' I say, picking up the vase of lilies. 'Lots of people are allergic to flowers.'

He points to Ink, who is settling herself next to the range, even though it has gone out. The kitchen is freezing, as is the rest of the house. 'She hasn't really been near you,' I say. Then I remember reading stories to the twins with Ink in the bed. Oh dear.

'Take a cold shower. I'll find some antihistamine.'

While he's gone, I look through the first aid box. All I have is some ointment, which is out of date. My thoughts stray to the shadow book. If I asked it for a cure for 'dog rash', would it show me the page?

Mike is back in the kitchen in jeans and a t-shirt. He hasn't shaved or put on his little wiglet thing. 'Why don't you drive to the chemist and get some stuff?' I say.

He grabs his keys and storms off, scratching his bum as he runs.

After I've washed and dressed, I send him a text: 'How are you feeling?' Then I spend the morning tidying up. There is a lot of cheap make-up smeared around the bathroom and a sink full of washing up in the kitchen. The least I can do is change his bedsheets. Then I eat cold apple crumble for breakfast and snap my fingers for a spark to light the fire in the range. My phone is on the kitchen table and, unusually, he has answered my message.

'Better,' his text says. 'It's the dog or me.' I don't think he's joking. I also have a feeling Ink did it on purpose, which is ridiculous, I know.

Kneeling beside her where she is keeping warm by the range, I have a word with her. 'Inky dog, did you give Mike a rash? Because if you did, you must stop.' Ink rolls on her back for a tummy rub, and I oblige. Mike could well be allergic. He's always had an aversion to animals. Perhaps it was his body's way of telling him to steer clear.

The cottage is clean and it is a beautiful, crisp sunny morning. I need to think, so I take Ink for a walk over the fields to the beach. When we get back, it is lunchtime, and

Mike's van is in the lane. I hope his rash hasn't worsened and made him feel ill. Allergies can be nasty.

The field is muddy, and I pull off my boots outside and wipe Ink with a rag. In the kitchen, Mike is stirring a tin of paint on the table. Apart from a few blotches, his rash has gone, and his eyes are dry. 'I've been thinking. Maybe you're right. We should give this bed and breakfast thing a go.' He's Mr Congeniality. I am relieved he's in a good mood, and when Ink trots across to greet him, I point to the range, and she turns about and settles herself for a nap with a huff.

I hang the garden coat on the back of the kitchen door. There is still a lot of decorating to do. The sitting room needs more gloss work, and the hall and stairs are in dire need of paint. With a bit of help, this place could be perfect. He's come back to help me get ready for the first guests. It's his way of making amends, and I'm touched. Perhaps working together on something will bring us closer.

'Did you eat lunch?' I ask, lifting the lid on the bread bin.

'I'm fine. Had a bowl of cereal. Ate too much yesterday.' When we were young, he was the slightly chubby one. Now it's the other way around. He's whip-thin, and I've noticed he is careful about what he eats. Me, I've been slightly fat since I had Jason, although taking these long walks with Ink has improved my figure. And the decorating. That's helped too.

'Sorry about this morning,' he says. 'You're right. We could make a go of this.'

The Mid Witch

'We could,' I say, feeling optimistic as our eyes meet. This might be fun.

He makes a sweeping gesture toward the garden. 'I'm going to convert the stables. Cut down the apple tree and build something low and sleek. I'm thinking wood frame contrasting with the old brick. Skylights, wet room. Be a real money spinner.' He laughs and says, 'First things first. Can't live with that bloody awful yellow in the sitting room. Got to get it sorted.'

I step closer and peer into the pot of sludge-coloured emulsion.

'What was it even called? Custard?' he says.

'Morning primrose,' I mutter.

'Lil!' He leans over the paint and kisses my cheek. 'You always did have terrible taste.'

As he picks the paint up, I see the shade is 'modern mole'. 'Gravestone grey', if you ask me.

'You're not re-doing the sitting room.' I follow him. He's already painted one wall. Cheeky bastard. The defiance that has grown in me in recent months bubbles up in a weird, calm anger. 'No,' I say.

He tilts his head, raises his eyebrows and speaks in an overly kind voice. His mouth is a gentle curve. 'Lilly, I've taken this afternoon off to get this done. So, you can either help or make some tea or something.'

'No, Mike. I'm done. You're not painting this room or any other. I've had enough.'

'What do you mean? I'm here, aren't I? Helping you?'

'No. You're just doing what you want, like you always do. I've had enough of your shit. You're leaving.'

'What! I thought everything was okay.'

'Until you fuck off again with the first woman who gives you the come-on. You're right, we don't have the kids to worry about anymore, and I'm sick of pretending we have some sort of marriage. I want that divorce.'

'Lilly.' He's laughing now, turning away, dipping the brush in the paint. 'You're going to divorce me because you don't like the colour of this paint. Sometimes you can be difficult to live with.'

And that's when I snap.

The old Lilly breaks off, and this other side of me that has lain dormant for a lifetime stands up in her place.

'How the fuck would you know?' I say. He paints with easy strokes. 'You haven't been here long enough to find out. I've spent my whole life waiting for you to come home and be a part of this family.'

He faces me, brush poised, exasperated. 'I'm here now!'

'Now is too fucking late. You're leaving!'

'What do you mean "too fucking late"? I thought this was what you wanted – to play happy families?' He's giving me that patronising look again.

'Our children have grown up and left home. It's too late to play that game.'

'We had a lovely day yesterday. The grandchildren–'

The Mid Witch

'Don't you dare talk to me about happy fucking families! Open-marriage Mitch! If it wasn't for me, you wouldn't even have a relationship with our kids. All these years I've tried to keep your philandering from them. Then you have the audacity to bring one of your fuck buddies to our son's graduation.'

'So this is about Charlotte.'

'No, Mike, it's about thirty years of disappointment and you not being able to keep your dick in your pants for five minutes. It's about every time you came home in between relationships with your promises and sweet talk and the "you're the only woman I ever loved" line – and just when I think everything is okay, off you bloody fuck.'

Mike's mouth hangs open.

'All these years, you've kept me hanging on with your lies about working away and your "I need a bit of space". And you know what? I'm middle-aged and menopausal, and I don't care anymore. Get out of *my* fucking cottage.'

Ink is standing beside me, and I put a hand on her head to steady my temper or whatever this is. Anger? Sadness? Sheer frustration?

'That's it then?' he says, face reddening. 'After all these years, you're going to end it now?'

'Don't you dare turn this back on me!' I point at the door. 'OUT!'

'Bloody typical. You start a row and drive me away!'

'You absolute cunt!' I yell.

'Spent my whole life caring for you, and this is the thanks I get! You're a bitch. You trapped me into marriage, and I've paid my whole life for one fucking mistake.'

My anger is a white wave of heat rising through my body. I stand fixed to the spot as the sensation fills me. My voice is quiet when I say, 'You practically raped me.'

'You were gagging for it,' he sneers.

'I kept telling you to stop. I wanted to wait. You carried on when I said no. You've been doing that my whole life. I can't do this anymore.'

Mike puts the paint tin down and balances the brush on top.

'Lilly, we were young. Young and foolish.' Again, the patronising voice.

'We were, but that doesn't excuse what you did. You made me.'

'Lilly, don't be ridiculous. I was a randy kid. You can't blame me for that.'

'You know what, Mike, I bloody can. Every time we've argued over all these long years, you've put the blame on me. As if it was my fault I got pregnant. That somehow I trapped you, and you've done me a big fucking favour by almost sticking around. The truth is, you're a shit. You were then, and you are now, and I want you out of my life.'

'I tried to make it right,' he begins, spreading his hands.

'No. No more lies and twisting the truth to fit the fairy tale in your head. Your parents insisted we got married.'

The Mid Witch

'Only because you wouldn't have an abortion.'

'Why don't you just fuck off!'

He's laughing now. Actually laughing. 'Nobody will have you. You've let yourself go. You're a grey-haired, overweight hag that nobody wants to fuck.'

Mike takes a step closer. He's never actually hit me. He's never needed to because we both know I'm scared of him. I've always had this grain of mistrust, though, wondering if one day he's going to strike. Normally, I cower and back off. Begin a new monologue that puts his point of view to the fore. Today I step nearer, and Ink places herself between us, her teeth bared.

He picks up the can of paint, and Ink rumbles a long, deep, threatening growl.

'I'm doing fine on my own, thanks. Now fuck off.'

He throws the paint at me.

It pours from the can and falls through the air. A wet wall of graveyard grey. Beside me, Ink leaps and twists. *No.* The thought is more than a word or a reaction; it's a command. I lift my hands in front of me as if to catch the liquid. The paint forms a ball, which I fling back. It spins through the air and hits him squarely in the chest.

I look at my hands, which are perfectly clean, and then at Ink, who wags her tail briefly at me. Mike is silent, watching the grey sludge ooze down him.

'The colour suits you. Now get out!'

Mike marches outside with as much dignity as he can muster.

Once in the garden, he regains some of his bluster. His natty sports car is parked in the lane, and he looks at it and then at his clothes. He undresses, and when he's in nothing but designer underpants, he walks toward me, no doubt expecting to come in and get changed.

I hold up my hand. 'Stop!' I yell, and Ink lends a massive bark to my order.

Mike's face changes from rage to fear. 'Lil! I can't get in the car like this. At least give me something to wear,' he pleads. Naked, he is quite orange.

I go indoors. I don't care if he's freezing his bollocks off in his Calvin Kleins. I want him gone once and for all. I grab a massive bag for life and run upstairs with it. In goes the fancy toiletries and wiglets, the neatly folded cashmere jumpers and his casual grey track suit. Shirts and socks, jeans and shoes. Soon the bag is overflowing, and I drag it to the doorstep.

'I want every bit of you out of my home,' I say.

Something in the cottage answers my plea. A vibration shudders through me and every room, and as I throw the bag at his feet, more of his things follow of their own volition. Clothes and shoes tumble down the stairs, through the kitchen and out onto the lawn. Books and old CDs fall from an upstairs window. Beige towels and curtains slide over the doorstep to join the ever-growing pile. Forgotten trainers and

The Mid Witch

old coats. The kitchen spits his cooking equipment out of every drawer and cupboard. His dirty washing and the stinking lilies land at his feet.

Then everything is still.

Ink and I stand on the doorstep star. 'I want everything gone by morning,' I say, waving a hand at the surprisingly large heap.

Mike has not moved. His eyes are large and wide as he stares right at me.

'Everything gone by tomorrow, or it burns,' I say, snapping my fingers and creating red sparks.

'What the fuck are you, some kind of witch?'

'You think?' I say. Then I turn my back.

Chapter Twenty

O nce the door closes, exhaustion grips me. I don't see what Mike does next. I don't care. I turn on the kitchen tap and drink straight from the flow. Ink laps water from her bowl, and then we stagger upstairs to bed, though it is not yet dark. I barely have time to register the nice clean sheets before I am deep asleep.

I wake with a start just before dawn. Somebody is banging on the door. Assuming it's Mike, I go to the window. All of his belongings, including the furniture, have gone from the lawn. He must have brought a van over.

The noise is not the door. Grant Fucking Rutherford is hammering another of his signs beside my garden gate. Fresh anger fills me, and I rush outside in my old dressing gown. Ink canters ahead in the gloaming, making little woofs of delight, and jumps smoothly over the garden gate. She's thrilled to see Grant and is doing her special skinny wriggle routine that she usually reserves for me.

'That's enough!' I say, and the same calm anger as before rises within me. I have not had the chance to process what exactly happened yesterday, and here I am again. Indignant and wild.

Grant hammers the board one last time and steps away from a sold sign. I am about to do something, I'm not sure what, when he speaks a strange word to the dog, making her stop her nonsense. Ink stands completely still. 'Lilith,' he says, holding up his hands as if I am about to shoot him. He's lacking his usual cocky expression. 'You're in danger.' My anger rises a little more. The lane is empty, and he has control of my dog. Is he the danger? If so, I'm ready to protect myself and Ink. I'm not sure how, but I have a power within me, strange and new.

'You have to trust me,' he says.

'How do you know my name?' Soft daylight filters through the damp mist. 'And why are you here so fucking early?'

He checks over his shoulder as if he's being followed. 'Lilith, what did you do?'

'Nothing. I threw my husband out. It's none of your business.' I'm defiant.

'You did something. Used your... instincts.'

'I don't know.'

'We should get inside,' he says, opening the gate.

At the cottage door, I go in, and he waits outside. Ink stands beside me. I put a hand on her head to steady my jangling nerves. I'm trying to piece everything together. Everything that happened yesterday and all the other things that have happened recently. Most of which I put down to a touch of middle-aged crazy woman.

He stands on the cobbles, mist swirling about him. 'You need to invite me in. If that's what you want,' he says.

'I don't know what's going on,' I say honestly. 'Why am I in danger?'

Grant looks back toward the lane. When he faces me again, he is more his usual arrogant self. 'You didn't think you could do whatever the fuck you did last night without consequences?'

'I don't know what happened.'

'You're turning into a witch, Lilith. Surely you know that?'

The idea is so preposterous when said aloud that I almost laugh. But Grant's expression is grave. More than grave. Frightened.

'I don't know anything.'

Next to me, Ink shakes herself, and there's a new urgency to Grant's voice when he says, 'Lilith, are you going to let me help you? We only have a short time. Can I come in?'

I've just got rid of one overbearing shit, and now here's another one. People say trust your instincts. Try to sense danger. Judge if something is not quite right. The house feels safe – it always does – but something lurks outside. Is Grant the danger? I don't know much about what is happening to me or why, yet I recognise that North Star Cottage has some sort of protective aura. Ink walks to the doorway and stands there, wagging her tail at him. For some reason, my dog likes him. I'm still unconvinced.

'Why should I trust you?'

'Lilith, we haven't got time for this!'

He rubs his face with both hands as if to wash away his anger.

'I'm a sort of witch,' he says. 'I've been tasked with protecting you. That day in the shop when you were mucking about and changing the faces of the ornaments... I had to make you stop. You can't do... *things* and think it will be alright. This *stuff*...' He's whispering now and leaning in the doorway, but he has not crossed the threshold. 'This stuff has consequences.'

I fold my arms.

'If you're my protector, why didn't you help?'

'I did help.' He looks at the ground.

'Help! I lost my job because of you.'

'I did help. I made you stop!'

'You could have spoken to me instead of acting like a dick.'

'There are rules. I'll explain everything.'

'If you're meant to protect me, why won't my house let you in?'

'It's an old place. It doesn't like men.'

I almost laugh. Then Ink's mood changes. She cowers, circles with her tail between her legs and whimpers. Goes to the doorway and back to me. I relent. 'Come in.'

Grant touches the doorstep star with the fingertips of one hand and says a few unintelligible words, then gingerly steps into the kitchen. It would be funny if Ink was not so clearly afraid. I close the kitchen door. The witch ball in the window is spinning, the surface alive with wispy black shadows in contrast to the bright day dawning outside.

Grant doesn't waste any time. 'Did your mother ever hide you?'

'Hide me?'

'Or your grandmother. Did they ever say "this is a hiding place" or put you somewhere to keep you safe?'

The Mid Witch

I don't know what he's on about.

'There will be a place that will keep you safe. Think, Lilith!'

'I don't remember!'

'Were you ever afraid?'

I shake my head.

'Close your eyes. Think about being scared.'

I do as I'm told, and Ink leans against me, and in that animal contact, I remember. 'Once, when I was very small, my mother put me...' I try to think where but have no idea. The memory is mostly feelings. Feelings that I have put aside all my life.

'Don't tell me. Tell Ink. Put your forehead on hers and think it. She's a good dog. She'll know.' I lean down and do as he says. Ink stands tall, and I close my eyes and remember. We stay like that for a moment so brief I can hardly grasp that the dog has learnt anything, but then she's through the door and waiting for me to follow.

'Good girl,' says Grant. I'm not sure if he means the dog or me. 'Go with her and hide. She'll know when it's safe.'

I follow Ink up the stairs and into the back bedroom that used to be mine when I was a child. It is the smallest room in the cottage, and I use it for storage. Ink makes her way between the boxes and junk to the back, where the ceiling slopes under the eaves. She stands with her nose against the wall, and then a panel slides, revealing a space. We crawl inside, and Ink shuts the door with a glance.

Old clothes hang from the walls, and a thick rag-rug covers the floor. All I have on is a massive t-shirt and my threadbare dressing gown. Shrugging on one of the coats and a hat, I feel around and find blankets. The space is just about big enough for us to lie down. I wrap us up, and we lie there in the dark. I hold Ink the same way I clutched Rufus, the big black lurcher, when I was last here. Then, as now, I do not know why I am hiding. Ink lies still, yet she is awake. Her taught muscular body is alert. Outside, a bleak, formless shadow lurks. She feels it too. A shiver runs through us both as we sense the dark force circling the cottage. Through the wood it floats and over the fields. Closer now, it prowls Church Lane and hovers at the garden gate.

In the garden are men's voices. Ink is listening, and she can probably hear what is being said. I wish I could see what was going on. I wonder if Maud is watching from her perch in the apple tree. As soon as I think this, I am within her – or she is within me. It's hard to explain, but now I see what the bird sees. The bare branches of the apple tree, black against the blue sky. The winter garden streaked with mist and sunlight. Two men speaking with Grant. They appear to be having a congenial chat about doing up old properties. Maud keeps cocking her head toward the lane, where the shadow lingers, although there is nothing to see.

The two men must have walked here. There is no vehicle. Maud sidesteps along the branch as the three men walk around the side of the house. The strangers might be father and son. They are happy in each other's company and seem perfectly normal. Perhaps they have nothing to do with any of this and the danger is in the lane, waiting for them to go. Then the younger man stoops to tie his shoelace. He places a hand on the ground, and the lurking shadow slides beneath the gate and slithers along the cobble path. Maud looks there – she must feel its presence as well. There is nothing to see. She tilts her head at the man, who is standing and turning. In a second, he will look right at me. Instinctively, I shut my eyes and pull myself away.

All of me returns to the hiding place with Ink. We keep still and breathe quietly as the threat seeps into the house and searches. It passes back and forth through the rooms. Dread fills us. Ink shakes. Her heart beats heavily. We are being hunted, and my brave girl is as afraid as I am. The thing takes its time, returning to each room over and again. When, at last, it leaves – slithering under the front door and into the woods – I sigh deeply. It's over. We're safe.

Then it calls me.

A siren call that pulls my soul.

Tuneless singing, full of promises and answers.

I put my hands over my ears, but the sound is within me and I cannot shut it out. Pleading and beckoning, it calls me into the woods, where the trees hang onto the last bright leaves of autumn. Ink presses against me, willing me to stay put. My mother's voice comes to mind as she pushed me in here all those years ago. 'Something will call you, Lilly. It will plead and promise, but you must not go. Stay here until the dog wants to leave. Hold tight to Rufus. He'll keep you safe.' I did as she asked then and I do it again now, putting both arms around Ink and holding her close. I bury my face in her smooth hound's neck and breathe in her warm fur. I think about the joy of her, scooting about the wood and running on the beach and through the fields. How she likes to sleep on her back with her long legs in the air.

Fear is exhausting. I sleep and dream of my mother and Rufus.

A gentle thumping wakes me. Ink is standing, and her wagging tail hits the old coats. Stiffly, I get up. The door to our hiding cupboard opens, and I follow her downstairs.

Grant is in my kitchen frying eggs and bacon on the range. Ink gulps down the food he has put out for her, then goes outside. We haven't eaten since yesterday.

Still wearing the coat and hat, I sit at the table, and he pours me a cup of tea and one for himself. It's almost dark. His clothes – old jeans and a t-shirt – are paint-spattered in morning primrose.

The witch ball hangs motionless above the sink. It reflects the room as if it is nothing more than a football-sized Christmas bauble.

I drink some tea while he dishes up, and then we eat in silence. This is bizarre. My thoughts are reeling. A week ago, I would not have predicted that I'd be eating a meal in my kitchen cooked by an arrogant man I actively dislike after recently expelling my husband from my home with magic I did not understand I had.

The door opens, and Ink returns from the garden and settles herself by the range with a huff.

Opposite me, Grant's shoulders are hunched, and he has dark circles beneath his eyes.

He takes our plates and puts them in the sink, which is already full of hot soapy water, then fetches a plate of toast from the warming oven and sets it in the middle of the table. He takes a slice onto a plate and spreads butter. I am warm now and shrug the old coat over the back of my chair and take off the hat. It is soft black felt, conical with a droopy point.

'I think this was my grandma's.'

'What did you do?' he says, neatly cutting the toast into triangles and pushing the plate toward me.

'I threw Mike out for good. When I got mad, things happened.'

'No, not that. You cast a spell, Lilith.'

'Did I? I was just mucking about.'

'You need to tell me everything you did.'

I am not interested in telling him because it feels like he's going to judge me or laugh. I stand and start dealing with the washing up. Maud flies to the window, which I open, and I give her some treats from her jar when she hops inside.

'When I was hiding, I saw you in the garden with two men. An older man and his grown-up son.'

'How? How did you see?'

'Maud showed me.'

'Who?'

'The Magpie. I call her Maud.'

'Like you were inside her head looking out?'

'Exactly that. Where she looked, I could see. But when the man turned, and I thought he would look at me – Maud – I shut my eyes and came back.'

'You have good reflexes. Have you done this before – looked from the magpie?'

'No. God, no. None of this stuff has happened to me before.'

'Nothing at all? No childhood memories of unusual abilities that you felt you needed to conceal?'

'No,' I say, and this is the truth. 'What is happening to me?'

'Happening? It's already happened, Lilith. You've turned into a witch.'

There's a wave of questions clamouring within me, and Grant frowns. 'Lilith, I need to take you to someone who will explain everything.' He gets up, lifts his coat from the hook on the back of the door and puts it on. He's leaving, and I don't want him to go. A short time ago, I was in fear for my life. 'They won't come back,' he says.

'Are you sure? And who? What were they?'

'You're safe here. Stay in the house and garden. Don't try any magic. I'll come back and get you as soon as I can.' He opens the door.

The Mid Witch

'Grant!' I stand up, and Maud flies to the top of the dresser and settles herself with a ruffle of her feathers. 'Thank you.'

He looks at the floor and smiles as he leaves.

After locking the door, I stand at the sink. Why do men always leave me with the washing up?

Chapter Twenty-One

The next day, I am drawn to the shadow book. My fingers tingle, and curiosity burns. I'd like to sit and read it, but I know I would not stop there. Before I could help myself, I'd be picking herbs and lighting fires. I don't even have an idea about a spell I want to cast or why. I leave the shadow book at the back of the under stairs cupboard with my other witchy things. I am like a child whose new toy has been confiscated.

Instead, I keep my mind on normal stuff and busy myself with the cottage. It's raining, which stops me wanting to mess about in the garden, and I feel safer inside. A new email informs me I now have two bookings for December, so I get on with finishing the sitting room. Grant has painted over Mike's graveyard grey, so I set about the gloss work, which is satisfying. With the radio on to stop my mind from straying, the day goes quickly. In the evening, I eat pasta and sauce and make a cake.

Grant does not return, and I don't hear from anyone all day. There isn't even any post. Why do men never give me their number? I want to speak to Grant. I need answers. For a start, how long will it take to contact the mystery someone? Days, weeks, longer?

Ink is very good and has pottered in the garden and slept by the range. We could both do with a nice long walk. Despite the rain, it is tempting to have a stroll in the dark. Then I remember the terrible, foreboding presence sifting through my home yesterday and the strange voice calling from the woods. Grant's exhaustion had been plain to see, even if he'd never spoken of it. No, I must be sensible. I get out my notebook full of everything bed and breakfast and check my to-do list. I spend the evening unboxing the three fire extinguishers I have purchased and hang them on the walls of the kitchen, sitting room and hall. This takes until ten thirty and I go to bed with a sense of achievement.

In the morning, the rain wakes me. A soft, restful patter on the window. I lie there cosy and warm with Ink pressed against me. Today I will move my things out of this room and get everything ready for the guests. I have a bit of a stretch and then get up. North Star Cottage is not overlooked, and I open the curtains wearing only the baggy t-shirt I sleep in that barely covers my bum.

Grant Fucking Rutherford is in my garden. He's pulled a chair onto the lawn and is sitting there in the early morning gloom, face turned up to the rain, in his underpants. I am so shocked to find a semi-naked man in my garden that I stand there gawping. He doesn't move. Slowly, I close the curtains. Then I notice all the wet, muddy footprints on the white sheets. Ink must have gone out to see him and then come back to bed. She doesn't like the rain. I peek through the curtains. Grant and I are about the same age, although he might be younger. He must go to the gym. In fact, he must go to the gym a lot. He has firm shoulders and toned arms with swirling black tattoos.

I turn away. *No.*

When I get this witch nonsense sorted out, I will find myself a nice man. Grant is obviously a nutcase. Some sort of health freak. He probably read that rainwater is good for the skin. Then again, nice skin. Smooth and dark.

In the bathroom, I catch sight of myself in the mirror. I'm

a mess and need a massive overhaul. Despite my dire need for tea and toast, I leave Grant in the rain – he's obviously enjoying himself – and take a shower.

I wash my hair and slap on a good handful of conditioner, and while it's soaking in, I have a go at the hard skin on my feet with the cheese grater thing and shave my armpits. Then I rinse off the conditioner and comb out my hair. These days it's the least of my problems. Long and steel grey with white streaks and loose waves. When I'm dry, I inspect myself in the magnifying mirror with my reading glasses on. I'm not a pretty sight. My upper lip has a luxurious growth of dark and grey hair. Five long black hairs and one white poke from my chin. Did I look like this yesterday – all middle-aged and furry? Or has this lot sprouted overnight? My trusty epilator needs charging, damn it. In the bathroom cabinet, I find a packet of wax strips and get to work sticking and stripping. Painful, yet necessary. Then I go in with the tweezers to tackle persistent offenders. Once done, I am barefaced and as red as a strawberry.

Next to my toothbrush is my HRT. I transferred the pills to a plastic container marked with the days of the week. Repetitive tasks are devilishly hard to remember, and this really helps. I am glad that I have not forgotten to take last night's pills, and that today is one of the two days I have marked with a dab of red nail polish to remind me to change the hormone patch. I wrestle the new patch out of its packet and peel off the protective layer, which is a fiddly, keep-my-specs-on moment. Now I have the thing grasped by the edge with my fingernails, I go into the bedroom so I can see what I'm doing in the long mirror.

These days, my bum looks like an aerial photo of arable fields on dimpled hills. I choose a bit of skin where the small rectangles of glue are faded and stick the new patch down. Then I rip the old one off and put it in the packet. The patches are described in the accompanying leaflet as discreet. This is true. The see-through patch blends perfectly with skin and is barely visible. If you were getting shagged from behind, I don't think a bloke would notice. That's what I thought when I stuck the first one on. I didn't know that the glue remains long after the patch has gone.

I have tried to remove the glue. Several options are available. Exfoliating mitten. Cleansing cream. The aforementioned cheese grater. Olive oil and washing up liquid. Nail varnish remover. Products that should not be applied to the skin and are meant for cleaning the bath. Nothing removes the evidence of the HRT patch.

I moisturise everything: feet, body, neck and face. When done, it is necessary to let the different unctions that stop me from drying up soak in. Normally, I do a few chores in the nude. Today I am mindful there is a wet bloke in my garden and keep away from the windows. I strip the sheets and the dog off the bed. Ink stretches and galumphs downstairs. I blast my hair with the dryer and hold a cold flannel to the skin on my blotchy upper lip. Then I pencil in my grey

The Mid Witch

eyebrows so that I don't look like Santa and get dressed in warm woolly tights and a nice sack with pockets and a pattern of foxgloves on a navy background. For some reason, I always feel happy in this dress.

At the top of the stairs, I hesitate.

Is this real? Or am I, in fact, losing my mind? The witch thing in the cold light of a late October morning seems like nonsense. Is it all my imagination? I touch my glue-scarred bum. Is this HRT making me hallucinate? Am I getting involved with another bad man? One who is messing with my mind? Let's face it, I have a very poor track record with men.

Mike was a bad man. A controlling bully who also managed to be absent for most of our thirty-year marriage. Then there's Philip Randy Landy, who is basically a nice bloke, but who is also a slut and gave me an STD.

Why is this obnoxious estate agent naked in my garden if not to take advantage of me?

I've had enough. Opening the hall window, I shout, 'Grant Fucking Rutherford, put some bloody clothes on and stop being so weird.' Maud squawks from the apple tree, and he leaps from the chair like his arse is on fire. When I see him again, he is standing outside my kitchen door, trousers on, buttoning his shirt. I try not to notice how the cotton clings to his wet muscles.

'Tea?'

Ink wags her tail from the dryness of the warm kitchen. I put some logs on the range and riddle the ash. 'Come in,' I say. He's annoying me now. He stoops, touches his finger to the doorstep star and comes in. His feet are bare. He's making more mess than the dog.

I put the kettle on and cut some bread. 'Toast?'

He puts on his shoes and socks. Not easy when you're drenched. I take his grunt as a yes. 'So, are you going to explain why you're practically naked in my garden at' – I look at the kitchen clock – 'ten-thirty in the morning?' He sips the mug of tea I've given him. Today he looks well. Not tired or worried. The word that springs to mind is vital. Grant Fucking Rutherford looks vital. I catch the toast when it pops up, hand him his on a plate, put butter and marmalade on the table and then feed Ink. We sit together in silence, eating toast and drinking tea while Ink makes a noisy job of her breakfast. Like a couple. Which is odd because I don't think we are even friends.

'I'm going to take you to meet another witch. Her name is Elaine Waters. She'll be able to answer your questions.'

No explanation about the rain kink then. 'Isn't this all a bit, you know, silly?' I say.

'In the cold light of day, the whole thing feels like a dream, doesn't it? You're wondering if you made it all up or have remembered the events incorrectly?'

'Something like that.'

He pushes his plate away and shivers. It's a wonder he hasn't caught his death. It's not as if it's warm summer rain. 'You're in denial. Common trait in witches like you.'

The Mid Witch

'Witches like me?'

'Old witches.'

'Thanks.'

He smiles. The same exasperated smile from when I was arguing with him about For Sale signs.

He thinks I'm an idiot. An old idiot.

'Didn't your family tell you anything?'

I fold my arms and sit back, giving him a hard stare. Obviously not.

'You've lived in this cottage and never wondered if your mother or grandmother were witches?'

'No. They seemed perfectly average to me.'

Grant takes his plate and mug to the sink. 'Come on. Don't want to be late. Get your coat.'

'Where exactly are we meeting your witch friend?' If he thinks I'm going off to some wood in the rain, he can fuck right off.

'Market Forrington. That bookshop at the top of the high street. The one with the coffeeshop.'

'Page's?'

'That's the one.'

Then I realise he expects me to get in the car with him. 'Why don't you give me her number? I'll message her, and we can arrange a time to meet.'

'Please don't be awkward. I'm not going to hurt you. Surely after the other day, we have some sort of trust. Elaine has cancelled her own plans in order to meet you.'

The witch ball in the window is perfectly calm, and the sun is peeping through the clouds. I just want everything to be normal. I want to take my dog for a walk and look for the rainbow. Not play this daft game of make-believe. More than that, I'm sick of men bossing me around.

'Snap your fingers, Lilith,' he says quietly. There's a twinkle in his eye. 'Go on.'

I snap, and sparks fly. They float in the air, silver and bright, and then fade away.

I go to the cupboard under the stairs and put on the black lace-up boots that were Belinda's and the long black coat. In the hall mirror, I pull on my grandma's conical hat for a joke. In the kitchen, I expect him to laugh, but he doesn't seem to notice. 'I'm not going without Ink.'

'Good instincts,' he says and waits while I put her coat and collar on.

His estate car is large and full of posts and For Sale signs. Ink sits on the back seat and seems perfectly at home. She must have been in a car before. I sit primly on the front seat with Big Bag on my knee. The seat is too low, and I can hardly see over the dashboard. I watch the drizzle and the wipers as we drive along in silence.

'So, what's with the sitting in the rain thing? Shower broken?'

He keeps his eyes on the road. 'Elaine will answer all your questions.' His jaw visibly clenches, and I realise I have asked something sensitive. I don't make any more conversation.

Market Forrington is bustling, as usual. We walk from the main car park to Page's, the bookshop café. I am relieved we don't bump into Call Me Charlie or Mike on the way. No doubt they are busy being entrepreneurs or some such shit. The café is at the back of the bookshop, and we thread our way through the stacked displays. Theo is there browsing historical fiction. With any luck, she won't notice us.

'Lilly! How lovely!' She wafts across, her smart grey coat flapping open to show her slim figure in fitted trousers and a soft, pale pink sweater. She's all pearls, silk scarf and a waft of expensive scent.

'Just taking the chance for a few bargains. Nothing like a good book on a dark winter night,' she crows while looking at Grant.

'This is Grant, er... Rutherford.'

'Of Rutherford and Grey?'

'At your service,' he says, oozing charm and smiles.

Theo simpers and offers her hand, which he takes in both of his. I almost roll my eyes. Apparently she's thinking of selling her flat, and while they talk shop, I take Ink's coat off as it's warm in the bookshop. She gives herself a shake, and I stuff her coat into Big Bag. Grant hands Theo one of his embossed business cards.

'I saw the sold sign, darling. Well done. Give me a call next week. We can go and look at flats together,' she says, air kissing my cheek. 'Cute hat. I thought you were Grandma Gwen.' She wafts off to pay for her stack of books. Grant looks wistfully after her. I think he'd like to give her more than a business card.

I pull off the hat and stuff it into my pocket. My hair dislikes this sudden interruption, and the static from the nylon carpet fizzes on my scalp and sends my long tresses into fluff mode. Should I put the hat back on?

Grant looks at my hair and then my face. 'She's your cousin?'

'Hard to believe? Truth is, we're not actually related. My mother's best friend, who I called Auntie Lyn – well, Theo is her daughter. Lyn and mum had so little family they sort of joined and made one.'

In the café, he finds a table at the back. I take off my coat and smooth my hair with my hands, which makes it worse. A woman in a green fur coat, probably in her mid-forties, is smiling at me. 'You must be Lilith! I'm so pleased to meet you!' She holds my hands in hers and looks into my eyes. Grant stands to one side. She and I sit. 'Double espresso and a glass of water, please, Grant. What would you like?'

'Tea, please,' I say, and Grant nods politely and goes to the counter.

'And this must be Ink,' the woman says, holding out her hands. Ink puts her head on her lap. 'Oh, you are a beautiful, clever girl,' she says, and Ink wags her tail in agreement. 'Oh, I'm so sorry, I'm Elaine.'

The Mid Witch

'Grant told me.'

'I hope he's been...' Just then, Grant is back with the drinks. He sets a little tray on the table and then waits, head bowed, eyes lowered. 'Would you like cake?' she asks. I am so amazed by the way Grant is standing there like a servant, I can hardly hear her. Some people in the café are staring at him. Elaine chats on about cake or perhaps toast. No: tea cakes. She sends Grant for hot buttered tea cakes, and off he goes. Elaine talks about the weather, the news and a book she might buy about growing herbs. Grant comes back with the tea cakes, and she sends him for a bowl of water for the dog and a dog biscuit. More talk of herbs. Drying them this time. Grant puts down Ink's water, and she takes one lap out of politeness then lies down to munch the biscuit.

'Ahh, now we are all set,' Elaine says, shrugging off the green coat and handing me a plate. Grant stands beside her chair. 'Go,' she says softly, and Grant swallows, glances at me and leaves.

Elaine butters a tea cake, and I do the same. 'Now, so much to talk about. You must have lots of questions. Let me just do this,' she rummages in her bag and brings out a palm-sized, smooth oval stone, which she places in the middle of the table. She moves it fractionally to the left and toward me, and it muffles all the chatter and ambient music and the noise of the barristers as if we are in a thick, soundproof bubble.

'That's better. Now we can talk in private.' Elaine drinks

her espresso in two gulps. 'So,' she says, patting my hand, 'how did it all start?'

I talk as if we're alone and she is an old friend. The café and the people fade away. Maybe it is the relief to speak at last about all the strange things that have happened to me in recent months, but once I begin, I can't stop. I tell Elaine about the sparks at my fingers and how Ink can open doors. The spell I cast in the firepit and how my magic came to me when I threw Mike out. When, at last, I sit back and look at my uneaten tea cake and lukewarm tea, I don't know whether to laugh or cry.

I expect her to unpick and criticise the spell I cast or ask me why I had no inkling that I would become a witch when my mother and grandmother were obviously witches. Instead, she leans back in her seat and stares at me. 'I can't believe he abandoned you in the pouring rain at night. What an absolute shit!'

We laugh together. Then she leans forward and takes my hand. 'I don't blame you for using magic on him. But you must understand that using your powers is dangerous in the modern world. Very dangerous.'

'I'm sorry.'

'No, don't be. You're a new witch. You didn't realise what you were doing. I've spoken to the coven on your behalf. And we've taken steps to ensure that no harm was done.' She shrugs and smiles. 'Everybody makes mistakes.'

I pick up my cup of tea. It is cold and uninviting. 'Let's

have a fresh pot,' says Elaine, putting her hand over the pebble. The noise of the café surges into our quiet space as she waves over a young man clearing tables. 'Could we have a fresh pot of tea?' she asks. He looks over to the 'please order at the counter' sign. Elaine touches him lightly on the arm. 'Yes, of course,' he says. 'Anything else?'

'And cake. You choose.' She smiles at him and off he goes. Elaine lifts her hand from the stone and looks at me with bright eyes. 'The thing is, a little bit of magic in an ordinary world goes unnoticed. A few spells to make the day easier are fine and something I'd encourage. But the big stuff... You need permission to cast large spells,' she says. The boy returns with tea and slices of chocolate cake and clears our dirty plates. I feel like I'm being reprimanded by a kindly school teacher.

'I'm sorry. My emotions got the better of me. Mike...'

'Oh no, it's not the business with Mike that's the problem. Grant smoothed him to be on the safe side, but it probably wasn't necessary. Most people that have an *encounter* generally give themselves a rational explanation. Put the whole incident down to stress, imagination, a faulty memory or alcohol.'

'Smoothed?'

'Oh, a simple spell that even Grant can do. It makes sure your Mike has a more feasible memory when he retells the incident.'

I stir the pot and pour us both a steaming cup.

'No, the problem was the spell you cast.'

'I'm not allowed to cast spells?'

'Yes, and no. You can do small magic. I'll get Grant to drop some reading in so you know the difference. I've been a witch all my life, and I've only ever cast two grand magic spells. Everyday life is easily managed with small magic.' She taps the pebble and then reaches into her bag and hands me a comb. 'Try this.'

Quickly I rake through my long grey hair, which stops its fluffy nonsense and falls once more into soft waves. 'Is it a magic comb?'

Elaine takes it back and drops it into her bag. 'No. It's anti-static.'

I sip tea and eat a forkful of chocolate cake, which is excellent.

'It's the spell you cast in the fire. Fire spells are often problematic and best avoided until you are a more experienced witch.'

'I didn't think I was doing anything. I didn't believe...'

'Well, that's the trouble. Your magic is within you, and you cast your first spell with untrained magic.' She slices her chocolate cake into neat squares with her fork. 'An unspecific spell in a very big fire!'

'I thought it was something for good fortune, health and happiness. Maybe love.'

'Mmmn, that's a lot of vague topics that you cast on a

waxing moon in October with fresh herbs and multicoloured candles – and on an ancient site.'

'Ancient site?'

'Oh, North Star Cottage has been a witch home for two hundred years. Possibly more. Which brings me to ask, where do you think your power comes from?'

'My mother?'

'Yes, of course. All magic is hereditary. It might miss a generation or two, but it always follows bloodlines. No, what I mean is, where does your magical energy come from?'

I stare blankly at her, and she adds, 'Magic is an ability we inherit, but it's like a battery that needs recharging.'

'I don't know.'

'Mmmmn. Well, you'll have to become more self-aware. Try to notice anything that makes you feel stronger – or whole.'

She pushes aside her plate, gets a small notebook from her bag and writes a list.

Grant is in the bookshop next to the café. Has he been there all this time? Elaine looks at her watch. 'Any burning questions?'

'What was that thing? The dark thing that came to the cottage?'

'Ahh, yes. Horrible. So sorry you had to go through that. The witch hunters. They sweep the country at regular intervals, looking for the unclaimed.' She smiles reassuringly, or tries to. 'We'll soon take care of that, and you'll be perfectly safe.'

'Unclaimed?'

'Those who don't belong to a coven.' Elaine squashes the last of the cake crumbs onto the back of her fork and pops them into her mouth. She is an efficient eater. My cake is hardly touched. 'Together, we are strong and safe, Lilith. Even in a modern world where most people view witchcraft as a fairy tale, we need the protection of others like ourselves. Besides, you're going to love meeting other witches, and the Allingshire County Coven are a really super bunch.' She pats my hand. 'Think women's institute with magic. Good mix of young and old with differing talents.'

She looks at her watch again. 'Jolly good. I will leave all the general explanations to Grant.' She's gathering her handbag onto her lap, and Ink, sensing we are about to leave, stands and stretches. The meeting is nearly over, and I still have so many questions.

'Is he a witch?'

Elaine laughs. 'No. Only women can be witches. But he is a loyal thrall of our coven, so feel free to ask him anything. I'll leave him at your disposal.'

I'm in two minds about Grant, unsure whether I still think he's an arrogant twat or whether I like him since he protected me from the witch hunters. Elaine notices my conflict.

'I know he can be a condescending prick, but he won't

step out of line.' She shrugs on her green, furry coat and tears the list from her notepad. The café is quiet now. We must have sat here for over an hour. 'After the other day,' she says, her voice a whisper now the stone is in her bag, 'you need a protector while you, you know, get the hang of things.' I follow her into the bookshop, where Grant waits. She gives him the list. 'See that she gets these books. I leave her in your care,' she says and then turns back to me. 'I'm setting you up with a workbook for newbies. It'll take you through the basics.'

'Thank you,' I say, and she reaches out and hugs me.

Chapter Twenty-Two

On the way home in the car, I can't stop smiling. I am found. I'm a witch, and I am found. This is the best news. Finally, I have a place where I belong. The sun is shining, and the future is bright. Soon I will join the Allingshire County Coven. I wonder if they make jam?

The Mid Witch

Grant parks his estate car in the lane near my gate and gets out. 'Thanks for the lift,' I say, hoping he doesn't expect me to ask him in for a cup of tea. All I want right now is to take Ink for a walk and try to process everything I learnt about myself in the past few hours. Grant opens the gate, and we go through into the garden.

'Are you going to stay in the house? If so, I'll go and get your books and grab some stuff from my place,' he says.

'What stuff?'

'Toothbrush. Change of clothes.'

'You're not staying here!'

'Didn't Elaine explain? I'm your protector now until you join the coven.'

Anger creeps upward through my core. Elaine did not explain this. The last thing I want is a man in my house. Especially this man.

'Well, you'll have to watch from afar because you're not staying here.'

'It's not safe to be on your own. Surely you realise that after the... *hunter*?'

His condescension makes my blood boil. He must sense it because he steps back.

'I'm fine. Get the books. I'll stay in the house.'

I watch him drive away, then chuck Big Bag onto the kitchen table, check the witch ball isn't doing anything strange and then set off with Ink. We go through the wood, and Maud comes too, flitting ahead and waiting for us on the bare branches of the trees. As the sun dips lower and the light fades, we head home over the fields. Ink has had a good run, and I'm happy. 'I'm a witch,' I say to Ink, who is trotting beside me along the cobbled garden path. Maud swoops down and sits on my shoulder. As I walk into the house with my animals, I realise I have not felt this whole and content since my children were small.

I re-light the fire in the range and fetch logs from the woodshed. I make tea, eat a bowl of cereal and wash up. Grant taps on the kitchen window.

'That's great,' I say, taking the armful of books and putting them on the table. 'Thanks for bringing them so quickly.'

'May I come in, Lilith?' he says politely. He has an overnight bag at his feet.

'No. Go home, Grant. I'm fine.'

'I'm your...'

'My protector. Yes, I know. But you're not living here. Give me your number, and I'll call if I feel under threat.' This time I'm talking to him like he's an idiot, and I must admit it feels good.

'Lilith, it's not safe.'

'No. I'm fine. Now go.' A little spark of anger rises in me, and my fingertips feel hot. Ink huffs at the draft. She turns circles and settles herself again with her nose tucked under her back leg. Her swan pose.

'Whether you like it or not, I have to watch over you, so

you'd better get used to the idea.' He stoops and brushes his hand on the doorstep star, waits a moment and then comes into the kitchen.

I don't have time to get angry. As he steps in, a gush of wind spits him out, and he lands on his arse on the cobbles. I shut the door on him and throw the old brass bolts.

Alone at the kitchen table, I read until I'm so tired I have to go to bed. When I wake, my head is swimming with thoughts about witches and witchcraft. There is a lot to learn.

I have moved into the back bedroom. Well, I'm sleeping there now. It used to be Belinda's room, and boy band posters adorn the walls. The cotton curtains I made – it seems like only yesterday – have little unicorns and clouds on them. When I open the window, the woods spread before me and I smell the sea on the chilly breeze. There's a man walking his dog in the distant field. I breathe in and close my eyes for a moment, and Ink nudges my hand with her cold, wet nose.

I put my dressing gown on, grab a bundle of laundry and go downstairs. Grant's blue estate is in the lane. He's here early. Or has he stayed all night? There's ice on the car windows. He must have been freezing out there, the stupid man. Should I take him a cup of tea? Or ignore the whole thing?

Ink opens the kitchen door and goes outside. Has a pee on the lawn and then trots along the path, jumps the garden gate and puts her feet on the car door and woofs. Grant's head emerges from the back seat in a woolly hat. I wave and hold up a mug and gesture to him to come in.

I riddle the ash to wake the fire in the range, add logs and switch on the kettle. The kitchen door opens, and Ink trots in. Grant is wearing a big overcoat and has a red blanket around his shoulders.

'Come in,' I say. He brushes his fingers over the star and leans on the range. I put a hot mug of tea in his hands and busy myself feeding the dog.

'I'm sorry,' I say, finding some eggs and cracking them into a bowl. The least I can do is make him breakfast. 'I didn't realise this protector thing was so serious.'

He shrugs and sips his tea, and I set the table. I make us scrambled eggs and toast, and we eat together while the radio plays. 'I had no idea you were in the car.'

He still doesn't say a word, and I'm not sure if he's sulking or too cold to speak. 'Look, stay. But you'll have to use a back bedroom. I've got bed and breakfast guests in a couple of weeks.' That reminds me: today is October 31st. When I take Ink for her walk, I will stop by my mother's grave.

'What's the matter?' he says.

'Oh, nothing. Just remembered today is my late mother's birthday.'

'Halloween. Good birthday for a witch.'

'Yes. I suppose so. She never mentioned it. The witch stuff. I just thought she was very superstitious. Like grandma.'

The Mid Witch

'Sometimes it amounts to the same thing. Was there anything unusual she did?'

'She had...' I clear the plates into the sink while I try to think of the word. 'Foresight. You know, hunches about things that might happen.' She'd set up the legal stuff so that Mike couldn't get his hands on the cottage.

'But she never told you that one day you might be a witch?'

I run hot water onto the dishes and then face him. 'I never had any magical stuff happen to me.'

'It can miss a generation or two. The aptitude. And midwitches are rare.'

'Really?' I turn back to the washing up to hide my smile. I've never been rare. I'm average. The thought makes me happy. 'I was reading last night about how magic can come at different times in people's lives. It didn't say much about the midwitch.'

He brings his plate and mug, drops them into the hot water and picks up a tea towel.

'What I don't understand is why now?'

'Well, that's what a midwitch is. A woman who develops witchcraft when she goes through the change of life.'

'Yes, I know that. What I mean is, why didn't you explain what was happening that day in Dunwicks?'

'I'm sorry you lost your job.'

'That's not what I'm asking. Why wait until now to tell me what was going on?'

He hangs the mug he was drying onto a hook on the dresser. 'Women like you... Well, I believe it's a tricky time in a woman's life. The er... The change.'

I lean into the sink, my hands flat, the water up to my elbows, and sigh. 'Menopause is the word you're looking for.'

'Yes, well. Often, the magic rises and then subsides,' he says.

'Probably because they feel like crap.'

'But unmatured magic happens in other types of witch. It's a fairly common occurrence. Lots of new witches have a few magical incidences. Some are so subtle they don't notice or choose not to. The magic and any abilities that might develop withers and fades to nothing. They might have...' He screws the tea towel into a knot while he picks his word. 'Tendrils. Threads of magic that are easily put aside.'

'What? And then they don't become actual witches?'

'Yes. The magic just goes away.'

'How do you know that won't happen to me?'

'I think you'll be alright.'

'But what if it starts to get weaker instead of stronger?'

'The coven has things in place so that witches can keep hold of their powers.'

I let the water out of the sink, and Grant takes off his hat and coat and stands with them over his arm.

'Look, I'm sorry you spent the night in the car.'

'It's not the first time.'

The Mid Witch

'Will you get into trouble if you fail in your duties as a protector?'

'Something like that,' he mutters.

'Haven't you got to go to work?'

'I can work from home.'

'From my home, you mean?'

He smiles slowly and raises his brows.

'Get your stuff. You can work in here where it's warm. Take a shower if you need to. There's plenty of hot water.'

We spend the morning congenially enough. He sits quietly with his laptop in the kitchen, and I put the sitting room to rights. Hang some nice flowery curtains that were my mother's. Roll up the tarpaulin that was protecting the carpet while I decorated. Hang pictures and drag in an old hearth rug. Position little tables and lamps and dust the big glass-fronted cabinet. The room looks cosy – or it will when I get some sofas to replace the ones I gave away. This is my next priority, and I curl up in the easy chair with Ink and search the free sites for furniture to suit the cottage.

Grant finds Ink and I half asleep in the winter sun. 'Nice,' he says, standing in the doorway.

'Thanks for re-painting the walls.'

He looks at his feet, and I realise it must be lunch and heave myself up. In the kitchen, I fill the kettle and slice bread.

'Did you sell any houses?'

'It's always slow before Christmas. I'll take that sign down later.'

I make us cheese and pickle sandwiches, and we eat in silence while he scrolls his phone and I read *Witchcraft for Beginners*. I can't imagine getting any of the spells to work, and I push the book aside. My first bed and breakfast guests will arrive in two weeks. Really, I should tidy the garden. Sweep some leaves. Mow the lawn before it becomes unmanageable.

'Have you tried any?'

Grant flicks through the first few pages.

'No.' I check the fridge, wondering what I can make for an evening meal.

'You should. It will give you some confidence and help with your disbelief.'

'They all seem a bit silly. Soup to soothe a troubled mind. Tea for the timid.'

I shut the fridge door and force a smile. 'Maybe it would be for the best if I let it, you know, fade away. I've managed this long without magic.'

'Have you?'

'I told you. I never had even an inkling until recently.'

'Yes, I know that, but my point is, was your life better? Before the er inklings?' He leans back in the chair and stretches out his long legs, crossing them at the ankles. 'Try one.' He pushes the book over to me. I don't want to, and I reach for his plate. He grasps my wrist, gentle and firm, and

The Mid Witch

looks into my eyes. 'Try this one, Lilith. Be brave. It's just a case of doing a spell that interests you.'

I pull back, and he holds me a little firmer. A book topples from the dresser and hits him on the head. He lets go. 'If it doesn't work,' he says, rubbing his temple and eyeing the dresser suspiciously, 'then we can try another spell. Or not.'

I slot the cookbook back into place and say nothing.

'What are you worried about? It's not as if this is the first spell you've done.'

'Elaine said the thing I did in the fire-pit was...'

'No, not that. The one that fixed your hair.'

I pass a hand over my head. 'It's that obvious? I thought it was a herbal remedy.'

'It was a spell to fix something that was wrong. Your hair was a mess.'

'Thanks.'

'... and you needed – wanted – it to work, and it did. You need a spell you find interesting.' He turns the book to face me, grins and taps the page.

I read aloud, '"A spell to summon a magical creature." Really? A unicorn is going to come and knock on my door?' I'm laughing now. The gardening would be a much more productive pastime than this nonsense.

'Well, you have two, and it is more normal to have three,' he says.

I put our plates and mugs into the sink. Maud is perched on the dresser with her head under her wing. She spends most of her time in the kitchen these days. Ink is stretched out in front of the range on a pile of old blankets. 'What sort of animal?'

'Probably not a unicorn. They're very rare,' he says. I look at the ceiling and sigh, which he ignores.

'Have you got any?'

'No,' he says. 'I had a dog as a kid. But he wasn't like Ink. He had no uncanny abilities.'

'What if Ink and Maud don't want a newcomer?'

'They won't mind. In my experience, a witches' familiars tend to get along.'

I read the spell, which isn't too complicated. It's all on one page, at least. I decide to humour him. Get it over with so I can press on with the gardening chores.

Grant helps me retrieve my witchy things from under the stairs. He places the old leather suitcase on the kitchen table and stands back while I rummage for the items I need. A beeswax candle. A small green-handled dagger. A pouch of sea salt. A clay bowl.

Ink follows me to the birdbath and watches with interest as I fill the clay bowl with the moon-blest water. She takes a few laps herself, and we go back to the kitchen. I anoint the candle with honey and set it on the doorstep next to the bowl of water. Then I sprinkle the salt with the dagger to make a circle around me as I stand on the doorstep. Grant leans on the range next to Ink and watches.

Self-consciously, I say the words. There are only two, and

I do not know what they mean, but I repeat them as I lift the candle. Now I feel silly because I have not remembered the matches. Not that I can ever find them. When I light the fires, the sparks from my snapped fingers fall onto paper, and paper is easy to light. I'm not sure I can get my spark onto the candle wick. I snap my fingers, and a good spark flicks out from my finger and thumb and floats in the air. A bright speck in the October gloom. I wave the candle wick into it without conviction, and it almost lights. I snap again, more forcefully this time, and quickly bring the candle to this bigger spark. The candle lights, and I almost grin at the pale yellow flame.

A few moments pass, and then, as per the instructions, I drip some of the wax onto my threshold. The wax falls fast and thick, spreads within the doorstep star and solidifies in the chilly air. Next, I take up the little green-handled dagger and scratch away the salt, opening the circle on the garden side. I repeat the words and step through the gap. The spell doesn't state what I should do with the candle, so I take it indoors and stand it in a jar in the kitchen window next to the overflowing geranium plant. Above it, the witch ball glows and spins gently in the rising heat.

'Right. I'm off to do some gardening. Shout me when the unicorns arrive.'

As so often happens when I walk into my garden, I change my mind about what I want to do. The unmown lawn is already ankle-deep and full of weeds and herbs. Once again, I cannot bear to cut this abundant life back. I find a few tiny foxglove and primrose plants. Perhaps I should let the lawn be and mow it next year after they have flowered. Next to the path is a holly seedling, so young the spiky leaves are soft and pale green. I winkle it free with the trowel from my garden coat and replant it in a space in the border. Another seedling, an oak this time, I relocate to the edge of the garden where Any-Job-Steve cleared a fallen tree. I find a stake to protect it from the beach wind that blows across the field.

I rake up leaves and put them on the compost, and when Ink comes to investigate, I remember again that it is Halloween – my mother's birthday. I pick a bunch of late Dahlias and carry them back to the cottage like a torch of flames to see if Grant would like to walk with me to the church.

I'm thinking about putting jacket potatoes into the range for our evening meal as I shuffle through the grass, still on the lookout for more seedlings. Ink stops and sits, and I follow her gaze. On the doorstep stands a large fox. I keep very still so I can watch her for a few moments before she runs away. The fox stays. Turns around. Sniffs the salt circle and then looks at me with bright green eyes.

Ink is the first to greet her. The two animals touch noses, and I step closer and crouch down, holding out my hand. The fox approaches me one step at a time, smelling the air and flicking her ears at every tiny sound. Slowly, she reaches my hand and sniffs. I have never been this close to a fox before. She is beautiful. Orange fur vibrant in the fading light. She is bright white under her chin and on her chest, and her tail is a magnificent plume.

The fox and I regard each other, and then her ears flick back at a sound from the cottage and she's off, streaking through the grass and into the border. The door opens, and Grant stands in the kitchen.

'Found something?'

I straighten up from my crouch, arranging the flowers in my hand. 'Dropped one. I'm going to walk to the church. Put these on mum's grave. Fancy a stroll?'

He nods and goes to get his coat while I put the spuds in. I don't tell him about the fox. He'll only claim she was a magical creature come to visit, which seems highly unlikely. We walk along the lane, and Maud flits ahead, going from branch to branch. The trees are almost bare, and we kick through the damp leaves. At the lychgate, I clip on Ink's lead and give her to Grant to hold.

St Gutheridge and All Angels is peaceful in the afternoon stillness. Grant follows me to my mother's grave and stands with Ink at a respectful distance while I change the flowers. The rain has already filled the flowerpot. All I need to do is take the dead bunch to the compost heap behind the stone wall.

Grant ambles along the mossy path behind me, and Maud perches on the head of a stone angel with broken wings. Now that I know I own the church and the grounds, should I take better care of the place? Employ a gardener, perhaps?

Ink streaks past me. Grant has wandered over to Galahad Thornbury's grave and is trying to read the poem on his headstone.

'You let her go!'

'Oh, sorry!' He holds up the lead and shrugs.

'We'll have to catch her!' We jog along the path. Ink is out of sight behind the yew tree. 'Ink, come! Ink!' I cry. The dog takes no notice. 'You should've hung onto her!'

'Not my fault she can slip her leash!'

I let out a long breath. It's no use calling her. The only thing that works is pulling her off.

We round the yew tree and see the dark shadow of my dog digging frantically where the wall bulges to encompass the graves of my long-dead ancestors. 'Every time!' I say.

'What's she up to?'

Grant seems to be finding the whole thing amusing. I start to laugh. It is pretty comical, to be fair. 'She's trying to dig up one of my relatives,' I say. 'In the summer, it wasn't really a problem, but now the ground is soft. Come on, better pull her off before she actually reaches bones.'

Mud is flying behind Ink in a steady flow when we get near. I'm shocked at the depth of the hole she has dug, and I feel in my pocket for my garden trowel. I'm going to have to fill this in.

'Right, come on, Ink. Time to stop!' I say.

The Mid Witch

Grant holds my sleeve. 'Hang on! Why don't you wait a minute and see what she's trying to find?'

'In a graveyard? Honestly, whatever she thinks is in there, I'd rather not know.'

He still has a hold of my sleeve, which is annoying. I shrug him off and give him a glare. Just then, Ink stops her frantic excavation. Her bum and back legs are sticking out the hole, and she is snort-sniffing and wagging her skinny tail. Oh god, what has she got? Ink backs out, and I brace myself for grisly human remains. She has something in her mouth. Something small. She holds onto it and gives herself a good shake, spraying us both with soil. Then she drops the disgusting relic into my hand.

Grant switches on his phone light so we can get a better look as I smear away the wet mud with my thumb. Ink has dug up a lump of green sea glass. Smooth and oval. Once, it must have been on the beach. Crazy dog. 'Good girl,' I say because she is clearly delighted. She sits bolt upright with an expectant look on her hound face. In my pocket, I find a few dog treats and give them to her and pet her soft head – the only part of her that is clean. This dog will need a bath when we get home.

'Right. That's that then. Now, no more digging,' I say, pulling out my trowel and trying to sort out the mess. 'Are you going to help me, you daft mutt?' Ink has already sauntered off and is sniffing about in the weeds.

'Whose grave was this?' asks Grant as he moves piles of

soil back into the hole with the side of his boot. It's more efficient than my trowel, so I let him get on with it.

'Bethany Blackwood,' I say, indicating the small headstone with the star like the one on my doorstep. 'She was my relative.'

Grant pats the mud flat with the ball of his foot gently as if he might disturb the grave's occupant. 'Bethany Blackwood is your ancestor?!' Moonlight illuminates his shock.

'Come on, those jacket potatoes will be like husks.'

Maud sits on my shoulder as we walk along the lane, and Ink trots between us. The sea glass is heavy in my pocket.

'You've never heard of her, have you?' he says as we go through the garden gate.

'Who?'

'Bethany Blackwood.'

'Nope.'

He doesn't say anything more because a small black cat is sitting on the doorstep.

Chapter Twenty-Three

T he cat has a sleek black coat and pale blue eyes. She stretches and then steps through the gap in the salt circle around the doorstep and winds between my legs. Ink ignores her and trots into the kitchen. I follow with the cat at my heels. Maud flits onto her favourite place on the top of the dresser and ruffles her feathers.

'Do you think she's a stray?' I say. At this, Grant looks up to the sky.

'You've just cast a spell to lure a witch's familiar, and now you're wondering if the black cat you've summoned is yours.' He stands outside, and I realise he dare not enter unless I invite him.

'Please come in,' I say, holding the door. He steps inside, and we watch the cat stalk about the kitchen as if she is taking stock. Ink lies by the range with a huff. 'I haven't any cat food,' I say as I take a damp cloth and wipe Ink's paws and muddy undercarriage. After all that digging, I thought she would need a bath, but most of the muck has gone.

'Tuna?'

'Tuna. Good idea.' I find a tin and fork some onto a saucer. The cat jumps onto the draining board as I do this, so I feed her there in case Ink interferes. I feed Ink, put the kettle on and make a pot of tea. Grant helps without being asked, fetching the jacket potatoes out of the range and getting butter and cheese from the fridge.

While we eat, the cat gives her long whiskers a wash, jumps down, laps water from Ink's bowl and then goes to the range. Ink is stretched out on her large pile of blankets. The cat walks over her and turns about a few times before settling into a neat round ball on Ink's flank.

'Hope you've got a big bed,' says Grant. And I can't help

imagining us all in it. Me, the animals and him. I push this ridiculous thought away.

I expect him to ask to see what the dog found in the grave, but he says nothing as he helps to clear up and then hovers by the door. 'It's okay. You don't need to spend another night in the car.' I show him Jason's old room – not one I have prepared for my bed and breakfast guests. I like this room; it is bigger than Belinda's and has a desk. I didn't choose it for myself because I prefer a window that lets in the moonlight. Now I know why.

The evening is weird. I would rather he wasn't here. He must sense this and stays upstairs. I hear him shower, and then the bedroom door closes with a bang. His laptop has disappeared from the kitchen table, so I stop feeling guilty about being unfriendly. He can watch a film or look at social media. He's here uninvited and I shouldn't worry. I get washed, pull on a tracksuit and go downstairs.

The animals – cat, bird and dog – peacefully sleep in the kitchen. The garden coat is still on the back of the door. I take the sea glass from the pocket and wash away the mud, giving it a quick scrub with the vegetable brush as if it is a potato. After making hot chocolate and lighting a candle, I sit at the table to examine it. It's pale green. Smooth and oval, about the size of my fist. Most probably, it came from this beach. On a whim, I wave it in the candle flame. It seems a witchy thing to do. Nothing happens. I submerge it in water. Hold it in front of a mirror. Drip wax on it and breathe over it. In the end, I decide to go to bed.

The clouds have cleared, and I put the sea glass on the windowsill and climb into bed with Ink. The little cat joins us and lets me pet her. I wonder if she can open doors like Ink or if I should leave a downstairs window open in case she wants to go out.

I wake in the night and remember I have forgotten to take my HRT. In the bathroom, I pop the pill into my mouth and slurp water from the cold tap. Moonlight fills the bedroom, and I stand by the window and admire the garden bathed in silver light. Everything is still and quiet. If Grant was not here, I would go out there. Have a wander about and a think. Behind me, Ink stirs, and the cat gets up, circles and settles herself.

The sea glass is pale grey in the moonlight. Holding it in the night's peace, I know my mother held it. I imagine her walking on the beach, the wind blowing her hair and flapping the long green garden coat as she collected stones and shells.

'Why did you put this one in Bethany Blackwood's grave?' I whisper and turn it over in the moonbeams. In all these long years, I never thought my mother a witch. Now, after all that has happened to me recently, each memory of her is tainted with new knowledge. What I had dismissed as superstition, I now see as witchcraft. When visitors left the cottage, she burnt dried sage and washed the doorstep star with rosemary-infused, moon-blest water. If anyone was ill, she would brew a cure with herbs and fruit on the range and ladle it into mugs. The drinks always tasted sweet and wholesome – and they worked.

The garden then as now was an overgrown jungle. The lawns were Mike's incursion. Like me, she never could see the value of one plant above another. Weeds and herbs flourished. Everything mixed together. Cabbages and roses. Rhubarb and marigolds. I sit on the window ledge and admire the abundance. That is what she would have seen as well. Whenever anyone admonished her for the state of the garden, her mild reply was that nature knew best. That was her all over – mild. She went through life unflustered, and never was she irritable or cross. By today's standards, she lacked ambition. She lived with her mother, Grandma Gwen, and never had a job to speak of. Sometimes she took in laundry or cleaned houses. We didn't have much, but then again, we always had enough. Looking back, I wonder we had any money at all. Did my father, whoever he was, provide an allowance?

I am older than her now. Even she could not brew a potion to cure the cancer that took her. If she had lived, she would have helped me. Steered me through this new witch phase with wisdom and kindness. I'm sad I must rely on strangers. She would have been proud to see me become what she had always secretly been. I snap my fingers as if to show the memory of her the sparkle I can make. Three times I snap, and a flurry of sparks flicker and float about. They are always beautiful in the moonlight. I watch them slowly fall. Some touch the stone in my hand, and when they do, I feel a change – a connection – and I know the sparks that come from my witch self are what the stone needs. I snap again and, this time, catch the sparks onto the stone. There is a warmth, and small letters on the surface stand out white like scratches. My mother's handwriting is unmistakable. There is one word – 'Beware' – and a fine and detailed drawing of a feather emerges.

When the word and the image fade, I am disconcerted. This is unhelpful. Who is she trying to warn me against? For a while, I lie in bed next to the sleeping animals, but this doesn't help to get me back to sleep. I wish there was someone I could turn to. Someone I could trust. But the trouble with the whole witch thing is that, no matter how hard I try, I cannot quite believe it myself, and therefore telling a non-magical person feels off. Dangerous, even. I consider Cressida, who would no doubt laugh and try to understand and secretly believe me delusional. The women I knew when I worked at Dunwicks Department Store would be kind and secretly scathing. Randy Landy would listen intently, fuck me senseless and forget all about it. This makes me smile.

I must have fallen asleep eventually because the next thing I know, I am jumping out of bed to a loud noise. I pull on my dressing gown and pad down the hall. Grant is banging on his bedroom door. Ink stands beside me, wagging her tail.

'Lilith! Unlock this bloody door!'

The Mid Witch

I turn the doorknob. The door stays put. 'There's no key in the lock,' I say.

'Look, you've made your point. But now I need to pee!'

'I haven't locked the door!' I give Ink a pat. 'Open the door!' I say to her. Nothing happens.

'Unless you want me to piss out the window.'

'Honestly, I haven't locked the door. There's not even a key.'

'For fuck's sake!'

It's probably because I'm tired that I find this funny and start to laugh.

He bangs on the door hard, and I am reminded of when Mike got a bit shouty and a door closed on him. He was furious for days. It was years ago. When we first came to live here. I don't remember the argument now, only that we couldn't get the door open for hours.

'Calm down,' I say. 'And don't pee out the window!'

I contemplate the door, and Ink sits beside my feet, ears pricked to see what happens next. This gives me an idea. 'Call the dog!'

'What?'

'Call the dog?'

'Ink! Come on, Ink. Come see me.'

Ink wags her tail and moves toward the door, which opens. Grant pats her head, but he's still scowling. He's wearing blue stripy pyjamas, which starts me laughing again. He stomps past me to the bathroom.

I go downstairs, put the kettle on and feed the cat and dog. Make a note to myself to do an online shop so that I can buy some cat food. The little cat purrs as she eats my last can of tuna, and I try to think of a name for her.

Grant appears in the kitchen, dressed in jeans and a black t-shirt. Before I can joke about his pyjamas, he says, 'I suppose you think that was amusing, locking me in my room since yesterday afternoon and ignoring my shouts.'

'Look. Let's get one thing straight. I didn't lock you up. And I didn't hear you. Honestly.'

The stubble on his unshaven chin is white against his dark skin. He is dishevelled – in a good way. I pour water into the teapot.

'You're not even going to apologise?' His voice is full of pained angst.

I set the pot on the table too roughly, and hot tea spills from the spout. My mood changes. 'You know what? I've had enough of men bossing me about.'

'I guessed.'

'... and never listening to what I have to say. I did not lock you up. You said yourself the house dislikes men.'

'You know you will not be able to do this bed and breakfast nonsense. It's too risky and...'

'That's enough!' I'm clenching my fists. I take a deep breath to calm myself. 'It's not up to you what I do.'

'When you join the coven, they will have something to say about it.'

The Mid Witch

'Why would they care?'

'Outsiders coming into an ancient magical space.'

'Well, this is how I intend to make my living. Bed and breakfast guests. So they will have to get used to the idea. Anyway, I can't see what harm it does. North Star Cottage has always been here. Anyone can wander along the lane and find it.' I wipe the spilled tea and get some mugs.

He sits on a kitchen chair and pulls on socks with shaking hands. Is he still furious or stressed from being locked up? 'If I'd heard you, I would have let you out. It's the cottage. It does... weird things.' He doesn't look at me. His phone trills, and he takes it out of his pocket and scrolls. I pour tea and plonk cereal boxes and milk onto the table.

'I'm not hungry, thanks,' he says as he texts. I sigh and glare at him. He's too busy with his phone to notice. 'You should get on with some more spells. I expect the coven will get in touch any day now.'

One side of the kitchen table is piled with my witchy stuff. I slide a book out and flip it open. Grant continues with his phone and doesn't even drink his tea. God, I hate moody men. Mike was like this. Able to carry on blaming you for stuff that was not your fault. Well, I've had a lifetime of apologising. Let him sulk.

I eat my cereal and pretend to read. Really, I'm watching him. I prefer him in casual clothes. If anything, he looks better. His t-shirt is not too tight but fits enough to show off his broad shoulders and muscled arms. Below his sleeve are the dark squiggles of his tattoos. They look like Celtic patterns, only they're not. He picks up his tea – which must be cold by now – and balances the mug on his leg. I'd like to know what is so fascinating on his phone. I'm musing about which social media or dating agency he's on when he brings the mug to his lips and I see it: on the inside of his bicep is a small tattoo of a feather.

Chapter Twenty-Four

He almost catches me staring. I jump up and put my dish in the sink and go upstairs. I'm desperate to check the image I found last night. I click sparks into the air, but although they land on the sea glass, no feather appears.

Perhaps the magic only works once or needs the combination of sparks and moonlight.

I pace up and down, holding the sea glass to my fast-beating heart. Then I stand in front of the long mirror. I'm still in my tatty dressing gown. I put the sea glass in the bedside drawer, beneath a pile of Belinda's books and notepads I have yet to tidy away. Then I take a shower. My mother has warned me. Taken the trouble to reach through time with her uncanny prescience to alert me to danger. She knew I would want to see the image again and find it different. I'm in denial. About witchcraft. About everything. Which is typical of me. I dry myself and tie my hair back and dress in warm tights and a dress with a pattern of tiny seashells. It's blue. I am confident in blue, I tell myself.

At the top of the stairs, I hesitate. But I need to be strong. My mother has warned me about Grant Fucking Rutherford, and he must go. I won't listen to any more nonsense about him trying to protect me. He's going. I chucked out Mike. I can chuck him out, too.

He has washed up and wiped the table. Now he is in the garden playing fetch with Ink. How annoying. Ink is swooping about in the unkempt grass like a black gazelle. It's tricky throwing out a man your dog likes. At the door, I pull on my wellington boots and step outside, and Ink bounds over. Maybe I should wait until later. When she's asleep.

This is how it was with the kids. Me trying not to upset

them and putting up with Mike's crap as a result. I take a deep sigh. No more, Lilly. No more.

'I want you to leave.' It comes out like an apologetic croak.

'What?' he says, standing there with a stick in his hand. He's much bigger than Mike, and I'm intimidated by his brooding look. He throws the stick, and I see a flash of the black feather tattoo. It strengthens my resolve. She told me Mike was no good, and I never listened.

'You're leaving. Right now. No more nonsense.'

'Now, Lilly. Let's talk about this. It's not safe. I'm sorry I was annoyed this morning. I can explain.'

Standing in the winter sun in front of him with Ink skipping about like a fool, I almost back down. I don't feel angry or magical. I'm a bit scared. Maud lands on my shoulder and gives my earlobe a friendly peck. 'No. I don't want any more explanations. I want you to go. Right now.'

I brace myself for a tirade of abuse, but Grant walks quietly to the kitchen door and waits. Ink follows him with her stick. 'Can I come in?' he says.

'No. Wait there. I'll get your stuff.'

Upstairs in Jason's old room, he has made the bed and hung his towel on the radiator. I put a few items of clothing from the back of the chair into his holdall and grab his computer bag. In the kitchen, I pick up his phone from the table.

He's standing where I left him. Thankfully, Ink has come inside and is settling herself by the range. I put his things on the other side of the step and then realise Maud is still on my shoulder.

'You're sure about this? It's only for a couple of days.' His voice is matter of fact.

'Then I'll be fine for a couple of days. You're leaving. Actually leaving, and no hanging about and sleeping in your car or any of that shit.'

'Right.' He takes his bags and walks off. I stand on the doorstep star and watch him drive away.

In the kitchen, I fill the kettle. I thought I'd feel elated or free or at least relieved. Oddly, I'm edgy and strangely alone. The witch ball is gently spinning, and on the smooth silver surface, a dark shadow moves. This was probably what it looked like this morning if I'd taken the time to notice. I water the red geranium and pick off some dead flower heads.

Ink is asleep. I am glad she is not troubled that Grant has gone. Maud flits to the dresser and begins preening herself. Outside, the cat is stalking something in the long grass.

It's early. I will take Ink for a walk to the beach when I've done a few chores. The beach always makes me feel better.

Stripping Grant's bed, I find the blue-striped pyjamas folded neatly under a pillow. Is this endearing or a bit weird? As I lift them, I can't help noticing the scent of subtle, slightly spicy cologne mingled with a nice body smell. I toss them on the bedroom floor and pull the sheets off the bed. Tonight, when the moon is out, I will have another look at the sea glass.

I spend the morning cleaning and clearing out Belinda's

The Mid Witch

old room. It's not good for my mental health to sleep in what is essentially a shrine to my daughter's childhood. She has a family of her own. Belinda has moved on, and I need to do the same.

Soon the landing is strewn with bags – some for rubbish, others for charity – and I am in tears over a box of forgotten toys I have found under the bed. A rag doll family that Grandma Gwen made for me when I was a child, which Belinda loved. Each one is no taller than my hand. There are seven people, two dogs and a cat. I put them in a line on the window ledge. Ink, who has slept in my bed all morning, lifts her head and gives a soft woof. Someone is coming. I hope it's not Grant spoiling for a fight. In the lane, a car pulls up. It's Theo. I sigh and go downstairs.

'Darling,' she says as she swoops into the kitchen in a cloud of expensive perfume. 'I came as soon as I heard!'

I don't bother to ask, 'Heard what?' Interaction is unnecessary with Theo. Her monologues are deaf. I fill the kettle as she hangs her coat under the stairs. Above my head, the witch ball gently spins in the draft, and more dark clouds skid across the surface. Outside, the weather is turning glum. I switch on the kettle, and Theo leans on the range to warm herself.

'... so anyway, I told Elaine I'd look after you as soon as I knew. Can't think why they didn't ask me. Then again, they assumed we were cousins. They think that this sort of thing is best dealt with outside of family. All nonsense if you ask me, so I played the known-each-other-since-childhood fact right down.'

She is leaning on my cooker in her designer jeans, crisp white shirt and long, dove-grey cashmere cardigan, and I cannot imagine anyone would think we were related. That's the only part of the conversation I have heard. I smile benignly and make a pot of tea. I could do with a cup. No doubt as soon as she has finished talking at me, she will waft off like she usually does, and I can get on. As soon as she's out of the way, I'll put a jacket potato in for my tea. Which reminds me, I need some cat food.

'Lilly!' She is now sitting at the table with my shadow book in front of her. I'd totally forgotten that all my witch stuff was lying about.

'What?'

'I see you've got your resources out. Good.'

My face is blank, and I'm suddenly exhausted.

'You haven't heard a word I've said! They said you were in denial. Now don't worry, we'll get all this sorted out.'

I pour the tea. What is she on about?

'Lilly! Listen. I know you're a witch, and it's okay. I'm here to help.'

We stare at each other for a long moment. Theo shrugs off her cardigan. Her eyes are bright as she says, 'I honestly think it is harder becoming a witch in middle life than it is when young. Youth is more...' – she presses her lips together – 'believing. When you're older, it's much harder to get your

The Mid Witch

head around it. Especially if no one warned you.' She raises her eyebrows over the rim of the mug as she blows on her tea.

'You know?!'

'Both our mothers were witches. That's why they were friends. And they were both members of the Allingshire County Coven. Although it was a small affair then.'

I don't know when I have ever listened to Theo so intently. It's like we are kids again. 'You see, I came into my magic quite early. I was only thirteen. But you'd shown no signs of any ability, so it was decided to keep it a secret. The whole witch thing. I think your mother was afraid you'd be jealous of me.' She cups her manicured hands around the mug. Her nails are long and silver-grey.

'You're a witch?'

She smiles for the first time. 'Always have been. Lilly, you must understand that what you are is quite rare. Most people who don't come into their magic in childhood or early adulthood never ever do. When we were young, I was desperate for you to be like me. So we could chat and share and, you know, be close. But they made me promise.'

When we were small children, we were the best of friends. Then it seemed like Theo grew up overnight, and I was still a little girl that wanted to play. She went to a private secondary school and made friends with popular, wealthy girls who didn't want anything to do with me, a kid who attended Marswickham Comprehensive.

Suddenly it all makes sense, and I am crying big hot tears

that drip onto the table. Theo rushes to my side, and we embrace, and I am more happy to get my long-lost friend back than I am about being a witch. 'I'm so sorry,' she breathes into my hair. 'They made me promise.'

We cling to each other like we've been shipwrecked, then break away laughing. I make us cheese toasties and fresh tea, and we reminisce about school and things we did in our childhood, before our teens. Before life got complicated. For the first time in a long while, I feel that everything will be okay, and I say a silent thanks to my mother for warning me about Grant.

After lunch, we walk Ink all the way to the beach and back. This, of course, rekindles more memories, and we are firm friends again when we return to the warm kitchen. The little cat is sitting on the step. She follows us in and jumps onto the draining board, clearly expecting food. I have hardly seen her all day.

'She's new,' says Theo, throwing her coat and cardigan over a chair. The kitchen is overly warm after the autumn chill.

'I cast a spell for another familiar, and she turned up.' I don't mention the fox.

'Oh, she's lovely. Pretty eyes. Well done, you.'

'I meant to order an online shop,' I say, moving cans around in the cupboard. 'I haven't got any cat food. I've fed her all the tuna.'

The cat sits expectantly, her tail curled over her front

paws, and Theo reaches out a hand for her to sniff. In a flash, the cat scratches her arm. Theo yelps. The cat hisses.

'Oh god, I'm so sorry.'

She pulls her sleeve down. 'It's just a scrape. Cats can be moody.'

Three lines of blood the length of Theo's forearm seep through her white shirt.

'Do you want to wash it? I've got some antiseptic somewhere.'

She is pulling on her cardigan. 'No, no. I'm fine. She's just a bit feisty. She'll settle down. What are you going to call her?'

Her name suddenly springs to mind. 'Claudia.'

Theo laughs her deep, posh girl's laugh. 'Perfect. Now, darling, the coven gets very funny about new witches being on their own in case they hurt themselves or draw more attention than they should. So somebody needs to stay with you until you get the hang of things.'

My expression must give me away because she laughs again. 'I could get Rutherford, the overbearing prick, back. Or you could have me.'

'Oh, no more Grant Rutherford.'

'Right. I'll pop home and get some stuff, and I'll stop by the shop and get cat food for Claw Dear!' The cat eyes her suspiciously from the draining board.

'How long will it take? I mean, I'm happy for you to stay.

But I'm trying to get this whole thing, you know, sorted in my head.'

'Oh, couple of days for you to try the basics. Maybe a week. Then I contact the coven. There is a brief initiation ceremony, and then the collective magic of the coven can keep you safe, and that's it.'

'Ceremony?'

'Think welcome party with a sign-up. Easy-peasy.' Theo already has her coat on and her bag over her shoulder. 'They're a really friendly bunch, the Allingshire Coven. Anything else you need?'

I open the fridge and check the milk situation. 'No. Maybe a loaf?'

'Great, I won't be long, and I'll grab us a takeaway to celebrate.' And she's off.

I head upstairs to check my guest bedroom. You can't put someone like Theodora Grimshaw in a back room full of junk. I put out fresh towels and then throw all the bags from my clear out of Belinda's room into Jason's and close the door.

Chapter Twenty-Five

Theo is singing in the kitchen when I wake. She used to sing all the time when we were kids, and I lie there smiling at the ceiling. I always sleep with the curtains open, and winter light fills the room. I must have slept in. No wonder – we sat up late, eating curry and drinking wine.

Theo is again the friend I knew. She's full of fun, and I am blissfully happy.

Ink and Claudia sit at the end of the bed listening to the singing, and I quickly shower and dress. Can't face Theo in my ragged dressing gown. I pull on comfy jeans and a shirt and jumper that I usually keep for best. I tie back my hair and take a moment to pencil over my grey eyebrows and dab on lipstick. Then I check my chin and top lip for whiskers and tweeze out the seven offenders.

The animals have waited at the top of the stairs, and we arrive in the kitchen together.

Maud is not on the dresser. She's not outside either, so I feed the dog and cat.

Theo has made breakfast: smoked salmon, scrambled eggs and a cafetiere of strong coffee, which smells amazing but tastes bitter.

I'm glad I got dressed. Theo is glamorous in champagne-coloured satin pyjamas and matching velvet mules.

'Gosh, this looks fab,' I say, giving my specs a wipe on my shirttail.

'Never practise magic on an empty stomach,' she says.

'Is that true?'

She laughs. 'No idea. But it sounds like good advice.' We sit and eat.

'You always wanted to be a singer,' I say.

'Well, we always have daft ideas when we're young. Everyone thinks they will make a great success of their lives.'

The Mid Witch

I stop eating and look at her. This is new. Or is this less self-assured Theo always there beneath the confident businesswoman she shows to the world? Before I can say anything more, she is clearing her plate into the sink. 'You take your time. I'll go and get dressed.'

I wash up, make myself a mug of tea and try to sort out all the witch paraphernalia that has piled up on one end of my large kitchen table. Theo returns before I get very far and makes more coffee. The witch ball spins with clouds – grey ones that scud across the surface like ghosts. Theo places a finger on it, and it stops. The clouds clear, and it just hangs there – a giant silver bauble.

'Which spell will you try first?' she says, placing the cafetiere and two mugs on the table. Ink comes in from the garden, leaving the door open, and stands beside me. I pat her soft head as I look through the books Grant brought.

'I've no idea.'

Theo waves a hand at the door, and it gently shuts. I've never seen anyone do magic, and I smile. This is real. We're both witches. Honestly, you couldn't make this stuff up.

Theo decides I should try a simple spell to warm water. She puts a small mixing bowl in front of me, fills it halfway from a jug of cold water, and sets the jug on the table. 'This is dead easy. Put your hands around the bowl and think about it getting hotter.'

I do as she says and imagine the water getting hotter.

Nothing happens, and I'm disappointed. 'Is there something I should say?'

'No. Just think about hot water. Try again. Close your eyes if it helps.'

The water is unchanged.

'Okay, dip a finger in the jug and then in the bowl.'

'Oh my god! The water in the bowl is warmer. Not much, though.'

'That's fine. Now try again and trust. My mother always said magic is 90 per cent belief and 20 per cent potency.'

Soon I can make the water hot. Actually hot. I am laughing with delight. 'Just think, no more cold cups of coffee,' she says. My tea has gone cold, and I wrap my hands around the mug and feel the tea heat. Brilliant. Next, I try the reverse. Hot to cold. Oddly, this is easier, and I can even create a thin crust of ice on the water's surface. We spend the morning doing what Theo terms household magic – useful, short-term stuff. I summon objects from high shelves. Open and close doors, even locked ones. Find objects she has hidden: keys, credit cards, a hairbrush. Banish unwanted smells: onions, vinegar, burnt toast. By lunchtime I'm exhausted. After a pile of sandwiches, we take Ink and walk to the beach. Ink is in a strange mood and trots beside me the whole time. I think she misses Grant, which is annoying.

Horseshoe beach has tall white-capped waves and lots of sea foam blowing on the wind. Ink forgets her troubles and runs about chasing the bubbles. 'Do you have any animals?' I ask.

Theo picks up a pebble and examines it. 'No. Not all witches have them.' She seems sad about this, so I don't ask any more. We walk around the beach, which doesn't take long, and then we climb the steep cliff steps and head for home. I remember picnics when we were small, with Rufus the lurcher digging in the sand. The Grimshaws never had any pets.

'You'll feel really tired after today. Tomorrow we can try some spells if you like,' she says.

Back at the cottage, I climb onto the old easy chair to rest. Theo lights the fire and covers Ink and I with a blanket. I only wake when she calls me into the kitchen for food. She's made a chicken casserole, although I'm not sure when. This morning, perhaps? After I've eaten, I confess my dire need for sleep and go to bed. Ink comes with me, and I am vaguely aware that Claudia is missing. I have not seen Maud all day.

In the morning, I don't try to impress Theo. We're friends again. True friends. I pull on my old dressing gown, go to the kitchen and feed Ink, who oddly is not hungry. She sniffs her breakfast and saunters into the garden. I hope she's not getting sick. 'Have you seen Claudia?' I say.

'She's in the shrubs, mousing, I think.'

I call from the kitchen door. The circle of salt is still faintly visible on the step, and the star is smooth with the wax I dripped. When I'm dressed, I will clear up the mess. Next week I have my first paying guests, and I wouldn't want them to think I'm a witch.

I put out cat food and a little saucer of milk. 'Don't worry, cats tend to come and go,' Theo says. We eat the bacon sandwiches she has made, and then I get dressed.

'What are you putting on?' she calls from her room as if we are still kids and she's come to stay the weekend.

'Leggings and a top,' I call back.

A light frost glitters in the morning sun as I fetch logs for the range. Ink is glued to my side as I go back and forth. She hasn't eaten her food, and when the log baskets are full and I've stoked the range, I get on my hands and knees to check her. She lets me examine her paws and run my hands over her body. I can't detect anything wrong. 'How are you, Ink?' I whisper.

'Right, where shall we start?' says Theo. Like me, she's wearing leggings and a loose flowery tabard, but on her the outfit is casual yet elegant, whereas on me it is comfortable. Then again, her clothes probably came from a boutique in Market Forrington, and I bought my stuff in a supermarket.

'Last night, I was thinking about the first spell my mother taught me. Want to try?' From her handbag she brings out an old, battered book that can only be her mother's grimoire. Lengths of faded ribbon mark the pages. She flips it open, and I gather what's needed as she reads a list aloud.

She has already cleared away all my paraphernalia into a neat pile so one end of the table is free for me to cast my spell.

The Mid Witch

I set the things before me: sea salt, a short white taper, honey, brown sugar, a crystal plate and two avocados.

'Great, you have a crystal plate,' she says when I come back from the sitting room with it. I also have a thin crystal candle holder from the china cabinet.

'Okay, first you have to cleanse everything,' she says, pressing the plunger on the cafetiere.

'Wait. What am I trying to do?'

She laughs. 'Sorry! Ripen fruit. Well, ripen anything – but in this case, the avocados. This spell also works if you want to speed up flowers – get them to bloom. Also useful for bananas.'

I follow her instructions. Wash the bowl and candlestick. Clean the surface of the table. Wash my hands. Dab a little honey and then sugar onto the taper. Wash the fruit and place it in the bowl and sprinkle a circle of salt around everything. Oddly, I'm not self-conscious, nor am I full of scepticism. I truly believe this spell will work. With confidence, I await the next instruction.

'Now take your wand and draw in your power.'

'I don't have one.'

'Oh, okay. Hang on.'

Theo lifts her large, expensive handbag onto her lap, fetches a tapered stick about 30cm long and hands it to me. It is smooth, dark with age, and the wood is pine. I know this because, in my mind's eye, I envision the lone tree growing on a stormy hilltop. Then the hilltop is bare, the pine tree gone.

There is more the wand wants to tell me, but I place it on the table and look away.

'What?' she says.

'I just remembered something.' I go to where the garden coat hangs on the back of the kitchen door. I fumble about in the junk accumulated in the space created by the worn-through pocket linings, my fingers sifting through folded-over seed packets, plant labels and garden string. Then I open my hand and simply think, and a smooth stick finds my fingers. It is old. Made from the yew tree that guards my garden gate. It is short, a mere fifteen cm in length. I bring it into the light. The wood is the colour of dark honey, and as I hold it, I remember my mother used it as a dibber for planting seedlings. No wonder everything grew.

Theo looks a bit irritated, so I return to the table with my short little wand and await more instructions. 'Are you sure that's a wand? You can always borrow mine.'

The wand is still speaking to me. Generations of women have held it. I see the yew tree and the branch it was asked to provide. The carving of it beside the firepit and the moon-blest water brought to the yew in thanks. I will do that, now this little wand is mine. I will take some moon-blest water to the ancient tree.

'Lilly!'

'Sorry.'

'Concentrate then.'

The Mid Witch

I turn my attention to the spell, although I almost don't need it now.

I do as I'm told, placing the fruit on the crystal plate and opening the salt circle. As instructed, I centre my magic and think of a place I felt replenished. Which is everywhere, really. Standing in the moonlit window. Pushing my hands into the sand on the beach. Touching the trees in my wood.

'Lilly!' she says again, and I light the candle. Without thinking, I do this by clicking my fingers and making a spark. I never can find the matches. Once the candle is lit, I hold the wand lightly in my hand and circle it over the flame and the fruit. There is a warmth in me, different from body heat. More like a pleasant feeling as I imagine the avocados are ripe. I wish them to a state of perfection – if that is what they want. I am asking rather than telling. Deep within myself, I know this is right.

My eyes are closed, and somewhere – from a distance, it seems – Theo says, 'Lilly, stop!' and then tuts. When I open my eyes, both avocados are a wrinkled heap. They've gone beyond ripe. Theo reaches out, no doubt keen to throw them away. 'Never mind,' she says. Then a tiny shoot sprouts from each. I lift them, and the shoots uncurl with two pale green folded leaves. A surge of happiness pulses through me. One of my first spells, and I made something grow!

'That wand thinks it's a gardening tool,' says Theo with a shaky laugh.

I pull on the garden coat and gather my seedlings. 'I'll

find some pots for them,' I say, and I can't keep the stupid grin off my face. Walking to the shed, I glance into the kitchen. Theo looks both bored and angry. Then again, she probably wanted the avocados for lunch, and teaching a new witch easy spells must be dull.

Ink comes with me to the potting shed. She is still out of sorts. I chat to her as I plant the avocados because I've read that dogs like the sound of your voice. She stands pressed against me, and when I'm done, I sit in the winter sun on the path outside the potting shed. She lays with her head and front paws in my lap, and I hug her. Maud comes out of the hedge and sits on my shoulder, but I cannot see the little cat anywhere. The horrible thought occurs to me that she may have been run over. Few cars travel Church Lane, which makes me worry she was not expecting traffic. After the spell, I am exhausted. Theo warned as much. The sun is surprisingly warm in this sheltered spot. I will sit for a while, and then Ink and I will walk along the Lane – just in case.

Much later, I wake freezing cold. Ink's shivering has roused me from a deep and troubled sleep. Around me, the garden is still and frosty in the fading light. I have slept here all afternoon. I stagger up and hobble to the cottage on stiff limbs. At the kitchen door, Ink is reluctant to come inside, even though we are both half frozen. I have to put down the plant pots and steer her in.

Theo is at the kitchen table with her phone, drinking coffee. 'Good walk?' she says. I've been gone all afternoon. It's nearly dark. If she'd looked from the kitchen window, she would have seen me. I settle Ink by the range, wrap her up and then fetch the plants and set them on the window next to the abundant geranium. The witch ball glowers darkly.

'I fell asleep.'

'What? Where?' She jumps up. 'You must be freezing. I thought you'd gone to walk Ink and, you know, process what's happening to you.' She fills the kettle.

'Have you seen the cat?'

'Claudia came in, ate some grub and then wanted to go out again,' she nods at the half-eaten food. 'I knew I should have kept her in.'

'No, that's fine, as long as you've seen her.'

'She probably doesn't like visitors.' She makes me tea and heats a can of soup. 'Anyway, good news. I called Elaine and told her about your amazing progress. She says she's sorting out a date for you to join the coven soon.'

I eat my soup in silence, more worried about Ink than anything else. Theo goes upstairs to shower, and I cook Ink some rice and chicken, which she reluctantly eats from a spoon.

'I've been chatting to Elaine again,' says Theo, fresh from the shower in a white kimono. 'She says it's not uncommon for witch pets to get a bit off-colour when new witches use their power.'

I smile my thanks and head to bed. My body aches like I'm coming down with something. Ink lopes after me, and we climb under the duvet together and snuggle up. Like me, Ink cannot sleep, even though we are both tired. I put the light on so I can read, but I can't concentrate. Theo comes quietly up the stairs and stands outside my door.

'Are you awake?' she whispers. 'I brought you a hot water bottle and some tea.'

'Come in,' I croak.

She puts the tea on my nightstand and gives me the hot water bottle. Then she draws the curtains and throws another blanket over us. 'We should take tomorrow off. Let you get your strength back.' She sits on the bed, and Ink rumbles a low growl, which makes Theo stand again.

'Sorry. I think she's a bit territorial about the bed.'

'Drink this. It'll settle you,' she says, handing me the mug.

I cup it in my hands and breathe in the warm smell of herbs and honey. 'Thanks. I'll just read for a bit.'

'Shout if you need anything,' she says and leaves, quietly closing the door behind her.

The tea is comforting. It smells like something my mother used to make when I caught a cold. I sit propped on my pillows, warming my hands on the mug. Who knew Theo could make healing teas? She's kind, and I am grateful that it is not Grant downstairs watching television in my sitting room. I can't imagine him being so sympathetic. I drink the tea and sleep.

In the morning, I lie in bed with Ink's head draped over my legs. Theo is already up. She sings in the shower. I swing

The Mid Witch

my legs over the edge of the bed, and Ink rolls onto her back, and I sit there, giving her tummy a rub. I feel better after the sleep, and Ink seems more herself. Pulling on my old dressing gown, I draw the curtains and look for Maud. It's a beautiful crisp November day. She's probably pecking fruit in the apple tree in the front garden. Yet somehow, I sense she is not. She is nearer. On the roof, perhaps? I close my eyes. Where are you, bird?

Now I am looking at the apple tree from the house. Maud moves her head, and I glimpse the window ledge, and then I am looking into the guest bedroom. Theo is in her underwear – matching lacy knickers and bra in a tasteful shade of pale pink. She is standing on a yoga mat and reaching to the ceiling. Then she bends slowly and rests her palms on the floor. Fascinated by her flexibility, I almost forget I am crossing the boundaries of decency by spying on her. It wasn't my intention. I was just looking for Maud. I pull away, intending to take myself out of the bird's eye, when Theo walks forward on her hands. It's then I see it: a small black feather tattoo on the inside of her thigh.

Maud flies away, and the ground sweeping below her makes me giddy. I pull myself back. Ink is sitting beside me, leaning her considerable weight against my leg. She's never normally this clingy. When I close my eyes, the image of the feather is etched on my eyelids in high detail, as if I saw it close up.

I take a shower and try to clear my addled mind. Ink stays

with me as I dress in jeans and a jumper. The house is cold, which means the fire has gone out in the range. I find big socks and tie my hair into a lump out of the way.

The effort of washing and dressing has left me wobbly and exhausted. I fetch the tea mug from my room and head down the stairs. At the bottom, I am dizzy and sit on the last step. Ink sniffs the dregs in the mug and curls her lips, showing her huge, hooked hound's teeth.

In the kitchen, I run the mug under the tap. Today the witch ball is almost entirely black, and the surface is shiny yet unreflective. Small slithers of silver peak through the darkness. My mind feels like this – as though I am trying to see in the shadows. A sense of foreboding lurks behind my extreme tiredness, and I know, deep within myself, that I am in danger. Perhaps the witch hunters are back? Does Theo have enough power to protect us?

'You're up! How are you feeling?' says Theo, breezing in. She fills the kettle, and Ink and I move away from her. The range has not gone out, but the fire is very low. I add the last of the wood from the basket and pull on the garden coat to get more logs.

'I keep forgetting to do that,' she says amiably. 'No, I'll go. You still look peaky. We'll have a restful day.'

At the back of the stove is the pan she used to make the tea. I carry it to the bin and tip away blackened herbs. Today the smell of the mixture makes my stomach roil. I sit at the end of the table and pull out the shadow book from under a

The Mid Witch

pile of stuff. I rub my specs on my jumper and wonder where the cat is. Poor thing.

Ink makes her low woof to tell me someone is here, and I move to the window. Grant is taking down the sold sign, and Theo is leaning on the gate. Snow as fine as dust swirls around them.

Theo sticks out her skinny arse. She's enjoying a flirt. Grant is having trouble getting his post out of the frozen ground; he's shoving it with his shoulder. I remember when he hammered it in. At the time, I thought it was a bit extreme. He goes to the back of his car, gets a sledgehammer and starts to whack the post. No doubt he is keen to show off his manliness for Theo.

Ink is standing by the door, wagging her tail. I'm surprised she hasn't gone to see him. Ink loves Grant and never misses an opportunity to show him. Maybe she can't open the door in her low state. I turn the handle, but nothing happens. The door is stuck. I place my hands on the wood and feel the powerful spell that has locked me in my house.

As if I have not had enough evidence, this changes my mind about Theo. She is my enemy. I don't know why she is or what she is trying to do, but it is not good. I watch her and Grant. Are they in this together? This seems likely. They both carry the same mark.

At last, the post is loose. Grant gives it a final heave to get it from the ground and throws it in the back of the car. Theo turns. Her face is furious. Perhaps they weren't flirting.

'Ink, lie down,' I say as I fill the sink with hot water and start washing up mugs and the pan. Ink goes to her pile of blankets with a huff.

'At last, he's taken away that sign,' Theo says, carrying in a basket of logs. Damp ones. She doesn't understand fires.

'I'll do that. You sit,' she says. I move away and try to think clearly. I could ask her to leave. It worked with Grant. But if she is capable of putting a spell on the cottage, what else can she do?

She chats on about the weather, Grant and estate agents as she makes us pancakes for breakfast. Ink watches her every move and curls her lip when she comes near.

Theo pours tea, sets the table and dishes up the pancakes. They look delicious. 'I'm sorry,' I say, pushing back my plate. 'I don't know what's wrong with me. No appetite. I think I'll take Ink for a walk.' I put on the garden coat. Ink is immediately by my side.

'Don't go if you feel rotten. I'll take her,' says Theo, unhooking Ink's collar and lead from the back of the door. Ink snarls, and a low, rumbling growl vibrates around the kitchen. The witch ball spins, and a cloud passes over the winter sun, darkening the room. Something flashes, and then my head spins. I'm falling...

Whether I wake hours or seconds later, I cannot tell. I'm sitting in the kitchen in my usual chair. Everything seems so normal, yet everything has changed. Theo is not here, and Ink is not lying by the range.

The Mid Witch

When Theo comes in from the garden, she has a bunch of herbs and a jar of water in her hands. 'Ahh, good. You're awake.'

'Where's Ink? What've you done to her?' I jump up and gasp, choking at a sudden tightness around my neck. I clutch for whatever is strangling me. My fingers find nothing. I pick at my neck with my nails, trying to grasp a thin wire that isn't there.

'Sit still, Lilly, before you pass out again.' She gives me a light shove, and I land on the chair. The strangling eases, and I suck in a deep breath and scream from sheer panic. Theo slaps me hard, smashing my spectacles into the side of my nose. I sit in shocked silence. Blood oozes down my cheek.

'She's outside. Stand slowly, and you can see her,' she says, nodding at the window. Ink is under the apple tree. The snowflakes are thicker now. Even from here, I can see her shivering.

'You can't leave her outside.'

'No. *You* can't. Just a little cooperation from you, and I'm gone, and you and your dog can get on with your boring little life.'

She sits opposite and pours herself coffee. 'Now I know you're tired, but all I need is a few more spells, and we're done.'

'Why?' I can't take my eyes off my poor dog. She's curled herself into a tight ball, trying to keep warm.

'Because I can only drain your magic when you make

magic,' she snaps. 'Really, Lilly! Did nobody ever teach you anything?'

'She'll die if you leave her out in the snow. She's just an innocent dog. She's a greyhound. They can't cope with the cold.'

'Oh, she's a big dog. She'll be alright. Here's your next spell.' She pushes her own grimoire over. A thin dagger marks the page.

'No! You fucking bitch. Bring her in. I'm doing nothing until she's safe!'

'Steady on, Limp Lilly. Remember who holds the choke cord,' she says, closing her fist. Around my neck, the thread tightens so sharp and thin surely my skin is cut. I feel with my fingertips and look for blood on my hands. My heart beats fast. I see Theodora Grimshaw as if for the first time. The mask of her feigned personality is put aside, and now she stares back at me, calculating and wicked.

I fold my arms across my chest and breathe deeply to calm my nerves. My mind is spinning.

The book moves closer on its own and stops in front of me, and Theo smiles thinly. 'The spell, Lilly. If it's too hard, I'll choose something simpler. Now come on, and the sooner this will all be over.'

What can I do for Ink? As I imagine how cold she is, I shiver. How long has she been out there? How long was I unconscious? She's hardly eaten for days. Before I can help myself, I am curled on the floor, shivering like Ink.

The Mid Witch

'That's why you should never have familiars. They are so weakening,' she says, hauling me off the floor and tossing me on the chair with surprising strength. I sit there, teeth chattering. Theo flicks a hand at the door. It opens. 'Call the hound in. But I'm warning you, if that creature comes anywhere near me, I'll kill it.'

I only have to whisper Ink's name, and she's there. I crawl onto the floor and lay with her by the range. Folding her in the warm blankets. I want to stay there, but Theo is rapping her knuckles on the table.

Bang.

Bang.

Bang.

The sound is so painful I sit back in my place and read the spell set before me. Theo cups her hands around her coffee, and I know she is warming it.

How friendly we were so short a time ago.

Chapter Twenty-Six

The spell is called agrimorta. I'm not sure what it's supposed to do, but I organise the things Theo has placed on the table. Hedge herbs and an odd-looking home-made candle wound with hair. Aromatic spices from the cupboard and a handful of yew tree needles, sharp and green.

The Mid Witch

I weigh each on the brass scales and add them to a big stone mortar bowl. It's hard work crushing the ingredients with the heavy pestle. My hands are still freezing, and I know I will not feel properly warm until Ink is.

'Will this spell take all my magic, then?'

'Oh, I wouldn't take it all, Limp Lilly. I'm not going to kill you! I'm a little wicked, darling, but I'm not evil. You can still be some sort of kitchen witch, like your mother.' She lifts her coffee, her eyes glittering at me as she blows on the hot drink. 'Anyway, look on the bright side. The coven will not be interested in your feeble abilities, and you can get on with your bed and breakfast nonsense. Brew a few sore throat remedies, bake true-love biscuits and other such twaddle.' She laughs.

'What if I tell them?'

'Well, firstly, you don't know who they are, and secondly, even if you did, they wouldn't care. You think I'm a bitch? You should've met the nice women of the Allingshire Coven.'

'What if they wonder why I didn't join? They know who I am.'

She shrugs. 'Most midwitches never amount to anything. They have a few spell sparks and their magic fades away.'

I don't care about the magic or the coven. Ink is sleeping by the range. She's peaceful now. As soon as Theo has gone, I'll cook her some more chicken. Maybe call the vet.

'And you can keep one familiar. Well, I know you have that pesky bird, but they don't count for much. The coven don't allow more than two for low magicals.'

'What did you do to my cat?'

'Well, despite the injury,' she says, pulling back her sleeve where three livid red lines run the length of her arm, 'I took her to the cat sanctuary. She won't miss you. I freed her from your thrall. She'd only just arrived, so it was easy to do.'

I pick up the strange candle made with different waxes and hair – hers, I assume. I light it with a snap of my fingers, the spark surprisingly bright for how tired I feel. Then I lean over the book and lift the dagger to read the necessary words aloud. Once again, I pronounce the strange language as best I can. The phrases repeat. They have a rhythm, and I speak as if I understand. My voice is calm. The vowels are long and musical. I drip the candle wax into the mortar bowl and stir. Then I pour everything into a metal dish and set this on top of a tripod with the hair candle beneath. I add more spices and drops of essential oils as the mixture heats.

Behind me, I sense Ink stand up. She wanders over to her water bowl and laps. I wish there was some food out for her.

'Concentrate, Lilly. Almost there.'

I stand so I can breathe in the fumes of the individual hedge herbs. I know where each grows around the boundary of my garden. The last scent is the yew needles, crisp and piney. Somehow, this smell provides clarity and strength. I'm still wearing the garden coat, and my mother's stumpy wand is in the pocket. I open my hand and the ancient yew comes softly to my palm. It belongs there, and I sense all the other Blackwood witches who have held it before me.

The Mid Witch

My hands are full. I have the dagger in my left and the wand in my right. I take another deep breath of the refreshing herbs. Around my neck, the cord tightens. I touch my wand to my throat, and a thin sliver of light falls onto the table and fizzes to nothing. Ink is on her feet again, and the kitchen door opens, bringing in a swirl of snow, a flutter of magpie wings and the green-eyed fox.

Fox and dog stand beside me, and the magpie perches on my shoulder. This is the wrong candle, I think, and blow it out. I summon a new one. While I am debating which colour, a black pillar candle floats to my waiting hand. Black is every colour mixed. Perfect.

With a flick of my wand, the new candle is in place. Another flick, and it burns with a clear light. The scent of wax mingles with the herbs. Snow swirls, and the witch ball twirls, sending shards of moonlight about the room. Theo cannot escape the fumes – not when I am strengthened by my creatures. She covers her face.

I step around the table, holding high the dagger and the yew tree wand. On my shoulder, Maud opens her wings. Ink and the fox step forward, teeth bared, eyes gleaming. There's earth under my feet and wind from the beach in my hair. Moonlight, snowflakes and the deep scents of the spell-casting give me strength. I draw in my power and cry, 'I am the midwitch! You will breathe my magic and harm me no more!'

Theo gasps in a great breath and coughs and sputters,

clutching her throat. I can feel her fighting me. 'Breathe,' I say again. This time she cannot counter my command. She breathes and cries, and I know her power over me has abated forever.

I lower my hands. The room calms. The door closes, and the swirling wind stops.

'Get your things, Theo. You're leaving.'

I've never seen her rattled, and I can't help smiling as she scuttles off.

I open the fridge, which is stocked with expensive food. When I was unconscious, she must have had a delivery. I open a packet of organic baked chicken, chop it up and put it into two bowls for the fox and the dog. Both animals stop eating when Theo returns with her bags, and Maud makes her crackling sound from the top of the dresser. The fox is almost as big as the dog. She's not a normal fox. As Theo creeps past, those green eyes stare, and I fancy that, unlike my dog, the fox has a dark streak for those she dislikes.

Theo hurries away with her fancy luggage. The suitcase wheels snag on the cobbled path. I stand on the doorstep star, flanked by Ink and the green-eyed fox, and watch her car lights disappear along Church Lane.

Chapter Twenty-Seven

November days get dark early. It's only four o'clock, so I phone the local cat sanctuary in Stonemeadow. They haven't seen a small black cat with blue eyes but will call if they do. I ring the vets. Again, to no avail. I'm angry with myself for believing Theo. That's the trouble with me. That's always been the trouble. Even when people are absolute bastards, I still want to believe they are actually nice. That they will tell the truth and be kind. I'm an idiot.

The fox has curled into a ball in the corner of the kitchen. Her red fur is beautiful, but my god, she stinks. Will she want to live in the house now? If so, she's going to need a bath. I stand near her, and she looks at me and then closes her eyes again. This wild animal does not want to be touched. I think she would let me stroke her – and her beautiful pelt is very tempting – yet she would rather I didn't. 'Thank you,' is all I say.

Ink is trying to make herself comfortable on her blanket pile. She's turning circles and scratching at her bedding. The fire has burned low and the temperature in the room is dropping. It's going to be another cold night. In the morning, I will search for Claudia in the lane and woods. For now, I must take care of these animals.

I put on my wellington boots and balance the big torch on the basket of damp logs Theo brought in. Then I haul them to the outside woodpile and put them back. Ink and fox follow me despite the cold. Inside the woodshed they scrabble about as I fill the basket with dry logs. Clearly, something is in here.

The woodpile is wrong. The logs are badly stacked. This is not my work – Theo was here. Carefully, I take apart the stack while Ink stands beside me, wagging her tail, and the fox watches from the door. Eventually, I find the little cat bound in a towel and tied with garden string.

The Mid Witch

'Oh, you poor thing,' I murmur as I lift her. At first, I think she's dead. Her ears are like ice and her eyes are closed. We all go back to the kitchen, and I cut the string and lift her free. Ink is on her hind legs, and before I can stop her, she is licking the little cat as though she is her pup. Claudia stirs, and so I put her by the range where Ink can reach her. As the dog continues, the cat comes back to herself. I feed her little bits of chicken, and she laps warm milk from a spoon. When they lie together, I realise I still have not sorted out the logs or stoked the fire.

Fox comes with me to the woodshed. But this time, she doesn't come in. She carries on along the path and stands in the torch beam by the garden gate that leads to the wood. Snowflakes swirl in the freezing night air as she turns her head to face me. We look at each other for a long moment, and then she is gone. Slinking under the gate to become a watchful shadow in the forest.

An owl hoots, and the trees rustle. I fill the log basket. The torchlight makes the frosty grass glitter.

North Star Cottage looks cosy, nestled in the overgrown garden. The light from the kitchen window is a warm glow, and the witch ball is a silver moon.

Chapter Twenty-Eight

There is a quietness to the day when I wake, and I know even before I get out of bed that the snow has settled.

Ink and Claudia follow me downstairs when I'm dressed, and we all go into the garden to admire the beauty of this new day. The sky is dark with more snow, and we wander around looking at the birds' footprints.

I stoke the fire, feed the animals and make tea and porridge. It crosses my mind as I scroll through my phone that I should do something about Theo. What she did was wrong. But her face was frightened as she scuttled away. She is no longer a threat. My power – I feel it now, like another heartbeat gently pulsing within me – is so much stronger than anything she has. I could get in touch with Elaine and tell her what happened. But I doubt Theo would try such a trick on another, and I know she can never do it to me again, so telling on her would be vindictive. I will leave things and let them settle. I am sure she has learned her lesson the hard way. And even though she's not, she feels like family. We go back a long way.

I have a video call from Belinda. School is closed, and it is lovely to see Amy and Sophie shrieking with delight in the snow. Belinda is relaxed for once and enjoying the moment and the gift of time off. Later, Jason sends pictures of a snowman with a rainbow scarf and asks if I'm okay.

I send a picture of Ink and Claudia curled up asleep together and tell him I'm fine. I have a quick chat with Cressida, and we make arrangements for a get-together the following week. I clean the guest room and change the bed, ready for my visitors.

Only two more jobs remain. I burn dry sage in a metal bowl and walk about the cottage to cleanse it of Theo's negativity. Then I break the ice on the birdbath and fill a jug with the moon-blest water, which I give to the yew tree.

The snow lasts four days, and I spend the time practising spells and walking. By the end of the week, only a few white lumps cling under the hedges. Occasionally a car trundles along Church Lane, proving that the roads must be passable again. The lane is occasionally used as a shortcut by locals who don't mind the potholes.

I'm tidying my log shed when Ink makes a soft woof. A car I don't recognise pulls up outside the gate. Have my bed and breakfast guests come early? Then Grant gets out of the car and stands by the gate.

I walk along the path with Ink at my side. I sense her hackles rise beneath her warm red jacket. We stop a few paces from the gate, and I summon the yew wand into my hand inside the garden coat's bottomless pocket. Ink is usually pleased to see Grant. Today she is not, which is telling.

The car is better described as a limousine. It is long and sleek with dark, tinted windows. Other eyes watch from within.

'What do you want?' I say, ignoring the unease in the pit of my stomach.

Grant takes a small step closer and brings out a tube from inside his smart navy coat.

'Are you Lilith Blackwood?' he asks, tipping a scroll from

the tube and unrolling it. He is like a medieval town crier with the scroll and a grim expression. I start to laugh.

'What? You know who I am.'

'Answer the question.'

'Yes, I am Lilith Blackwood.'

'Last of the Blackwood witches?'

'As far as I know.'

He unrolls the scroll a little more and reads aloud, and when he does, his voice changes into that of a woman's – like he has become the mouthpiece for another's words. I sense her authority as he speaks.

'Lilith Blackwood, you are hereby commanded to attend trial by your superiors for your crimes.'

'What! What crimes?'

He ignores me and carries on. 'Will you attend of your own free will? Or do you wish to be coerced? You are warned that there are persons here who can and will coerce you if you refuse to cooperate.'

Again, I feel the unfriendly gaze of the unseen occupants in the car.

'Refusing to cooperate will be judged against you,' he says in his own voice, as if I am having trouble understanding.

In my hand, the wand is hot, and a part of me would like to do something, though I'm not sure what. I only know I am angry and wrongly accused. Through the dark evergreen branches of the yew tree, the sky is bright blue.

'Please get in the car, Lilith.'

Grant's voice has returned to normal.

'In the car? No. Absolutely not.'

Is that a small smile at the corner of his mouth? It is already gone. I suppose the bastard thinks this is amusing.

'Then you'll have to make your own way. Here's the address.' He puts a piece of paper in the letter box on my gate and steps back.

'When?'

'As soon as you can get there within the next twenty-four hours. Refusing to attend will deem you guilty.'

Grant opens the car door and turns back to me. 'It really would be easier if you got in.' I ignore his condescending tone and fold my arms, and he drives away with exaggerated calm. When the car is out of sight, I go to my mailbox.

Back in the cottage, I make tea and sit at the kitchen table, then read the note. All it says is 'Allingshire County Hall, in Barrington'.

Most of the time, I don't notice or care about my lack of driving skills. Today, I know there are few trains running because of the bad weather. I don't fancy trudging through the sludge to catch the bus from Foxbeck, and I doubt it is running, anyway.

I call Any-Job-Steve. Turns out he's not at all worried about being employed as a taxi service and collects me in an hour. By then, I have changed into a warm dress and boots and put on my best winter coat. I've wiped the mud off Ink's jacket and put a snack and drink for us both in Big Bag. My phone is charged, and as an extra precaution, I have also packed the yew wand. There is already too much in the bag, but I squeeze in a hat, gloves and a small torch.

Steve is pleasant company and chats about his Christmas plans on the long drive to Barrington. I don't feel like talking. My mind is too full of trouble. The main problem is that I don't know what I'm in for. Is this meeting petty nonsense because I sent Grant away? Or is it to do with Theo? Has she decided to retaliate for losing?

'Now, what time shall I collect you?' asks Steve as he pulls up outside the County Hall.

'No, it's a one-way trip. I'm staying with a friend,' I lie and hold Big Bag up. It's easily mistaken for an overnight bag. I thank him and pay, and Ink and I watch him drive off. After I take Ink for a pee on some grass, we go in.

County Hall is built in the same style of Victorian grandeur as the University. We pass through carved oak doors and stand beneath a dusty chandelier in the entrance hall, wondering where to go next.

'Good. You've arrived. This way, please, Ms Blackwood.' A young woman in a flouncy satin skirt, ankle socks and high heeled sandals leads us up a curved staircase and along a corridor. Her bare legs must be freezing. Her sharp heels make spike marks on the carpet as she sashays. She takes us into a small cloakroom, and I hang my coat and Ink's on the pegs.

'We don't usually allow dogs in the Hall,' she says as we

follow her. More stairs and a hallway. Outside a door marked *Strictly Private*, she holds out her hand for Ink's lead. 'I will take the dog now,' she says.

Ink shakes herself, sniffs the carpet and then sticks her long nose up the woman's skirt. The woman shrieks and steps backwards, staggering in her stilettoes, and grabs the edge of an ornate picture frame to steady herself. She teeters off without a backward glance.

'You shouldn't do that,' I whisper. 'Not when your nose is so cold.'

One deep breath. Then I open the door, and it begins.

Chapter Twenty-Nine

The high-ceilinged room is empty except for a pale blue rug and a circle of mismatched chairs.

Beyond the three long windows, snow falls in thick flakes. I'd like to be home beside a good log fire. I hope this nonsense doesn't last long.

A door opens, and in comes Grant, who holds the door for Elaine Waters, the witch I met at the bookshop café. She is followed by ten more women – at least, I assume they are all women. I also assume they are Allingshire Coven witches. Each wears a long cloak with a hood pulled low over her face, and they seat themselves and chat in hushed tones. Everyone ignores me. I am the elephant in the room. Grant clears his throat and intones, 'Ida Carmichael-Grey.' All the witches stand in silence until this new woman is seated. She looks directly at me, and it feels like she is only centimetres from my face. She, too, is cloaked, but her hood is pulled back.

'So, you're Lilith Blackwood.'

'Yes.'

'Come closer.'

I walk toward the circle.

Am I expected to stand in the middle? If so, somebody will need to move to let me in. Perhaps that is the point. Ink walks with me step for step, and I put my hand on her head to steady my nerves.

'Bringing your familiar with you for protection speaks of guilt if you ask me.' The voice comes from the circle, but I cannot tell who spoke.

'Do you know why you are summoned before a quorum?'

'Tell me.'

'Ahh, she professes ignorance. Typical of a power seeker.' The same voice? Or will all the speakers be unidentifiable?

The Mid Witch

Fear replaces my irritation, and Ink leans into me. Her warmth is a comfort. I wish I'd kept my coat on.

Ida Carmichael-Grey ignores the comments and gives me a hard stare. 'You are accused of attempting to absorb another witch's magic by the use of a forbidden spell.'

'Agrimorta,' someone mutters, and the others hush her.

'That's not what happened.'

She holds out her wand to stop me. 'You are also accused of pretending to be a novice witch when, in truth, you are far from that.'

'No,' I say.

'You began the forbidden spell and attempted to take another's power on the pretext of giving her some of your magical energy.'

If Theo was here, she would explain that this was not the case. The good part of herself would prevail.

I wouldn't even mind if she bent the truth a little and maybe said that we were experimenting and things got out of hand.

But that's me. Ever the optimist when it comes to people's characters.

I don't have a chance to speak because Grant is bringing in another woman.

It is Theo.

She is wearing a soft grey woollen dress with a pink silk scarf around her neck, and she takes small steps in flat ballet pumps and leans heavily on Grant's arm.

Gently, he leads her to a chair and helps her sit.

I gape.

'Yes, Mr Rutherford was able to undo your hex so that Ms Grimshaw could tell us the truth.'

Theo looks at Grant, and he at her. Oh my god, are they shagging? They are. I have a flashback to Theo with her arse in the air by the garden gate and Grant all manly with his hammer. I've been set up.

'You simpering, manipulative bitch!' I say.

The witches all turn toward me. I cannot see their faces, but I can feel their stares and the thrill that runs through them. I have not one friend in this room. Only a dog. If I don't defend myself, I am lost.

I walk closer, and the nearest witches shrink back. Some of them start a sneering chant: 'Take her power. Take it. She is unworthy.'

Ida Carmichael-Grey holds up a hand for quiet, and the witches settle into silence. I approach Theo. I want to look into her eyes. Before I can get near, though, I meet an unseen wall. I hold my hands out and touch the smooth, ungiving surface of this invisible cage.

'You are accusing me and have not heard my side of the story,' I say, wrapping my arms around myself and stepping back. Ink shakes.

Theo stands. She holds Grant's arm to steady herself as she pulls away the pink silk scarf. 'Isn't this evidence

The Mid Witch

enough?' she wails. All the witches gasp. Around her bruised neck is a blood-red line.

I am open-mouthed. 'You must have done that to yourself,' I say, but my words are lost in Theo's pitiful weeping. Grant tenderly hands her back the scarf, which she wraps around her neck.

Ida Carmichael-Grey raises her eyebrows at me. 'Seems you have partaken in more than one forbidden spell.'

'That's not what happened. She did that to *me*. She...' Ink, sensing my rising panic, barks. I get on my knees and hug her to me. 'Sh sh sh. It's alright. It's all going to be alright.' Ink growls.

'Control your familiar, Ms Blackwood. Let us hear your version of this sorry business,' says Ida Carmichael-Grey, crossing her legs and folding her arms. I stroke Ink, calming myself as much as her. When I stand, I keep a finger hooked into her collar. The hooded figures face me. Some shift in the chairs, and I sense the weight of their judgment. All I can do is tell them what happened.

I start at the beginning – when I first felt my magic. Ida Carmichael-Grey taps the arm of her chair. 'No. This is not what is in question here. This quorum has convened to ascertain whether you made forbidden magic. Nothing more.'

I begin again – this time, when Theo arrived. 'Why did you send the thrall away?' asks a voice from the circle. Who spoke? They are all completely still.

'What thrall?'

'Grant Rutherford was tasked with keeping watch over you.' I still cannot tell who speaks.

'Oh.' He's a thrall? I remember now and recall his strange behaviour in the café when I met Elaine. 'I sent him away.'

'Why was that?'

The image of the feather tattoo comes to mind. Not the one on his arm, but the one on the sea glass. If Theo and Grant have this mark, perhaps they all do. 'I'm recently separated. I was uncomfortable with a man in my house.'

'Did Mr Rutherford act inappropriately?' says the voice.

'No, he did not. But I felt uneasy.' The circle of women murmur and turn their heads to Grant. He looks at the floor. Oddly, I feel sorry for him.

'Carry on, please.'

I tell my side of the story, but some things I keep to myself. My magpie seeing Theo's tattoo, for instance, and the green-eyed fox. I stick to the spell-making. As I speak, Ida Carmichael-Grey closes her eyes. Is she having a nap?

There is a long pause when I'm done. The heads turn toward Ida and wait. 'We will debate,' she says, but she looks at Grant, not at me.

When Ms Carmichael-Grey stands, so do they all. They file out of the room, and when only Grant and I remain, he says, 'Follow me.' He takes Ink and me through a low door hidden in the wood panelling. A narrow corridor leads to a room that he unlocks with a key. Ink and I go inside, and before I get the chance to speak, he has gone, locking the door behind him.

The cramped, windowless room has a trestle bed with a blanket. Pale light comes from a single bare bulb in the ceiling. I sit on the bed and instinctively get the yew wand out of my bag. It is just a piece of wood. Ink stands by the door and then circles, and I know she is attempting to open it. Like me, she wants to get out. Like me, she is powerless. I snap my fingers for a spark, and nothing happens. Sitting on the bed, I am normal. Normal and afraid.

Chapter Thirty

Time drags. I cuddle with Ink under the blanket. All we can do is listen. The old building creaks and something scuttles in the wall cavity. Traffic whooshes on the road far below, and now and again, indiscernible voices seep into

The Mid Witch

our prison. Ink shivers and wines. Poor dog. Being trapped is horrifying for her.

When footsteps approach, we leap up. The key turns, and Grant comes in with a tray. He pulls a flap of wood from the wall – a table.

'What's happening? Ink needs to pee. So do I.'

'She'll have to use the floor. You can go in here.' He sets a bucket with a towel over it in the corner. Really? A bucket!

He turns to go. 'Grant! Wait. She's so frightened in here. Can't you take her somewhere safe? She's scared. She used to like you.'

Ink is pressed against my leg and is shaking. Grant looks at me properly for the first time and then reaches out and strokes her head. The touch changes everything. Ink wags her tail as if she recognises him again. She doesn't want to leave me, though. 'Go, good girl. You'll be okay. It's only for a little while,' I say, clipping on her lead and handing it to him. He talks to her and smooths his hands along her back, and eventually she allows him to lead her. As he closes the door, her nose pokes through and his hand gently guides her away. My heart is breaking. 'I can't believe you think I did any of this,' I say.

'Magical truth is hard to find,' he says, and the key turns.

Without Ink, I am bereft. Alone, this bleak room is a coffin. I lie on the bed and put off peeing in the bucket for as long as possible. Eventually, I have to go, and when I lift the towel I find a roll of toilet paper, which is a relief.

Under the tray cloth is a packet of sandwiches and a bottle of water. There are also dog biscuits and a bowl. I hope Ink is alright. Grant is obviously a prick and is most definitely shagging Theo, yet I know deep down he will look after my dog. Which is strange. I drink some water, but I can't face any food. Even the snacks I brought with me are unappetising now.

For something to do, I tip out the contents of Big Bag and sort everything. I put the rubbish, receipts, tickets, tissues and sweet wrappers in a pile in the corner. I pull hair out of my hairbrush and put lipsticks and eyebrow pencils into an empty make-up bag. I pack everything back in. My phone is dead. I wish I had something to read. Not that I could concentrate.

The light goes out, so I get into the bed and muck about with the torch for a bit, then turn it off to conserve the batteries. I wish I could sleep.

When I hear footsteps, I am on my feet. The light comes on, and the door opens. It's Grant, but he walks back along the passage without stopping to say anything. I grab Big Bag and follow. I want to ask about Ink – Is she okay? Where is she? – but there is no time. We are back in the high-ceilinged room, and the quorum is assembled. The long windows are night-black, and the hooded witches watch as I walk in.

'Well,' says Ida Carmichael-Grey, 'we have heard both of your stories and taken the time to deliberate the matter.' She leans back and folds her arms. 'The trouble is, Ms Blackwood, as compelling as your story appears, there is one fatal flaw.' At this, the witches begin to mutter, and she glares around the circle until they are quiet. 'Theodora Grimshaw does not possess the magic required to cast the spells you accuse her of. She is little more than average.'

'She took my cat,' I say. I never told them about poor Claudia.

'And that's another thing. Ms Grimshaw does not even have enough power to attract her own familiars – much less manipulate yours.' Ida Carmichael-Grey is smiling. She is a most benevolent and patient witch. My skin creeps, and in my chest, a dark shadow grips me. What will they do? With these people, I am alone. Normal law doesn't reach here. I am entirely at their mercy.

'I have not lied.' My voice is feeble. Surely one of these witches is on my side? Elaine watches me calmly. She and Ida Carmichael-Grey are the only ones undisguised.

'You have been found guilty by this quorum of Allingshire County witches.'

'You're wrong. You're just choosing to believe one of your own rather than an outsider...'

'Ms Blackwood, I can assure you that we have considered very carefully–'

'Why don't you all stay away from me and let me get on with my fucking life? You want to know what I think? What I really fucking think?' I wave my arm to encompass the room. 'All this hooded cloak and dagger shit is archaic. You can't sit here in your circle and pass judgment like you're the law You're not. You have no right to lock me up like I'm a criminal. And you know what? I've had enough of this shit.' I pick up Big Bag and head for the door.

I'm walking so fast when I hit the invisible wall, it almost knocks me out. I stand for a moment, holding my face. When I take my hands away, my nose is bleeding.

'Where magic is concerned, we are the law, Ms Blackwood, whether you like it or not.'

I'm still too angry to be scared. I face them. 'If you are truly lawful, then I demand a proper trial or a retrial. I am telling the truth. You lot wouldn't know the truth if it bit you on the arse!'

I put Big Bag down and rummage for a packet of tissues to sort out my nose. Despite my recent tidy-up, I still can't find anything. I almost resort to tipping everything on the floor when I find them. By the time I've mopped my face, all the witches are arguing. Every voice is muffled, and their heads bob as they put their thoughts to Ida Carmichael-Grey.

I have been so focused on the circle that I didn't notice Grant and Theo. They sit at opposite ends of the room.

Theo interrupts her injured bird routine to smile at me – brief and triumphant. Can she hear what they say in the circle? Or is she just sure everything is falling in her favour?

Grant acknowledges me looking with a flick of his eyes.

Where is Ink? I hope she is safe.

His face is impassive, unreadable. Then I notice his hand.

The Mid Witch

Almost imperceptibly, he turns his hand as if turning a key in a lock.

That's it.

The words he said as he locked the door.

'Magical truth is hard to find,' I say, and the witches fall silent.

All eyes are on me. Yet I suspect they do not see me. Not really. I need to be in the centre of their circle. Over here, I am an outsider. I march forward, and everything slows down. I am heavy, moving through thickened air, and it takes every fibre of my inner self to ease between two chairs and place myself in the middle of the circle.

The cloaks shimmer around the witches' bodies, and I understand that their disguise is an illusion. From here I can see a barrier flickering around the room, encompassing all of us. I lift my hands and look at my feet. Threads of light bind me. I never knew. I'm in danger of my life.

Ida Carmichael-Grey has her wand pointed at me. She is still and composed. This is not her first witch trial. I put my hands on my head and then move them away and out – an instinctual move to shake off the bonds. The threads flick away and fragment. Another sweep of my hands would wipe away the annoying cloaks, I'm sure, but my interest is not with them.

I address Ida Carmichael-Grey. 'I demand a re-trial.'

'Your trial is over.'

'Then you are no better than the average human accusing

me of things you cannot prove. Condemning me because you fear my power.' I turn about, focusing on where the eyes must be in the hidden faces. 'I bet there is not one among you without an ancestor who was executed because the truth was what the judges wanted to see and not reality.'

The last person I turn to is Elaine. She stands before I have the chance to confront her. 'I propose a truth seeker,' she says.

To my left, another witch stands. Then, to my surprise, so does Ida Carmichael-Grey. Then they all do.

Chapter Thirty-One

It takes three days for the truth seeker to arrive. In the meantime, I'm kept under lock and key but in a better room. This one is in the loft space of the County Hall. I have the use of a toilet and sink, and there are books to read. They push food through a hatch in the door. I don't see or speak to anyone. Not even Grant. This room is also windowless, which is very depressing. When I'm not reading, I lie in bed and imagine my garden, the beach and, of course, the animals. I don't want to cry, but I do. I try to connect with Maud, but this place is like a lead box: nothing gets in and nothing gets out. I hope the cat is alright and that my family is not wondering where I am. No doubt the bed and breakfast guests arrived and found North Star Cottage locked and empty. My business has not even begun, and I will already have bad reviews.

When the door opens, I am unsure what time of day it is. Grant is unshaven and looks as dishevelled as I feel. Almost.

'Is Ink okay?'

He nods. 'Get your stuff. It's time.'

I follow him back to the room. Now the chairs are in rows. The witches file in, cloaked as before, and Ida Carmichael-Grey sits to one side. Her wand lays across her lap like the cane of a Victorian school teacher. Then a tall, thin man enters. He is young with high cheekbones and dark hair tied up in what trendy people call a 'man bun'. He pushes his hands into the pockets of his jeans and waits. Is this it? This youth is going to decide my fate? And where is Theo?

'Ms Grimshaw is unwell,' says Ida Carmichael-Grey to the young man.

How very convenient.

'But if it pleases you, seek the truth in this witch.' Ida

The Mid Witch

points her wand at me, and it pricks between my eyes like a thorn.

The young man approaches me, and all the witches lean toward us in anticipation. I hope this kid knows what he's doing. I get ready to tell my story again.

There is no need.

Gently, he takes my head in his hands. Long fingers move over my scalp. He tilts my face and looks into my eyes. His eyes are brown like mine. Our gazes lock, and I know I cannot look away until he does. He breathes in and brings his face closer. I am limp – hanging like a rag doll in his grasp. Time slows and stops. Only he and I exist in the whole world, and as he looks and looks, cold chills streak through me.

Then it's over. He lets go, and I stagger to get my balance.

'Truth,' he says. 'Some omission. But truth overall.'

Ida Carmichael-Grey nods. Then she stands and hands him a gold coin, which he pushes into his pocket. 'Any others?' he says.

'She's sick. But this is enough. Thank you.'

He leaves, grabbing a padded jacket from the back of a chair as he goes. 'She's a midwitch...'

'We know that now,' says Ida Carmichael.

I expect the quorum to chatter and mutter, but everyone is quiet. Ida stands and waves at them to remain seated.

'Ms Blackwood, the seeker finds you truthful.'

I pick up Big Bag. All I want to do is go home. Get my dog and go home.

'However,' she says, 'whatever happened between you and Ms Theodora Grimshaw we will never really know. An untrained witch with your abilities is not safe to be left at large.'

'You still don't believe me!' I sound like a petulant child. Days without my HRT have left me weepy and vulnerable. If I ever get out of this, I'll stash some spares in Big Bag.

'Let me finish. I am happy for you to go free on the condition you agree to train. Your abilities may be considerable, but you are still a novice.'

'You're sending me to Hogwarts?'

'This is no laughing matter, Ms Blackwood. You will make a pledge or suffer the consequences.'

'I am happy to make the pledge,' I say.

'Very well. Come with me.'

She takes me to a library where two witches are waiting. One is young, and the other is much older than me. There's no way to tell whether they were part of the quorum.

We stand at a round table where an ancient leather-bound book rests on a carved wooden stand. They take out their wands and point them at the book. 'Your wand, Ms Blackwood.'

I rummage in Big Bag and eventually find it. Their wands are long and elegant, beset with carvings and jewels. Mine looks like a bit of stick. It is a bit of stick. I point it at the book.

'This is the collective Grimoire of the Allingshire Coven,'

The Mid Witch

Ida Carmichael-Grey says, tapping the cover. 'Are you ready?'

I nod.

'Here we bind our magic in the presence of three.' They speak together. 'A pledge is made by this midwitch to learn the laws of magic to the best of her ability and power henceforth she will commit to the coven for her protection and ours.' Briefly, they tap the tips of their wands onto mine, and a pulse surges up my arm as though I have grasped an electric fence. Then they move away.

'That's it, Ms Blackwood. You may go.'

'What happens next?'

'You'll hear from us.' Ida smiles thinly and nods toward the door.

From the library, I find the staircase and go down until I reach the cloakroom. My coat and Ink's are still there. I'm cold, and I wrap up and check my phone, which is working again. It is Sunday. I have been here four days. There are messages from Jason and Belinda and Cressida. I take a moment to reply with smiley faces, relieved that everyone is happy and well and none the wiser as to my troubles.

In the mirror, I am washed out and grubby. My hair hangs in lank grey strands, and there are dark circles under my eyes from worry and lack of sleep. From the depths of Big Bag I pull out my grandma's old black conical hat and put it on. It's surprisingly warm. I think I've been cold forever.

There is nobody about as I trot down the sweeping staircase and pause at a window. Snow has settled and Barrington looks like a Christmas card. A thousand questions rush through my mind. Are the trains running? Where is Ink? Is Claudia alright?

When I reach the last staircase, Grant is waiting at the bottom. Ink bounds up the stairs to greet me. She goes nuts. Running about in circles. Wriggling like a lunatic and making her happy growl. I hold her and cry with relief. When she's calmed down, I put on her coat.

'Thank you for taking care of her, and for…'

He shakes his head very slightly. He has broken rules to help me. The words he told me to say changed everything. Gave me some of my power back or made them see me. I'm not sure which. Possibly both. I have so many questions.

'Can I give you a lift home?'

'No. Thank you. I'll be fine.'

He shifts from one foot to the other. 'It might be tricky getting back. The trains are off and…'

'Really, I'm fine. Thanks again.' I push through the oak doors. I want to scream, 'You're sleeping with that bitch! Why on earth would I get into a car with you?' But I don't.

Outside, it is bitterly cold, and Ink and I walk past the shop fronts full of Christmas decorations. I catch sight of myself in the window. Yep, I look like a witch. Maybe this hat was a bad idea.

A brass band plays carols on the corner, and a small crowd listens, stamping their feet in the cold. I'm not in the

The Mid Witch

festive mood. All I want is North Star Cottage. I flag down a cab. It's going to cost an arm and a leg, and I don't care. The cab driver is grumpy about driving out to Foxbeck and frankly unimpressed with having a huge dog in his cab. After what I've been through, I take it in my stride.

In the warmth of the taxi with the radio playing, I have a quiet cry. I'm almost asleep when we arrive. I direct him to Church Lane and then pay with a card, which also annoys him.

Maud is on my shoulder as soon as I'm through the gate, and little Claudia is on the doorstep star. God, it's good to be home. I light the fires in the kitchen range and the sitting room to get the place warmed up. There's no hot water, so I boil the kettle for a wash at the kitchen sink. When I feed the animals, I notice that someone has left a cat food dispenser filled with dry food. It must have been Grant.

I eat cheese and biscuits, take my HRT and go to bed early. God, I've missed sleeping with my dog.

In the morning, there is hot water. I get myself sorted. Tackle my hair. The stuff on my head that needs washing and the stuff on my face that needs ripping out. My hairy legs can wait. I slap on an HRT patch. The old one must have fallen off out of exhaustion. In the wardrobe, I am delighted to find that my favourite sack dress is clean, and I sling it on with some warm tights and a jumper. Bliss.

After we've eaten breakfast, I check my emails. The bed and breakfast guests cancelled because they didn't want to travel in the snow. What a relief. I reply and wish them a happy Christmas.

I decide to walk to Foxbeck and get some groceries from the little shop. I pull on the garden coat and grandma's hat, wrap up Ink and set off. It's cold and sunny. Maud flits ahead of us tree by tree along the lane. Ink dashes about in the snow like a mad dog, sniffing everything.

There are no tyre tracks on the road. Only nature has travelled this way since last night's snowfall. It's a new beginning, and it's beautiful and fleeting, and I crouch so I can put my hands into the snow and soak up the power of life in the frozen water.

A jay flies past, dropping a feather as he goes from one line of trees to the other. I hurry to catch it as it flutters down. I'm alongside the Church lychgate, and the blue and black striped feather seems a good omen. I tuck it into my hat.

'I'm a midwitch, mum. Did you know?'

I think perhaps she did.

Ink bounds out of the ditch and places something at my feet. I have to laugh. She's found her toy. With her skinny tail in the hook of happiness, she waits in anticipation. Front paws flat. Bum in the air. Silly dog.

There's a tingle in my fingers. I can throw the pink cock remarkably far. Ink is delighted, and we have a brilliant game all the way to Foxbeck. What else is magic for if not to play fetch the dildo with your dog?

The Mid Witch

Bonus Mid Witch story

Thank you for reading. If you can take a moment to leave a review I'd be very grateful.

Grab your free Mid Witch short story here:

www.djbowmansmith.com

Acknowledgments

I would like to thank my husband for his unfailing support and my two daughters for their constant encouragement and my editor Anna Sharples for her eagle eye and sound advice.

Find her here: www.sharpsightedgrammar.co.uk

About the Author

DJ Bowman-Smith writes witchy paranormal women's fiction. She's passionate about giving mature female protagonists the strong voices they deserve.

She lives with her husband on England's south coast and has two grown-up daughters. When she's not conjuring up magical mayhem on the page, you'll find her creating her own artwork (because apparently one creative obsession wasn't enough) or baking because her husband loves cake.

She finds much of her inspiration in the everyday: overheard conversations, people watching and walking Evie whippet on the beach. She says magic is everywhere, if you know where to look.

Deborah loves connecting with readers who share her passion for stories with grown up protagonists and midlife humour, so don't be shy about finding her on social media or joining her mailing list—she'd love to connect.

Printed in Great Britain
by Amazon